She lay there like the other girls. Her body, like theirs, had seven stab wounds. ~~hair~~ was cut short, but she appeared to have worn it short anyway, and there were no loose strands ... Her eyes, wide open, seemed to be staring at the sky. Such ... surprised look. ... victims. It was the hardest thing of all to take.

Victims. Bert often stumbled over ... though he'd spoken it quite naturally ... a human sacrifice to the gods.

We need different w... ing no room for confusion and ... the car. They'd have to wait for the results of the autopsy. Meanwhile ... as plenty to do. The machinery of a police investigation was going into action again.

THE STRAWBERRY PICKER

MONIKA FETH

Translated by Anthea Bell

Definitions

472644

THE STRAWBERRY PICKER
A DEFINITIONS BOOK 978 0 099 48846 0

First published in Germany by
Bertelsmann Jugendbuch Verlag under the title *Der Erdbeerpflücker*
Published in Great Britain by Definitions,
an imprint of Random House Children's Books

Bertelsmann Jugendbuch Verlag edition published 2003
This edition published 2007

3 5 7 9 10 8 6 4 2

The Publication of this work was supported by a grant from the Goethe-Institut.

Mixed Sources
Product group from well-managed
forests and other controlled sources
www.fsc.org Cert no. TT-COC-2139
© 1996 Forest Stewardship Council
FSC

Set in 10/15pt Garamond by
Falcon Oast Graphic Art Ltd.

Definitions are published by Random House Children's Books,
61-63 Uxbridge Road, London W5 5SA.

www.randomhouse.co.uk

Addresses for companies within The Random House Group Limited can be found at:
www.randomhouse.co.uk/offices.htm

THE RANDOM HOUSE GROUP Limited Reg. No. 954009

A CIP catalogue record for this book is available from the British Library.

Printed in the UK by CPI Bookmarque, Croydon, CR0 4TD

My thanks to:

... Gerhard Klockenkämper, whose wide technical knowledge
was a great help in my research,

... my husband, for always being ready to listen,

... our son, for being what he is,

... the village where we live,

... last summer's strawberry pickers for the idea.

Monika Feth

1

It was one of those days when you could almost smell the heat. Skin burned brown by the sun. Sweat breaking from every pore the moment you moved. The kind of day that made him feel edgy and irritable. It was better not to annoy him on such days.

The others were used to that by now. They let him work in peace, didn't speak to him, even lowered their voices when he passed them.

He couldn't understand why some people always had to be talking. They didn't distinguish between what was important and what wasn't, just let their petty, silly, excitable words spill over everything. Even as a child he'd found out how to defend himself against that kind of thing by just switching off. He liked to see someone else's lips moving while not a sound reached his ears. Like a fish, he thought. Like a fish on dry land.

He used to get beaten for switching off like that. These days no one noticed that he'd gone underground. Most people were as pathetic and stupid as the silly things they said.

Another hour, then it would be time for the lunch break. He'd get that over with quickly and then go back to work.

He knew where this restless feeling would lead if he didn't take his mind off it. He knew what happened when his hands began trembling. Like now.

Oh God. He stifled a groan. Two women turned to look at him. He hardly knew them, and stared darkly at them. They lowered their eyes and turned their backs to him again.

The sun was blazing down from the sky.

Burn these thoughts out of my body, he thought. Please! And these feelings!

But the sun was only the sun.

It had no power to grant his wishes.

Only a fairy had that power.

Young, beautiful and innocent. Most of all, innocent.

A fairy just for him, not for anyone else in the world.

*   *   *

As I drove along, the wind blew the scent of fresh strawberries in through the open window. And the heat, which had come far too early this year. My skirt was sticking to my legs. There were beads of perspiration on my upper lip. With all its faults, I loved my beat-up old Renault, but there were days when I longed for a newer model with air conditioning.

When I'd turned the bend in the road I could see them – the strawberry pickers in the fields, bending over the plants or walking carefully between the rows, carrying crates full of punnets. Spots of bright colour on the wide expanse of green. The sun turned their skin brown.

They were seasonal workers, some of them from Poland, some from elsewhere, some from the most remote corners of Germany. The last adventurers, an annual invasion. The villagers shut their doors and windows against them.

In the evenings the strange men and women, boys and girls met by the well in the middle of the village, drank, smoked, talked, laughed. They kept themselves to themselves, didn't greet their neighbours, didn't even smile at them.

A lot of proverbs make sense. *As you sow, so shall you reap*. The villagers had sown distrust, and now they were reaping the cool reserve they deserved.

I drove up the long, winding drive to the house. White gravel crunched under my tyres. Like a movie, I thought. All much too perfect, much too good to be true. Suppose I woke up and found I'd only been dreaming?

As soon as you came close to the house you could positively smell the money that had gone into every detail. The old watermill had been carefully and expensively restored. The architect had even used the millstream in his design for the interior, tapping it for water to run along a narrow channel through the entrance hall.

The sun shone down on two-hundred-year-old red-brick walls, made the gravel gleam, was reflected back from the glass front of the extension, which looked like something thought up by a sci-fi author.

My mother's house. Every time I came to visit, its beauty enchanted me again.

I opened the door and went into the hall. Welcome cool air met me. So did our cat Edgar, who owes his name to my mother's love of the stories of Edgar Allan Poe.

I picked him up and cuddled him. Enormous quantities of cat hair drifted to the floor. I put him down again and he washed one side of himself and stalked over to the stairs ahead of me.

Everything inside the house was equally exquisite and expensive, designed by someone who knew what he was doing. The sun cast soft afternoon light through the tall windows of the hall and made the wood of the staircase glow. The rattan chairs on the terrazzo floor made you want to be in Italy, like the plainly whitewashed walls and the round, monastic window niches.

The staircase was a work of art in itself. The steps actually seemed to be floating in the air. The joiner who made them was famous for using the minimum material to create the maximum effect. He did it very well. It was the same with everything here, every room and every piece of furniture. On principle my mother had chosen the best and the most expensive. She could afford it.

Once Edgar reached the top of the stairs he padded along the upper gallery, purring. He knew I always went to see my mother first.

There wasn't a sound from her room. Perhaps she'd fallen asleep. I carefully opened the door.

My mother was sitting at her desk in front of a stack of paper, reading glasses on her nose. She turned to me and smiled. 'Jenna! How nice!'

My mother's a writer. A crime writer, to be precise, with a list of very successful books. Ever since she turned her back on what my grandmother and her reading group would call 'real literature', her books have sold like hot cakes. They've been translated into over twenty languages, and production companies scramble for the movie rights.

'Sit down. I'll be through with this in a moment.'

You can interrupt my mother any time, whatever she's doing, unless she's making a note of an idea or sketching something out. I'd got accustomed to it ages ago, and I didn't mind any more. I used to. I always felt the words mattered more to her than I did.

Edgar had already jumped up on the sofa and was waiting for me to sit down. He curled up on my lap, closed his eyes, purred and dug his claws affectionately into my thigh.

I can still remember life before my mother was so successful. We lived in the town of Bröhl then, in one of a row of houses. The front gardens looked like well-tended family graves, planted up with evergreen shrubs, rhododendrons and annuals. Here and there water gurgled over the nice clean stones of a water feature and ran into a lily pond containing several fat goldfish.

My father had his office on the lower ground floor, behind windows surrounded by ivy. A brass plate was fixed to the right of the front door at about eye level, saying THEO WEINGÄRTNER. FINANCIAL ADVISER. The plate was polished till it shone. Many of my father's women clients checked their make-up in it before they pressed the bell.

We had a cleaning lady who came in twice a week, and a window cleaner came once a month. My mother wrote and wrote.

After her study on the first floor, her favourite place was the garden, which looked like a showpiece feature for a glossy mag like *Homes & Gardens*, with just the right mixture of formal beds and wild corners, the sort of thing that gardening magazines like.

My mother coped with writer's block by working in the garden. Perhaps there were times when she'd have liked to discuss a problem with my father instead of digging it into the soil or tying it up to a trellis, but he couldn't muster any interest in the conflicts my mother described on paper and the words she used for them.

When he talked about my mother's profession, which wasn't often, he called it *scribbling* and described her as a *scribbler*. He did it with a friendly wink, thus making light of the whole idea. He couldn't bring himself to say *writer* or *author*, because that would have meant he took her career seriously.

And he went on acting the same way even when my mother first began to appear on chat shows, and journalists turned our house upside down doing photo-reportage pieces and making short films about her.

But the royalties from the publisher earned even my father's respect. They paid for perks like the new BMW, a modern, better-planned design for my father's office, a new computer for my mother, the conservatory she'd wanted for ages.

My mother's writing had little to do with our daily life. She did it on the side, so to speak, and we didn't get to know much about it.

There'd be a day when she remarked, in the kitchen, that she'd just finished her new manuscript. A few weeks later her editor would come, and the two of them would sit in the conservatory discussing the manuscript and scattering pages everywhere, so it was difficult to walk about without creating hopeless confusion.

Later still the postman brought proofs, the jacket design and then the finished book.

My mother needs her writing. She needs it to help her stand up to everyday life, she says. She always did. Perhaps she needed it even more back then, because she had to stand up to my father too.

He doesn't like surprises; he's keen on having a perfect life in a perfect home and with a perfect career. Sometimes I feel he's like someone living in an outsized doll's house where nothing is ever moved and everything stays neatly in place.

My mother, on the other hand, is naturally chaotic. I'm sure that when she was a child her doll's house was a mess, and it was only logical for her to get other people to look after the house.

She turned more and more to the garden. It was her own manageable, self-contained universe where she could do just as she liked. Success was obvious and mistakes could easily be put right.

And it was the same with writing. My mother could create a complex world where only she had power over her characters and their story. People were born, people died, and my mother pulled the strings. It all went on quietly, behind the closed door of her tiny study. Sometimes she talked about it, and her eyes seemed to sparkle. But usually she kept her writing experiences to herself and we discussed other things.

A magazine once described my mother as a woman who was addicted to writing but had learned to hide her addiction well. Life wasn't enough for her, said the journalist; she invented another life in her stories.

Another life. Perhaps my father could have gone there with her if he'd wanted. But he didn't want.

And what about me? No one asked me what I thought.

My mother took refuge in reading tours too. She'd travel around for weeks on end, calling me from Munich, Hamburg, Zürich, Amsterdam. There was always a list of the hotels where she was staying beside our phone. *Mama: can be reached at . . .*

While she was away our cleaning lady became housekeeper too: she spent the day with us and did all the housework. She cooked as well: good home cooking. My father ended up ten kilos overweight.

My mother became famous. I gradually acquired special status at school. Even some of the teachers looked at me with awe. I began selling my mother's autographs, and I did pretty well out of them.

It was in the evening, when shadows fell into the house, that I missed my mother. Not that I'd have wanted her to be at home all the time. Far from it. But I was used to hearing her going up and down the stairs. Reading part of a manuscript aloud under her breath. Phoning. And I missed the scent of her perfume, lingering invisibly in a room where she was or which she'd just left.

We grew rich. My parents bought the old watermill in Eckersheim with twenty thousand square metres of land, in the idyllic setting of a landscape conservation area, and hired a well-known architect to renovate and convert it. My father would have preferred a villa on the outskirts of Bröhl, but he didn't get his way. He got a secretary.

Her name was Angie and she looked like an Angie too: mid-thirties, ash-blonde ponytail, fingers covered with rings, skirts too short and too tight. My mother spent every spare minute on the building site; my father had no spare minutes at all, because he and Angie were so deep in his work.

I was left somewhere in between. I just hung around, didn't work hard enough at school, and all of a sudden I grew up. I was fifteen.

A year later my parents divorced. My father didn't move into the converted mill with us. He stayed on in the old house with Angie, who was pregnant.

'There.' My mother took her glasses off. 'You've come at the perfect time. I'm dying for a coffee. Do you have to dash off?'

'No, I can stay as long as you want. Sure I'm not disturbing you?'

She put her pen down. 'Yes, but at just the right moment. I'm stuck. I switched the computer off ages ago. You know what it's like when you're staring at the last sentence like a rabbit hypnotized by a snake, and you suddenly realize a whole hour has passed?'

My mother didn't expect an answer. Rhetorical questions are her speciality. She stood up, bent down and gave me a kiss.

I was as familiar with her perfume as with her voice or the warmth of her skin. Calypso. She never wore anything else. It was light and fresh and smelled of summer. My mother had it made specially in a perfumery, mixed just for her, and she had chosen the name herself.

That was the one extravagance she'd allowed herself since becoming a rich woman, except that she paid a small fortune for striking rings, necklaces and bracelets, and then didn't wear them because she thought they looked too conspicuous.

'Something wrong with me?' She patted her short black hair, which had silver-grey threads in it.

'Nothing at all!' I smiled. 'You look great. As usual.'

She took my arm and led me out of the room. 'You too.'

That was a downright lie. But perhaps she didn't even notice she was lying to me. Perhaps she was lying to herself. Persuading herself I was beautiful, like her.

But I'm not, and I never wanted to be. I wouldn't change the way I look, even if it's nothing to write home about, not for any beauty in the world. I'm me, which is more than many people can say about themselves.

We went downstairs. Patches of sunlight shone on the kitchen floor. Our other cat, Molly, who is black and white like the squares on a chessboard, was lying stretched out on one of them. Molly, who owes *her* boringly ordinary name, inspired by no one and nothing, to me, greeted me with a chirping 'Miaow', rose and rubbed round my legs. Then she and Edgar disappeared through the open terrace door into the garden.

My mother made us coffee in the rather elderly espresso machine. I noticed again how she was getting to look like my grandmother, though she often said crossly that Grandmother and she were like fire and water, and nothing seemed able to change it.

'How are you getting on with the new book?' I asked, perching on the edge of the table, which was warm from the sun.

'This one's going to cost me years of my life.' My mother has a way of combining the most dramatic statements with the most ordinary of gestures. Concentrating on what she was doing, she put coffee cups, sugar and a dish of orange biscuits on a tray and carried it all out onto the terrace. 'I wrote better when you were still living here. I miss the peace and routine of our life then.'

'So it's not me you miss?'

I regretted the words the moment they were out. Was I still annoyed to be just a rather unimportant part of my famous mother's life? Did it still hurt to know that basically she didn't need me? That any kind of daughter would have done for her, a daughter picked at random, interchangeable?

'Forget it.' I dismissed my question with a gesture. 'I didn't mean it seriously.'

She was looking at me, hurt. 'Can't you stop being so over-sensitive, Jenna?'

That was rich, coming from her! My mother could spend hours arguing over a single syllable.

I dropped into one of the garden chairs, leaned back and took a deep breath. If I were ever to feel sorry I didn't live there any more it would be because of the view. I was looking at gently rolling countryside with grazing sheep. They belonged to a neighbouring farmer. Here and there a crooked old fruit tree stood defiantly in the grass, as if it had been forgotten.

No one had touched this landscape. Mercifully even my mother hadn't thought of laying out a mini park here, or having a designer do it for her. Like me, she appreciated its magic and left the garden untouched.

The murmuring of the millstream made the idyll complete. I clasped my hands behind my head and closed my eyes.

'When are you off on a reading tour again?' I asked.

My mother waited for me to open my eyes before she answered. 'I have just a couple of readings planned, no tour. You know I always use the summer holidays for writing.'

Summer holidays. Everything revolved around her writing. Even the seasons. And the writing had loomed even larger since she and my father divorced. As if it protected her from the world, from loneliness, from her feelings.

I looked more closely at my mother. Suppose her whole self-controlled outer appearance was just a façade? A perfect suit of armour. I sensed her nervous energy. It actually seemed to flow over the table. She was always like that at the beginning of a new book. Putting out feelers, sounding out everyone she met, every word, every sound and every noise, every smell. There was no point trying to tell her anything at moments like this, because although she might be physically present her thoughts were somewhere else entirely.

'It's a funny thing about this novel,' she said, hesitating briefly. 'I still don't know who my central character's going to be, and I've already finished the first chapter.'

I nodded, not knowing just what to say. Anyway, my mother doesn't usually expect any answer when she's talking about her work problems. She's just thinking out loud, using whoever she's talking to as a mirror.

Mirror, mirror on the wall, who's the cleverest of us all?

No, wrong fairy tale. I didn't have the talent to be a Snow White. I could choke on a single poisoned sentence.

We drank our coffee in silence.

'So what did you come for?'

Good question. What did I come for? Perhaps I'd known, but by now I had forgotten.

*   *   *

The dead girl lay in the undergrowth, naked. She was on her back. Her arms hung down beside her body. Her right leg was bent at a slight angle; her left leg was stretched out.

Her hair had been cut off. One loose strand still lay on her shoulder; others had blown away and were wrapped around the stalks of plants or caught on the rough bark of trees.

Her eyes were wide open, staring at the sky. As if, at the moment of death, her principal emotion had been surprise.

Some children had found her. A boy and a girl, brother and sister, the boy ten years old, the girl nine. Their parents had forbidden them to play in the wood. They played there all the same, and had been terribly punished with a sight they would never forget.

They ran away screaming. They stumbled, still screaming, across meadows and pastures, clambered over fences, crawled under barbed wire. As they were taking a short cut through the brickworks yard, one of the workers stopped them. He listened to what they told him through their tears and sobs, called the police and took the children to the police station, where the secretary made them cocoa and rang their mother.

The corpse turned out to be that of an eighteen-year-old girl. She had been raped. Seven stab wounds were found on her body. The first of them, straight into her heart, had killed her.

The murder victim came from Hohenkirchen, near Eckersheim. She was still at school and lived with her parents. One of the police officers who went to the crime scene was able to identify her. He knew her parents and volunteered to break the news to them.

Her mother collapsed at the door. The woman's husband led her to the living-room sofa and put a blanket over her legs. Then he clapped the policeman on the shoulder and offered him a drink.

People sometimes act that way when they're in shock. They do the strangest things. Once the police officer had met a woman who, on hearing that her husband had died in an accident, went into the kitchen, ladled cold chicken soup into a plate and ate it as if she hadn't had a good meal for ages.

The girl's name was Simone. Simone Redleff. The entire village went to her funeral. It was the biggest funeral anyone had ever seen in Hohenkirchen.

The whole of her school year came. The girls had handkerchiefs pressed to their mouths, the boys surreptitiously wiped tears away with the backs of their hands. They were all still in shock. Death had come too suddenly, out of the blue. But that wasn't the worst. The worst was its terrible, unsparing violence.

You often heard of dreadful things like this, but at a distance. If such violence could happen to someone they knew, the mourners seemed to be thinking, where would they be safe themselves?

In the chapel of rest, they played pop songs chosen by a friend of the dead girl. The tunes, among all the flickering candles and the flowers smelling of death, filled the room with desperate sadness.

Outside, the sun shone down as if nothing had happened.

But nothing would ever be the same again.

The murder of 18-year-old Simone Redleff, as Detective Superintendent Bert Melzig of the Bröhl CID said at the press conference, has many features in common with the murders of two young girls a year ago in the north German towns of Jever and Aurich. Neither case has yet been solved. Melzig would not give any detailed information while police inquiries are still in progress.

* * *

He was worn out, but all the same he didn't sleep long. He liked the half-dreams that came into his mind between sleep and waking, but he hated and feared them too. At the moment he feared them.

He tried desperately to think of something else.

He couldn't do it. The images kept coming back like boomerangs.

He still felt the excitement. No other emotion was anything like as strong.

Oh, girl, he thought, why did you let me down?

Because on closer inspection she hadn't been a fairy at all, not even really pretty. Her voice had sounded squeaky with fear, like a bird's. It had infuriated him. He hated shrill voices. You could hear the fear in them.

He hated the sweat of fear too.

Her hands had been all slippery.

Not that he really believed in fairies. He wasn't a child any more. And a fairy would have been more powerful than he wanted.

She had to be *like* a fairy. Like the fairy in the storybook he had as a child. Slender. With soft, shining hair. Beautiful.

Big eyes. Long lashes.

You didn't see details at a distance. You saw them only when you were really close to each other. And by then it was usually too late. He kept finding something that took him by surprise, something he wasn't prepared for. Even a mole in the wrong place could spoil the image.

The girl in Jever had smelled of tobacco smoke. She'd even offered him a cigarette! She'd smiled flirtatiously, put her head back and blown smoke in the air, never guessing that she'd already signed her death warrant.

Groaning, he turned over onto his other side. He was glad he'd taken a room at this little inn and wasn't staying at the farm with the others. The room was small and ugly, and instead of a bathroom it had a shower cubicle so small that he could hardly move in it. It was right under the roof and hot from the sun in the evening. The window looked out onto the chimney next door. But the rent was within his budget and he didn't have to give up his freedom.

Above all, he could dream safely.

His dreams were not the sort you could have in a hostel dormitory. It was difficult to hide the uneasiness that often made him wake suddenly, drenched in sweat. And he couldn't risk talking in his sleep.

No, it was better here. Almost perfect.

If only he could drop off to sleep.

He needed his sleep to get through the days. To maintain his façade. Of course the cops had been snooping around, asking the strawberry pickers questions. And they'd be back. As soon as they had some definite clue.

He turned onto his back and clasped his hands behind his head.

But they wouldn't find anything.

They wouldn't get him.

They'd never done it yet.

He smiled in the darkness.

Soon afterwards, he was asleep.

2

After school I went straight home. I didn't feel like hanging around in the café having a coffee with the rest of the physics class. Suddenly it struck me that maybe I'd been looking for life in the wrong places too often.

Somehow I'd grown out of school. I ought really to have been taking my final exams this year. I hated having had to stay down in Year Eleven, so that now I had another year to go. Timetables, exam papers, the smell of whiteboard pens, sweat, the same faces all the time – it was getting me down so badly I sometimes felt like just hitting out.

I found the mornings at school so deadly dull that I had difficulty not falling off my chair.

Formulas. Numbers. Poems. Truisms.

Noise. Teeming crowds in the school yard. Bad air.

I don't know what architect gave his bad taste free rein in our school building. Probably one who was never a school student. A nightmare of glass and concrete, it was an oven in summer and an ice house in winter.

I just couldn't wait to get out of it again.

I lost half an hour in a traffic jam for which there was no obvious reason before I finally turned into Lessing Street. My resident's parking permit was no use if there wasn't a space free. I drove all around the block twice, cursing, then someone moved out and I squeezed my Renault into the space.

The staircase smelled of an exciting mixture of cabbage, coffee and fried bacon. I opened the windows of the only landing on the way up, but I knew someone would slam them shut again the moment I'd closed the door of my flat behind me.

You chose this life, I told myself on the way upstairs. This is exactly what you wanted.

In the watermill, the rooms were always at a pleasant temperature – refreshingly cool in summer, comfortably warm in winter. No worn wooden steps, no peeling plaster, no wilting house plants on the windowsills, no bikes in the hall, no kids' buggies outside the doors, and no hastily scribbled obscene graffiti on the walls. There'd been a new one added recently, the only one to show a touch of class. I liked it. HOLY VIRGIN MARY, YOU CONCEIVED WITHOUT SIN, TEACH US HOW TO SIN WITHOUT CONCEIVING!

Someone had tried to scrub it off and failed. The letters were only slightly blurred. One day the stairwell would be redecorated, and then as time went on new graffiti would be added.

'Anyone at home?'

No reply, but I hadn't been expecting one. I put my school bag down in my room and went into the bathroom. I noticed that the loo seat was up just in time before sitting down.

Merle was always bringing home characters who thought it was beneath them to put the seat down. Where men were concerned she had rather primitive tastes. Although she was one of the most independent people I knew, she adored dominant guys. She despised herself for that, but there was nothing she could do about it. Although I didn't get the impression that she was seriously trying to.

Recently she'd found herself well on the way to monogamy. It was a thorny path to take, and now and then she still rebelled.

The kitchen was in the usual state of chaos. None of us got up early enough in the morning to leave without a panic, let alone have time to restore order. It didn't really bother me, but tidying up was usually left to me because as a rule I was home first, and that annoyed me.

Merle had an afternoon job with Claudio's Pizza Delivery Service, either driving the van or working in the kitchen, depending on what was needed. Caro was having problems with her boyfriend, Gil, again, so we hardly ever got to see her.

I was hungry and felt tired, but if there's one thing I hate it's eating at a table with dirty dishes on it, so I started clearing up.

Merle usually made herself muesli in the morning: grated an apple, mashed a banana, squeezed in half a lemon. I threw the fruit peel in the bucket for bio-compost, scraped dried apple fibres out of the grater, and put both grater and lemon squeezer to soak in hot water.

Caro had hot cocoa and toast and ham with a soft-boiled egg. Pieces of eggshell lay beside her plate, and most of the breadcrumbs had fallen on the floor, where they crunched under my feet. She hadn't finished her cocoa, and now there was a skin on it which reminded me of my grandmother's throat. That in turn made me feel guilty because it was ages since I'd been in touch with my grandmother.

I liked tea for breakfast myself, and Finnish crispbread with cheese. I'd wasted five valuable minutes that morning looking for a book I'd mislaid, so I didn't have time to put the cheese slices in the fridge. The few hours since then had been enough to make them turn transparent and start curling up at the edges. They'd be no use even for cooking now. I could only throw the cheese away.

For the hundredth time I thanked heaven for the second-hand dish-washer we'd finally decided to buy a few weeks ago, after much discussion. It swallowed up the dirty dishes and I just had to pass a damp cloth over the table and the work surfaces before the kitchen was reasonably fit for human habitation again.

I conjured up scrambled eggs with mushrooms and tomatoes, made myself a camomile tea and was just about to start eating when Caro shuffled into the kitchen.

'Aha,' I said, with some annoyance. 'So the rats come creeping out of their holes.'

Caro looked at me blankly.

'Just half a tick too late to help me tidy up.'

Caro yawned. She ran her fingers through her tousled hair. Dragged herself over to the fridge. Opened it. Took out a yoghurt. Found a spoon. Sat down at the table with me. All in slow motion.

She was wearing her shortest skirt and a sleeveless T-shirt, both black, and on top of them the grey linen blouse I loved, but she wouldn't part with it except on loan, and not very often then.

'I had a visitor,' she said.

'Meaning you weren't at school.'

Caro had been bunking off lessons all the time recently. Sometimes she didn't even get out of bed in the morning. Sometimes she started off and then turned round again. It was all but miraculous that she hadn't been thrown out of school yet.

She made the face that said: I hate it when you talk like a mother. Then she began spooning up her yoghurt.

'Visitor?' I asked. 'Anyone I know?'

'Nope.'

'Serious?'

She shrugged.

So it was all off with Gil again. I opened the book I'd put beside my plate. If she didn't want to talk, fair enough, I wouldn't make her. I was glad to be left in peace anyway. The morning had been a strain. Six long, bleak, lost hours, and who was going to give them back to me?

Caro got busy with the espresso machine my mother had generously given us when we moved in. 'Want one too?'

I shook my head and pointed to my teacup.

When Caro was sitting down with her espresso again, and reached for the sugar, the sleeve of her blouse rode up, revealing an ugly red mark on her left forearm.

'Caro . . .'

She quickly pulled the sleeve down again.

It was a long time since she'd last been self-harming. When had she begun again? And why?

'Want to talk about it?'

'Nope.'

'But if you did want to . . . ?'

'. . . I'd turn to you and Merle. In confidence. I promise I would.'

She was always telling us that, but nothing ever came of it. You had to take her by surprise, overcome her resistance and get her talking before she knew what was happening. It didn't always work, but mostly it did. Every time we found out a little more about her. And piece by piece we put the jigsaw puzzle that was Caro together.

She came from a broken home – broken past mending. Well, her parents and her younger brother, Kalle, still shared the same flat, but none of them had anything to do with the others. They all went their own way.

Her father beat her mother. Her mother beat the children. The children beat up other children. It had always been like that. A vicious circle of violence, and Caro herself couldn't break out of it. Although she didn't harm anyone else, she harmed herself.

'I wish I could fall in love,' she said dreamily.

'You do. All the time.' Caro was in a permanent state of infatuation. She'd hardly got used to one boyfriend before she was holding the door open for the next.

'Not like that. I mean for real.' She put a sugar cube in her mouth and crunched it. 'For ever and ever, understand? All soppy and genuine. A great love. Till death us do part.' She rolled her eyes. 'And as the fairy tales finish: if they aren't dead yet they're still alive today. Amen.' Laughing, she fished another sugar cube out of the bowl. With her figure she could afford to eat them. She was slim as a reed, and normally she picked at her food like a sparrow.

'You want to settle down?' I drank my tea, which had no sugar in it. It tasted as if I'd poured hot water over dried grass.

'That sounds so weird. Settle down. But call it that if you like. OK, maybe I do want to settle down. Any objections?' She gave me a provocative glance across the table.

'If you told me you'd got a job as a high-wire artiste in the Krone Circus, I'd have fewer problems imagining it.'

'I'd never take a job in a capitalist circus like that. Or if I did join a circus somewhere I wouldn't be a high-wire artiste or a fire-eater or anything like that, I'd be a clown.'

That just suited her. With her short hair and big eyes, it wouldn't take much more to create the perfect illusion.

But why was she self-harming again?

'Don't change the subject,' I said. 'What about Gil?'

She put her empty yoghurt pot down on the table and tipped it over with her forefinger. The spoon fell out, clattering. 'What about him?'

'Do you want to settle down with him?'

She shook her head. 'We split up. Last week.'

'And you found a replacement right away?'

'So?' She looked at me aggressively. 'Do I have to go about in sackcloth and ashes for weeks on end?'

I didn't like it when she forced me into preaching morality. 'Did I accuse you of anything?'

'You? You're accusation itself! Just look at you!' She knocked the yoghurt pot off the table. It landed on the floor, rolled over the tiles and ended up next to a large dust-ball.

'It so happens I like Gil.' I realized that my scrambled eggs were cold now. I blamed Caro for it. 'I think he deserved a chance.'

'He had it.' Caro stood up to make herself another espresso. 'More than one too.'

'He didn't have the ghost of a chance.' I pushed my plate away and drank some tea. It tasted even nastier lukewarm. The aroma of the espresso rose to my nostrils. 'Can I have one, actually?'

Caro slammed the cup down in front of me in an unfriendly way. 'What makes you think that?'

'Because you're so dead set on your longing for that one great all-embracing love that you wouldn't recognize real love even if it was standing in front of you.'

'If love can stand in front of anyone,' said Caro, with a nasty smile.

I didn't answer: I drank my espresso. This was one part of Caro: cold cynicism. The other parts were warmth, affection, sympathy. But there wasn't much of that to be seen at the moment.

Merle and I had decided to let it wait. Sometime or other Caro's buried good qualities would surface again. Till then we had to keep it cool. We had time. And it was worth waiting for Caro.

'How about a visit to the travel agency?' I asked. Caro was all for it. We often did that – picked up lots of brochures and planned adventurous trips that we couldn't afford. Maybe we really would go on them some day, when we had enough money.

At first Caro and Merle had been surprised to find that I wasn't rolling in money, since I was the daughter of best-selling author Imke Thalheim (my mother had always written under her maiden name, and she went back to it entirely after she and my father divorced). Later they realized that the reason was my pride. I couldn't bear being more dependent than necessary on my parents.

On the way to the travel bureau Caro linked arms with me. It was nearly the holidays. The last summer holidays before our final exams next year.

'Suppose you just broached the subject with your mother after all?' Caro saw my expression, and dismissed her own question. 'Only asking! I mean, the poor woman hardly knows what to do with all that cash, right?'

'Oh, Caro, forgive me!' I stopped walking. 'I've obviously done you an injustice. You don't think only of yourself after all. You have this totally unselfish desire to help my mother get rid of her money!'

Caro nodded gravely. 'I just can't bear to see anyone suffer.'

We looked at each other and spluttered with laughter. There was no way at all I was going to ask my mother for money, but I didn't have to explain that to Caro. She knew.

* * *

The days went by monotonously, all the same. That was a good thing. He needed a quiet basis for his life. So that he could stay in control. As long as possible.

His desire was like an animal getting greedier all the time.

But there were parallels. He thought about the films he liked. *Dr Jekyll and Mr Hyde. Nosferatu. Frenzy.* Bram Stoker's *Dracula. The Silence of the Lambs. The Night of the Werewolf.* And all the rest of them.

After seeing each of those films he'd felt a little as if someone understood him – and somehow justified. For a long time he'd felt he needed to talk to the directors of those films. Or one of the actors. But then he saw a documentary about Hitchcock. He heard that fat, inhibited, anxious-looking man say things that disappointed him deeply. And the world owed *Frenzy* to that elderly mummy's boy?

And what could he have said to Klaus Kinski, who'd played the lead in *Nosferatu*? A self-centred megalomaniac who ended up wasting his creative powers on vulgar stuff to titillate his audiences?

But each of those directors had known him. Better than anyone else in the world. They'd never met him in the flesh, yet with their films they'd gone to the essential heart of him, they'd known about his most secret, hidden hopes and fears. And put them on screen.

He was old-fashioned about films, didn't like many modern ones, thought carefully which to buy on DVD. He was proud of his very private collection, just as he was proud of his very private library. Dostoevsky's *Crime and Punishment*, Mary Shelley's *Frankenstein*. Patrick Süskind's *Perfume*, Akif Pirinçci's *Felidae*.

He couldn't watch the films because he didn't have a DVD player. But he had to own them all the same. It gave him a sense of being at home to have them with him.

He didn't like porn. He hated the emptiness that those books or films left in his head.

Good books, bad books. Good people, bad people. It was thanks to his mother that he could tell the difference between heaven and hell, God and the Devil. His mother and her years of absence. His hard childhood had taught him everything. However evil disguised itself, he'd know it under any mask.

There were only a few people like him. Those few were artists. They wrote books, painted pictures, made films.

And he admired them from afar.

At a suitable distance.

They were like him, yet different. People from a more elevated sphere. He'd never have been bold enough to get close to them.

And perhaps it was better to guard against disappointments anyway. Or he might have felt about some of them the way he did now about Hitchcock and Klaus Kinski.

Not coming too close meant, paradoxically, that he could stay near them. He didn't want anything to destroy his image of such people.

They were driven. Obsessed. Like him.

They all knew about those red dreams in the night. It was difficult waking up from the dreams. They knew about the burning thoughts that ate your brain away.

You could tell from their pictures, their books, their films. They were frightening.

Like looking in a mirror, he often thought. As if you saw yourself reflected there hundreds of times. Like in the halls of mirrors on fairgrounds. Your own face reflected to infinity, cruelly familiar.

He felt hungry. He often forgot to eat and didn't notice until his stomach ached. He looked at his watch. Nearly nine. Perhaps he ought to go to the little café in the village. He didn't feel like cooking anything for himself.

He really liked cooking and was quite good at it (as far as was possible on the two primitive hotplates here). If he'd had the staying power he could have trained as a chef. And then got a job on board a ship.

Perhaps that would have changed everything. Perhaps it would have driven the restlessness out of him. Perhaps the sight of endless expanses of water would have soothed him, made him a better person.

But deep inside he knew he was pretending to himself. He was the way he was. He couldn't run away from that, hard as he kept trying. He'd fought countless battles against himself. And lost them all.

He went out into the corridor and closed the door behind him. He didn't meet anyone on the way down, just heard the usual sounds coming from the rooms. Most of the guests here, nearly all reps or casual labourers, spent their evenings in front of the TV set. They led a sad life, a life slipping away, always on the move, never at home anywhere. Their marriages didn't last long, and even if they didn't end in divorce their children grew up without a father around the place.

A piece of paper covered with clear film listed the house rules and hung by the front door. Its tone always annoyed him.

This door is to be kept closed after 8.00 p.m.
Smoking outside the rooms is strictly forbidden.
TV and radio sets are to be turned down to a reasonable volume.

And so on, and so forth.

The style of it suited the landlady, a loud-voiced, shrill-spoken woman in her mid-forties. Life with an alcoholic husband had dug early wrinkles into her face. She felt responsible for everything, poked her nose in everywhere.

Her narrow lips turned down at the corners, she seldom laughed, and if she did it was a curiously abrupt and cheerless sound. Her clothes smelled of old sweat mingled with the aroma of an over-sweet perfume.

He wondered whether to tear the house regulations down, but left them where they were. He didn't like the handwriting. He felt as if touching it would soil his fingers.

Outside, the heat hit him in the face. It was almost as concentrated as the heat in his room. He'd have to keep the ventilator running overnight, even though its whirring kept him from sleeping well.

Perhaps, he thought, he ought to go out and do something instead of sitting around in the café or his room. Perhaps he should drive to Kalm. Or Bröhl.

He'd go to Bröhl, he decided. He could eat an evening meal in the town at his leisure, watch the people out walking, take a stroll himself in the castle grounds or around one of the nearby lakes.

He went to his car and started the engine. Whatever financial difficulties he was in, he'd never give up his car and the freedom of movement it gave him.

He rolled down the window on the driver's side, although that would upset the air-conditioning. The wind ruffled his hair and carried the fragrance of strawberries in from the fields. Fresh. Aromatic. Sweet.

He breathed deeply.

Sometimes feeling happy didn't seem so difficult.

He switched on the radio. Tina Turner. Why not?

And he sang along, tapping out the rhythm on the steering wheel with his fingers.

Even forgetting sometimes didn't seem so very difficult.

3

The police are following up over four hundred leads in the murder case of eighteen-year-old Simone Redleff from Hohenkirchen. However, there is no hot trail at the moment. A reward of 5000 euros is offered for information leading to the arrest of the murderer.

Talking to our reporter, Detective Superintendent Bert Melzig was optimistic that this appalling murder would be solved. There's no such thing, he says, as the perfect crime.

Meanwhile it turns out that there is a very clear connection with the similar murders in north Germany (see our reports). In each case the victim's hair was cut off, and in all three cases the necklaces worn by the girls were missing. It can almost certainly be assumed, says Melzig, that the murderer took the necklaces as fetish objects.

* * *

Bert Melzig crumpled up the newspaper and threw it on the table.

'What a load of bollocks!'

He poured himself another cup of coffee and took it out on the patio. With a groan, he dropped into one of the chairs around the garden table. As soon as he was sitting down he felt like jumping up again, and restrained himself with difficulty. He had to look after himself: he wasn't all that far away from a heart attack. Or so Elias said, anyway. Elias was his best friend, tennis partner and doctor.

Not that Elias annoyed him by harping on about it – he just dropped a comment now and then, and those remarks settled all the more persistently in his friend's mind because they were casual.

'We all have to die of something,' was Bert's stock answer, also casual.

'That's right. Some sooner, others later.'

Typical Elias. He always had the last word.

Bert sipped his coffee. His wife had taken the children to see her parents. She'd said she wanted to get away from her daily routine for a weekend. He, on the other hand, needed peace and time to do some thinking, so they'd decided to spend this weekend separately.

Thinking. Bert's mouth twisted wryly. He'd intended to do so much. But yesterday evening, just after Margot set out with the children, he'd opened a bottle of red wine. And then another. And that put paid to any thinking.

Now this newspaper report first thing in the morning, the Saturday edition. As if a sore head wasn't punishment enough.

'The bloody press,' he growled. 'The curse of modern times.'

Talking aloud to himself was a bad habit, but he couldn't help it. He'd done it from childhood. Thoughts were clearer spoken out loud. Everyone who knew him, particularly his colleagues at work, was used to it. If he thought out loud in front of them they didn't look surprised, but left him alone and waited.

'And I really do treat those reporters fairly. I regularly give them information; you'd think I might at least expect an accurate story in return. Is that too much to ask?'

Even dead drunk he would never have said there was no such thing as the perfect crime. Of course there was. Always had been. Countless murders, rapes and abductions were never solved.

Nor had he told the press there was no hot trail at the moment. That was pure speculation, although unfortunately it was true.

They were always putting words he'd never said in his mouth. And although he knew that responsible and well-researched articles were a rarity in the age of tabloid journalism, he was always disappointed to find himself dealing with people who took such liberties with the truth.

That comment about the absence of any hot lead would only feed a stupid but widespread prejudice. Yet again the police would feature in the public eye as a bunch of inefficient fools.

'The one plus in all this is that the murderer will feel he's still safe,' muttered Bert. 'And if he feels safe, he may make a mistake.'

Mention of the missing necklaces and the cutting of the girls' hair, however, was a catastrophe. Something like that could set off copycat incidents and blur any real clues.

His mobile rang. The need to be available at any time was so ingrained in Bert that he never thought of switching the thing off, even at home.

A glance at the display showed him the call was from his boss. That put the lid on it.

'Melzig here.'

He heard his voice sounding abrupt and unfriendly, but he didn't feel like pretending. On a Saturday morning, at least, he'd have liked to have just a little privacy.

'What's all this I read in the paper, Melzig?'

Bert couldn't stand people who rang and didn't say who they were, simply talked away and expected you to recognize them by voice alone. For a brief moment he was tempted to pretend he couldn't identify his caller, but he didn't. He also refrained from giving the answer that was on the tip of his tongue: if *you* don't know what you're reading, who does?

'I've no idea how they got wind of it,' he said instead.

'But someone must have—'

'None of my team, sir. I'll swear to that.'

'As I thought. But I want you to find out who gave the press that information.'

The boss sounded more conciliatory now. He was well known for exploding at the tiniest thing, but he quickly calmed down again.

'Could have been one of our north German colleagues,' said Bert. 'Or the victim's relations, the Redleff family. They've been practically under siege, as you know.'

He could sense his boss nodding. Could see his double chin disappearing into his tight shirt collar and quivering at every movement. If the boss wore a shirt early on a Saturday morning, that was to say. They didn't know everything about each other, which was just as well.

'How are you otherwise, Melzig?'

This question always brought the conversation back to everyday life.

'Fine, sir. Can't complain.'

The answer, like the question, was always the same.

It's odd the way we treat each other, thought Bert. As if we all thought and spoke in prefabricated clichés. Suppose I really was in a bad way. Would I tell him? Or would everything still be fine? Would I still say I couldn't complain?

'See you Monday, then, Melzig. And get a move on with this case, right?'

Oh, great, thought Bert when the conversation was over. As if it were that simple.

On Monday he'd ask the Redleffs what they had told the press. And then he'd have to spend time finding out how the press had known that there were necklaces involved in the other murder cases too.

It was possible that the north German police officers had been a little too talkative, but Bert didn't think so. Mind you, there was always liable to be a leak somewhere.

The wind was rather chilly today. Shivering, Bert hunched his shoulders and crossed his arms over his chest. Somewhere out there was a man who had to be stopped in his tracks.

The thought did not inspire him, it depressed him.

* * *

When Caro woke up she saw that he wasn't lying beside her any more. He must have left in the middle of the night. Silent as a shadow. Unnoticed.

He didn't want to meet Jenna and Merle – he'd said so several times. Not yet. Any more than he wanted to meet Caro's family. Although it had never entered Caro's head to introduce him to her family – least of all them.

It was different with Jenna and Merle. They weren't just friends, they were far, far more. Caro didn't trust anyone. Hadn't trusted anyone for years. With Jenna and Merle she'd taken the first hesitant steps in that direction.

Not that he had anything against the girls, he said. It was nothing personal. He just didn't want to meet them or anyone else who was part of Caro's life.

Not yet, he'd said. Later. Sometime.

Heavy-hearted, she'd accepted that, because anything was better than losing him.

Even on his first visit to the flat Caro had noticed how strangely he behaved. She'd assured him they would be alone. All the same, he'd looked around cautiously as they entered the hall.

Like an animal tensed to spring, she'd thought. A panther, perhaps. Or a leopard. Wild, wilful and beautiful.

They hadn't known each other long, and they met far too seldom. He hardly ever had time. But every time they did meet it was like lightning striking.

Caro had never before gone weak at the knees at the mere sight of a man. She'd thought that kind of thing only happened in novels. He was hungry for life. Untamed. Not worn down to size by the years. You could see it in the expression of his eyes.

He was a free spirit, and when they were together a little of that rubbed off on Caro. Wasn't that what love was supposed to do? Change you? Show you new dimensions?

Caro turned over and looked around the room. It seemed larger from her bed. Or perhaps that was just because she felt so lonely.

He could at least have said goodbye, she thought. A kiss, a touch. She wouldn't have needed more. But just taking off like that?

It was the way he always disappeared. Abracadabra.

In fact he did look like David Copperfield, although he was stronger, and you could see from his body that he was used to heavy work. But at first sight he could have been the magician's twin brother.

A less gentle version of him.

Caro had never been attracted to gentle characters. She liked their company, went to the cinema or out dancing with them, ate a pizza afterwards and talked through the night with them, but deep inside she was untouched.

She always told herself that kind of man was better for her. Frank, honest, reliable, loving, faithful.

But also boring. Most of all, boring.

She'd tried it once. His name was Marvin; he was an exchange student from the USA, and had gentle brown eyes that always looked slightly surprised. It was all right with him for a while, but then she began imagining someone else while they were kissing.

She'd never forget how hurt he was when she dumped him. He didn't eat, hardly slept, and lost so much weight that his clothes hung loose. Then he went back to the States and it was as if they'd never met at all, or if they had it was in a dream.

Caro got up. She turned the radio on, but switched it off again quickly when she heard the presenter's voice. So much cheerfulness and jollity early in the morning was more than she could take.

She slouched into the kitchen, where Jenna and Merle had left the usual chaotic aftermath of breakfast. Sighing, she began to tidy up. Perhaps they'd both appreciate that.

Every sound echoed in her head, leaving a small, sharp pain behind. Why had she drunk anything when she knew it didn't agree with her? And one of those cheap red wines that made her feel really unwell. It was all she had found among their provisions.

At first he hadn't wanted any, and just drank to keep her company. The alcohol didn't seem to affect him, but it did her. She had talked and talked. And giggled. Until he put his hand over her mouth.

It had been a large, broad hand. Her whole face had disappeared under it. Suddenly she'd felt cold and pushed the hand away.

Then he'd laughed.

And she had put her arms around his neck and snuggled close to him, feeling loved and comforted.

He could change the mood in a room from one moment to the next. And a person's mood too. Because he really was a magician. Abracadabra.

Caro smiled as she stacked the dirty dishes in the dishwasher. Perhaps she'd found what she was looking for at last. Perhaps she could stick with him.

She looked at her watch. If she hurried she'd be in time for the third lesson. 'Not a bad idea,' she said out loud, and began whistling. It really wasn't a bad idea. The way things were going, the teachers would soon lose patience with her.

In the shower she put her face under the jet of water and stretched. It was too soon to believe in it yet, but it did look as if she had really and truly fallen in love.

'In love,' she whispered. 'In love, engaged, married.'

* * *

He hung up, pushed the door of the phone box open and took a long stride out into the square, which was quiet and pallid, as if frozen in the sunlight. He wiped the sweat off his forehead with the back of his hand and felt as if he'd been doing nothing else for years. As if his life consisted of that one mechanical gesture.

The phone box seemed to have stored up the heat of an entire summer and the odours of countless human beings. He had held the door open with his foot as he talked, but that hadn't been much use, for there was no wind at all. Not a breath of air moving.

'Nathaniel,' his mother had said, 'where are you? Please, dear, tell me how I can reach you.'

He heard the tremor in her voice that announced the usual flood of tears, and hung up quickly. Her complaints got on his nerves. He didn't want anyone to be able to reach him, least of all her.

Nathaniel. She was one of the few people who still called him that. He would have liked to forget his name, the way he'd happily have forgotten his whole childhood. But now and then he was brought right up against it again. Escaping the past was a trick he hadn't mastered.

He must stop calling her. In fact he wasn't even sure why he did it at all. Out of a sense of guilt? Out of habit?

Disappearing was simpler than he'd expected. You just had to take care not to stay in one place too long. And not to leave any traces behind. Then it was easy.

He shouldn't have called. She was certain to be moving heaven and earth to find him. He could so easily let something slip talking on the phone. A few hours later and she'd be here.

'Sense of guilt? That's ridiculous!' He'd got used to talking to himself out loud, asking himself questions and answering them. There were fewer and fewer question. Life here was so simple.

Get up. Work. Sleep. The day was passed between those landmarks.

He loved being out in the fields, watching the light change, feeling the wind, sun and rain on his face, sensing the muscles under his skin. The work did his body good. He noticed that from the way the women looked at him, and their readiness to get involved with him. And of course he also noticed it from his hunger for them, which wouldn't go away.

'Hey, Nate!'

He turned at the sound of the voice. Only one person called him Nate, and here he came. He was limping, dragging the leg that had been shattered in an accident years ago, his jeans were encrusted with dirt and his hair hung over his face in greasy strands.

'Bloody hot!' said Malle, putting his hair back behind his ears.

No one knew Malle's real name – perhaps he didn't even know it himself. His surname was Klestof, and he spoke German with a slight, indefinable accent. But he wasn't telling anyone where he came from.

They went in to eat together. As they entered the canteen the noise the others were making surged towards them like a wave. Malle greeted people to the left and right of him. He was an odd mixture: basically good-humoured, friendly and helpful, unless he'd been drinking.

Then he might get argumentative, and if he did that he often hit out.

And when Malle hit out it was devastating. The dangerous thing about him was that, under the influence of alcohol or in very difficult situations, he lost all control over himself. He could swing between contradictory feelings like grass swaying in the wind, giving way to every mood. It didn't exactly make him popular, although that was the very thing he wanted: to be liked by everyone.

The menu was turkey schnitzel with potatoes, peas and carrots. They took their food and looked for a table. No one was going to sit down with them if it could be avoided. Nathaniel didn't mind.

Frozen vegetables. The turkey too tough, and so dry that you could hardly swallow it without water. The potatoes overcooked and watery. Dessert was a pale yellow blancmange with strawberry sauce.

Money for meals was deducted at source from their weekly wages. You couldn't rely on itinerant workers. They might disappear as suddenly as they had arrived, sometimes in the middle of the night. Nathaniel had known some who went off without their pay.

'Miserable pigswill,' said Malle. 'Could cook it better myself.' He pushed his plate away and reached for the dish with his dessert.

Nathaniel was glad he was able to adapt to almost any situation, adjust to practically anything. He knew he had to eat in order to do the heavy physical labour, so he ate. It was faster here than in a café, where the food might have tasted better, and it was cheaper. In addition he could get back to work quickly. An hour at midday was all he needed to stoke up his strength again.

The others were different. Most of them were unhappy with their working conditions. Not for nothing had the farmer who owned all the strawberry fields around here become the richest man in the village. He paid starvation wages and put the workers up in small dark rooms for which, of course, he also deducted a high rent from their pay.

His wife was the kind of woman Nathaniel avoided. Heavily made up, showy clothes, early lines showing on her face. She didn't say a civil word as you passed her. Nathaniel had never seen her smile.

However, he had seen the way she looked at him, and he had quickly looked away. If she took a fancy to him, that was all he needed! To have her start chasing him! He could do without complications of that kind.

Malle had finished his dessert and was cleaning out the dish. Nathaniel pushed his own helping over.

'Really? You don't want it?' Malle had reached for the dish and was digging his spoon in before he had even finished the question.

'You have it,' said Nathaniel. 'I'm not very hungry today.'

He'd eat a few strawberries. It was more important to keep Malle in a good mood, get him feeling they were friends. He might need him some-time, and if he did then Malle would be in his debt and couldn't refuse to help.

He'd always done well with those tactics. They'd saved his skin several times.

You're a bastard, thought Nathaniel, grinning to himself. That's right, you're a bastard.

4

Merle and I had been shopping. We were planning to cook together. Caro had been going to join us, but then she phoned and backed out.

'She really didn't give any reason?' asked Merle.

'No,' I said.

'I don't understand why she's making such a secret of this new boyfriend.' Merle cut the green bit out of the cherry tomatoes, a job calling for a delicate touch. 'She's not usually so . . . so peculiar.'

'How do you mean, peculiar?'

'Well, we might at least have had a glimpse of him.'

'Oh, nonsense! First, Caro knows she can rely on us, and second, her taste in men is quite different from ours.'

'Not necessarily.' Merle put half a tomato in her mouth. 'I could easily have fallen for Gil.'

I looked at her and grinned.

'Oh, well.' Merle grinned back. 'Would that have been progress or not?'

'You bet it would!' Gil had been too gentle a soul for Caro, and certainly for Merle. Personally, I'd liked him a lot. He was like the brother I'd always wanted. It was hard for me to think of him in the past all of a sudden.

The water was boiling. I opened the packet of spaghetti in too much of a hurry, and it fell out on the work surface and lay there like sticks in a game of Pick-up-Sticks. I gathered it up again.

'Anyway, he was something special,' I said. 'Which is more than can be said of most of the characters who turn up here.'

Merle was making vinaigrette, and seemed to be deep in thought. Then she half turned to me. 'That murder a couple of weeks ago . . . it really bothers me. I mean, I knew the girl. Well, I didn't really know her, but she crossed my path a few times. At the nightclub and sometimes in the pizzeria. She was always smiling. I . . . I just can't imagine her being dead.'

She kept going back to that subject. It really seemed to be weighing on her mind. And at just that moment the spaghetti was ready to be drained. I felt callous, talking about a murdered girl and still cooking at the same time.

'Is the salad ready?' That was life. One girl dies, another looks forward to a good meal, and we all try to come to terms with these contradictions.

A few minutes later we were sitting opposite each other at the table.

'Imagine it,' said Merle. 'You trust someone and then he goes and murders you.'

By now they'd found out that the girl had been to the nightclub. She'd been out driving her father's car. The police assumed that she'd invited her murderer into the car herself. Perhaps she'd met him at the nightclub, perhaps she'd known him for some time, or perhaps he was hitching a lift and she picked him up.

'It's horrible.' I was only picking at my spaghetti. My appetite had disappeared.

'What would you be thinking about in those last seconds?' Merle was painting patterns on the edge of her plate with tomato sauce, using the prongs of her fork as a brush. 'When you know you're going to die?'

'In accidents,' I said, 'you're supposed to see your whole life pass before you like a film in a few minutes or seconds. Maybe it's the same with a murder?'

Merle shook her head. 'I think you'd just be frightened. Horribly, dread-fully frightened. Kicking and hitting out to defend yourself and suddenly feeling you aren't strong enough. Maybe you'd begin to pray.'

'Pray?'

'When there's nothing else you can do.'

'Stop it, Merle. I don't want to think about it in all this detail.'

'You'd rather bury your head in the sand?'

'No, but I don't want to see dead girls in front of me evening after evening.'

'OK.' Merle lapsed into silence for the rest of the meal.

'Did you notice that Caro's started self-harming again?' I asked her as we were drinking an espresso afterwards.

Merle nodded. 'Something to do with the new boyfriend, I guess.'

'Maybe we ought to lie in wait for him if she's not going to introduce him to us,' I said.

'By night and in a dark corner, hoping he'll need to go to the loo?' Merle grinned. 'Thanks a lot. I'd rather wait for Caro to make the first move.'

As if on cue, we heard the front door of the flat open and close. Caro came into the kitchen and dropped into her chair, glancing at our plates.

'Any left?' she asked. 'I'm ravenous.'

She beamed at us hopefully. She looked happier. Happier than I'd ever seen her before. As if she'd become a new person overnight. And she was hungry!

Perhaps we were doing the man she loved an injustice. Perhaps he was good for her.

'Of course there's some left,' I said. Merle was already on her feet, fetching a plate from the cupboard.

Why shouldn't Caro be happy for once in her life?

* * *

His colleagues in north Germany had been friendly and forthcoming. They had let Bert see their files, shown him the material they had, and accompanied him to the scenes of the two crimes. They had photocopied the expert opinions of witnesses for him, explained the stage they had now reached, and were ready to discuss anything and everything.

Those murders were now twelve and fourteen months in the past. Hardly anyone mentioned them any more, and the press had dropped the subject.

The police had exhausted all possible avenues of investigation, and had come to no concrete conclusion. A nightmare for any good CID officer.

Two murders within such a short time, thought Bert on his way home again, and then the next not until a year later. Does that fit the pattern of a serial murderer? He answered his own question in the affirmative. Several things had to coincide for the murderer at the same time: motive, victim, location and opportunity. If any one of those components was missing he couldn't act.

But maybe they were dealing with a highly intelligent murderer. One who not only carefully avoided leaving any trace of himself but was deliberately acting in a way that didn't conform to the statistics. As a rule the intervals between serial murders grew shorter rather than longer.

In both cases the victims had been young girls: one seventeen, the other twenty. They had both been blonde, with long hair. Both had had their hair cut off. Both had been wearing necklaces that were not found on them.

Both had been stabbed. Seven times in each case.

My God, thought Melzig, horrified, how can a man in a frenzy control himself like that? Or hadn't he been in a frenzy? Was it possible for a man to rape and murder a girl as if carrying out some cold ritual?

Bert felt differently about every criminal, and his feelings tended to form at the very beginning of an investigation. This one frightened him, and that was unusual. It had never happened to him before.

The photographs of the crime scenes showed the same expression on the faces of the two dead girls as he had seen on Simone Redleff's. There had been incredulous astonishment in their wide eyes.

One of the girls was called Mariella, the other Nicole. It was important to Bert that the victims had names. And that those names were frequently mentioned in newspaper reports. It made the victims less anonymous, made them human.

They could have been anyone's daughters, sisters, granddaughters, nieces or girlfriends.

It was quite different with the murderer. He had no profile. He was nothing but a menacing shadow, a danger that could be imagined lurking in every corner.

Missing necklaces. Seven stab wounds. Hair cut off. Bert had read up old cases and found no pattern. His north German colleagues had done similar research, without success.

Every murder was terrible, but serial murders were more than terrible. Bert had never before had a serial murder to investigate. But he had studied them, always hoping never to have such a thing on his own patch.

He could understand, if not excuse, many murders. He had investigated cases of murder committed out of jealousy or greed, had solved cases where someone killed for revenge, or for fear that another criminal offence might come to light. He had encountered sex killers too.

But a serial murderer was something alien to him. He couldn't manage to think himself into such a person's mind, and that was exactly what he had to do over the next few weeks. He had to change his viewpoint, discover the pattern from outside, and then slip into the murderer's skin. Think and feel as he did. And catch him like that.

My language is getting aggressive, he thought. And as he was still brooding over it he realized that this particular murder case was going to change him.

He drove to the next lay-by and got out of the car. A short walk in the open air would do him good. There was a wood just beyond the lay-by, and he plunged into its shade, hands dug into the pockets of his jacket.

The smell of decaying leaves and the fields of crops beyond the wood brought a flood of memories to his mind. Bert had spent his childhood in the north. A strict, joyless childhood full of darkness and anger.

He had never wanted to go back to that part of the country again.

Only now did he notice how much strain he'd been under since arriving here. He clenched his fists. Realized that it was raining and his hair was getting wet.

But his face was wet not with rain but with tears.

He hastily dashed them away and hurried back to his car.

The case had already begun to change him.

* * *

He hated crawling around among the plants in the rain. Although he wore protective clothing, he could feel his own things getting clammy underneath. The straw spread between the rows prevented the moist, heavy earth from clinging to his boots, but his hands looked as if they'd been in a mudbath.

The others seemed to feel the same. They were in a dejected mood. No one laughed, no one cracked jokes. They worked calmly, concentrating, hoping no one else would come too close to them.

In rain, the fruit lost its fragrance. Even the colour faded. Strawberries, thought Nathaniel, must have been the favourite fruits of the sun god in ancient Greece.

Rain or no rain, he didn't mind how he earned his money. The main thing was not to be forced to sit at a desk. He was a man who liked to keep moving. Other people sat down to think; he couldn't think unless he was in motion. The wind in the fields often blew his head clear again.

Work must make you sweat. One of his grandfather's principles that had branded itself on Nathaniel's memory. The old man had explained the world to himself and other people with such maxims, although he said very little else. Never before or afterwards had Nathaniel known anyone so silent.

Grandfather had preferred to let his hands do the talking. And his belt. And if that wasn't ready to hand then a stick, a wooden spoon, a coat hanger or a heavy chain from the workshop – anything like that would do.

Every time, Nathaniel had made up his mind not to cry. And every time he had burst into helpless tears. That seemed to make the old man even angrier.

But the sense of humiliation had been worse than the pain. Nathaniel could still taste it on his tongue today.

Grandmother didn't interfere. She had accepted everything her husband did, for as she saw it he was a virtuous and upright man. And virtue and rectitude, she had learned in church, often went hand in hand with harshness and rigour.

Usually Nathaniel had to follow Grandfather to the barn to be punished. The barn was behind the house, and out on the road no one could hear what was going on in there.

Nathaniel had often wondered whether Grandmother really knew nothing about it. He had tried to read her eyes. But his grandmother had been an unapproachable woman who always kept herself under control.

Work must make you sweat. Order is half the secret of life. Never put off till tomorrow what you can do today. Ingratitude is the way of the world. What Hans doesn't learn now he never will learn.

You could have filled an encyclopaedia with the old man's maxims. He didn't just churn them out – he expected Nathaniel to act in line with them. If he didn't, Grandfather took his belt off.

Like mother, like son.

It hurt.

'Take that!'

It hurt badly.

'Once and for all, I'll show you!'

The leather strap stung his skin.

'You're not going to bring shame upon us, not you too!'

Afterwards Nathaniel would lie in the dim, dusty light of the barn. Leo the dog, who had slunk away into a corner in fear, came hesitantly out, licked his face and lay down beside him. They could lie like that for hours. No one was bothered; no one came to see if they were all right.

Leo was kicked and beaten too.

They both led a dog's life.

* * *

Caro looked at herself in the bathroom mirror. Everyone said she was too thin, but she still felt she was dragging a body that was much too fat and heavy around with her. The mirror showed its top half to her, down to the waist. She could see the cuts on her arms, and the scars of the old injuries.

Tears came to her eyes. She felt helpless when he wasn't with her. A prey to everyone, most of all herself.

'I'm going to feed you up,' he'd said. 'Until you're round and you feel good.'

But he liked to hold her so much too. His hands were large and assured. She nestled close to him and felt safe and protected.

'You're like a child,' he'd murmured into her ear.

A child. That was just what she never wanted to be again.

* * *

This time everything was right. She was like a young animal. Her beauty lay hidden under an angular, awkward outer husk and was there just for him. He was discovering her gradually, taking his time.

He read no answers in her eyes. They were full of questions. He was ready to answer them. Sometime. He'd do anything for this girl.

Very gradually he began making peace with himself and the world. It was a difficult process, and might well take half his life. Anything was possible. So long as she was beside him.

Innocence. Caro was just another word for it.

* * *

The strawberry pickers were out in the fields again. The farmer was just leaving a third trailer by the side of a field; the first two were already heavily laden. A girl not much older than me was carrying a full crate along. In spite of its weight she walked so lightly that it looked like a dance.

None of the men looked at her, though they all ought to have been craning their necks. A pretty girl, even in her work clothes: shapeless dungarees with a limp T-shirt under them. She had tied a scarf over her hair to protect it from the sun. A few blonde strands peeked out.

I took all this in at a glance, then I drove past and had to turn into the road leading to my mother's house.

The watermill lay alone in the heat of the afternoon. It was as if a flickering aura surrounded it. I'd read somewhere recently that old parsonages and mills were haunted considerably more often than anywhere else. That reinforced my feeling that the building had a long history behind it, and in spite of all my mother's research we hadn't found out nearly everything there was to know.

My grandmother's car, a red Charade, was there already, and you could see how carelessly it had been parked. Grandmother loved driving, but whenever possible she avoided parking in a small space or reversing.

I parked next to it, and as I got out I was met by Edgar and Molly, rubbing round my legs and purring. They both followed me into the house, where the familiar pleasant, cool atmosphere awaited me.

Grandmother was sitting on the terrace in the shade of the green sun umbrella that made her face look paler. All the same, she looked terrific. She's seventy-five, but most people would say she was sixty at the most.

She held her cheek up to me. I kissed her and felt her soft skin under my lips.

'Now, sit down and tell me how you are,' she said, looking hard at my face.

There's nothing you can hide from her, so I didn't even try. 'Fine, except that my school report wasn't exactly a big hit.'

Grandmother dismissed this impatiently. 'I'm not interested in your marks, I was asking about your life. You ought to know that by now.'

I refrained from telling her that marks make up a large part of a student's life, and wondered what I could tell her instead.

'What are your flatmates up to these days?' she asked.

Grandmother had met Caro and Merle at our house-warming party and immediately took them under her wing. She had talked Caro into eating two slices of her home-made buttered almond cake, and told Merle, who's always tired because of her job, that she ought to get more sleep.

'That's one amazing lady,' Merle had said later, and Caro had asked me if she could apply for the post of Grandmother's second granddaughter.

'They sent love,' I said.

'Is Caro still harming herself?' asked Grandmother, narrowing her eyes. She sometimes bore a strong resemblance to a crocodile lying in wait.

'You noticed?' I was genuinely surprised.

Grandmother raised her eyebrows. 'I may be old, my child, but I'm not senile. I can put two and two together. So?'

I nodded. 'Even though she's just fallen in love and seems really happy. Something's sent her off the rails again. But she doesn't talk about it, or at least not to us.'

'A brave girl,' said Grandmother. 'A pity there aren't more like her about.'

My mother came out of the house with a tray, gave me her cheek to kiss and began laying the table.

'How's the book going?' I asked her.

'A chapter since you were last here.' She smiled with satisfaction. 'Not bad when you think how the entire world's ganged up on me. Workmen in the house all the time. The boiler in the kitchen went wrong, the gutter had to be repaired, the pump in the tank gave up the ghost, and then a gardener cut down the diseased maple.'

'A good gardener doesn't cut down sick trees, he saves them,' said Grandmother disapprovingly.

'Actually there was no saving this one,' my mother told her. She was wearing a plain black linen dress and a cognac-coloured blouse, with a pendant I hadn't seen before – a very thin metal disc the size of a saucer hanging from braided leather thongs.

'Goethe couldn't write unless he was perfectly calm,' claimed Grandmother. I didn't doubt for a second that she had just thought that one up to show my mother her own limitations.

49

'Poor man.' Unimpressed, my mother cut the strawberry tart. 'And before you ask,' she told Grandmother, 'no, I didn't make the pastry case myself, I bought it. Goethe had his Christiane to cook and bake for him. I'm not that lucky.'

'Well, Goethe was a poet,' said Grandmother.

'And all I write is crime stories.' My mother put a piece of tart on Grandmother's plate and smiled affectionately at her.

'Which I love reading,' I said, coming to her aid.

'But you girls won't be writing essays on thrillers like that for your final school exams,' said Grandmother. 'Whereas Goethe's *Faust* . . .'

'Oh, do stop going on about it, Mother. Eat your tart and enjoy this fine weather.'

'Strawberries.' Grandmother picked up her plate and inspected her piece of tart. 'Do you buy them here in the village?'

My mother nodded. 'And please don't say you think the strawberry farmer is a modern-day slave-driver. We've argued about that for hours already.'

Grandmother ended the argument by beginning to eat. 'That murder,' she said after her first cup of coffee. 'It dwells on my mind.'

My mother nodded, glancing at me. 'I'm glad Jenna has moved into Bröhl. I wouldn't like to think of her out and about in the dark near here.'

'Do the police think the murderer's still around somewhere?'

My mother shrugged her shoulders. 'They don't even know if he's a local man. After all, the other two murders that may also have been his work were committed in north Germany.'

'So it doesn't matter where I happen to be out and about after dark,' I tried to joke.

They both looked daggers at me.

'This is no laughing matter,' my mother reproved me.

'The reason why she has no understanding of the gravity of the situation,' Grandmother said snidely, 'is because she grew up in a house full of corpses.'

'Thank you so much,' said Mother sharply.

They're both brilliant with the spoken word, each in her own way. Neither of them is ever at a loss for an answer. Their clashes have real class, but it's better not to come between them.

'Do you mind if I just go and buy a few strawberries?' I asked. 'Caro and Merle are keen to have some. I promised to bring them back.'

They shook their heads, secretly sharpening their beaks to carry on the argument.

It was a day straight out of a picture book so I decided to walk. Edgar ran after me to the end of the drive, and then stayed sitting in the middle of the path like a statue.

The mill was a good way from the village. In the old days it had been the local emblem, and all official festivals took place here. There were some faded old photos of them which the chairman of the parish council had given my mother as a present when we moved in.

The village lay deserted in the silence of the afternoon. It made me feel as if I hadn't grown up here and didn't really belong. The old, almost deaf dog who was always keeping watch over the little church was so fast asleep that he didn't notice me passing. The cats stretching out in the sun on the windowsills and front steps of the farmhouses ignored me.

If their owners had been outside they'd have behaved much the same. They'd have eyed me suspiciously, waiting for me to speak first, would have responded with a nod or a mutter and then watched me go on. A mother whose crime stories can be seen on television doesn't exactly get you a warm invitation to share in the life of the village.

But I didn't want to anyway. I liked the village. I loved the plain, simple farms, the paved paths, the picturesque corners tucked away here and there, the sound of the tractors, and I'd got used to the smell of drains, pigs and chickens. I liked the open fields, the scent of strawberries, the villagers themselves and even their tight-lipped manner. So long as they kept their distance. I didn't want to get involved in their petty quarrels.

The woman who came to clean for my mother often told us about those. Scuffles at festive occasions, threats, telephone persecution. 'Funny things do happen.' That was the way her stories always began.

My mother never objected to these conversations. She often said that if they didn't exist then you'd have to invent them. 'That's life,' she said. 'Imagination can never compete with it.'

The other people who lived in the village didn't come near the mill. Times had changed. My mother could have been living on an island.

For the first time I realized how isolated she was here.

There wasn't a soul to be seen in the strawberry farmer's yard either. The walls cast long shadows. It was so hot that my hair was sticking to the back of my neck. I pressed the bell next to the window of the sales room and waited.

After a while the window opened. A girl of about my own age looked out.

'Yes?'

I ignored her unfriendly manner. 'Two kilos of strawberries, please,' I said.

Without a word, she put four blue plastic punnets filled to the brim on the windowsill. I could see lavishly flowered wallpaper behind her and an old-fashioned, dark kitchen dresser.

'How much?' I asked. A few years in this village and I'd forget how to talk in complete sentences.

'Five euros.'

I paid, the window was closed and I went back into the sleepy village street.

The strawberry pickers were all in the fields; they'd swarmed out like big colourful birds.

The words sound like poetry, I thought. Strawberry pickers.

I'd forgotten to bring my mother's shopping basket, and held the four punnets stacked in front of my stomach, a very unsteady arrangement. The berries were plump and red. Their aroma surrounded me like perfume.

The old dog outside the church had woken up. He thumped the tip of his tail on the ground, not very hard, and looked at me as I passed.

'Hi, you,' I said, and he seemed to have heard me, because he whined quietly.

If I hadn't been balancing the punnets in front of me I might have patted him, in spite of his dull black coat. Probably no one else did. I felt his eyes following me and tried to shake off my rising sense of guilt.

At home, I put the strawberries in the kitchen and went back out onto the terrace. The little walk had done me good. My toes felt warm and dusty in my sandals. My body felt as if it had soaked up the sun. I put my head back and closed my eyes.

Mother and Grandmother had finished their exchange of hostilities and were talking peacefully. The birds were twittering in the trees. A sheep bleated now and then. You could hear a tractor chugging in the distance.

Sometime, Caro, Merle and I had decided, we'd go and spend a year in London. But until that time came I was glad to be living in pretty little Bröhl, and coming out here into the country now and then.

The hustle and bustle of a big city was wonderful for a few hours, but after that it made me nervous. I often felt as if I'd been born too late and I really belonged in some quite different century.

* * *

Bert was looking at his wife as she moved busily around the kitchen. He enjoyed watching her while she was cooking. Her movements were so economical, so assured, so attractive.

She didn't like it when he said thoughts like that aloud. She didn't like him to talk about her in general. It embarrassed her to be at the centre of his attention.

It had been her reserved manner that particularly attracted him in the first place. Her composure that almost bordered on coldness. *Ice Maiden*, he had called her to himself. And his burning wish had been to break through the layer of ice behind which she took refuge.

Break through it, he thought. Even then I spoke of love in terms of violence.

It had taken some time for that layer of ice to melt, and it had never entirely disappeared. The moments when they had been completely united with each other might never have been anything but an illusion.

Bert drank his coffee and immersed himself in the newspaper again. He only skimmed it in the morning, to glean basic information on major events. It wasn't until the evening that he got around to reading it thoroughly.

A difficult time, thought Bert, complicated, noisy, fast-moving. And if you can't keep the pace going you're dismissed from the game, and other players bring it to its conclusion.

'Broccoli or salad?'

He looked up, bewildered. 'What?'

'I asked if you'd rather have broccoli or salad.' Recently Margot's voice had often taken on a reproachful tone.

'I don't mind.'

At the beginning of their relationship they'd had long discussions about the best way to divide their roles between them. They had settled on Margot staying at home with the children, while Bert would provide for the household financially.

Margot herself had wanted it that way; she didn't like the idea of giving up responsibility for the children. Even to him.

But lately she had been wondering, with increasing frequency, whether they had made the right decision. As a former bookseller, she couldn't just go straight back into her profession. She would have to work her way into it all over again, and it would be a long time before she was anywhere near up to date with modern developments.

They avoided serious discussions of the subject. Since the children came along – meaning more or less for the last ten years – they'd hardly had any conversations of the old kind. Weariness, exhaustion, frustration left them silent. They often dropped off to sleep over a book or in front of the television set.

'Salad, then,' said Margot. 'That will be quicker.'

'Shall I give you a hand?' asked Bert.

'No need. But you could tell me about your new case – that would give me something to think about.'

Bert put down the paper, got his thoughts into order and began talking. He liked discussing his cases with Margot, and seized every opportunity to do so. She asked the right questions. Questions of the kind that occur only to someone who isn't involved.

Her questions often put him off his stroke, but almost as often that turned out to be a good thing, because it made him change his point of view and look at a problem from a different angle. After these conversations he sometimes saw things more clearly than before.

He told her about Simone Redleff and the girls from north Germany, seeing it all before him again. Those dead young faces. The places where the bodies had been found. Photos of the girls when they were alive, showing them happy and laughing. All those pictures were pinned up on the wall of his office.

'Terrible,' Margot kept saying.

He would have liked to go over to her, put his arms around her and forget there were people in the world who killed other people. Would have liked to kiss her the way he had kissed her the first time ever, when he felt as if the world had stopped going round. Instead, he went on talking.

'Could it be someone she knew?' asked Margot when he had finished.

'Hardly. We've looked at the alibis of everyone who might have been involved with her.'

'So you're assuming it was a stranger?'

He nodded.

'A stranger who also committed the murders in north Germany?'

'With the three cases so like each other – yes.'

'Then he certainly doesn't live in north Germany, and he certainly doesn't live here.'

'How do you work that out?'

'It would be much too dangerous for him. He'd take care not to commit a murder near where he lives himself.'

'We're talking about a serial murderer, Margot.'

'Who's dominated by his urge to kill. I know.' She had a lettuce leaf in her left hand, a paring knife in her right hand, and was waving both in the air. 'But don't you think it would be a mistake to underestimate him?'

'I don't underestimate him.' Serial murderers were often phenomenally intelligent. History could show plenty of examples. 'He could – I'm just thinking out loud – he could have been laying a false trail by committing a murder near his home.'

'False trail?'

'To confuse us. I mean, it's obvious for us to assume that he wouldn't kill in his own neighbourhood. And if he turns this assumption upside down . . .'

'You can't think the way he does, Bert.'

'But I have to! I don't just have to think like him, I have to feel the way he does too. Because I can't rely on him making a mistake and falling into my trap of his own accord.'

'You sound like a poacher in one of those corny sagas of country life that keep getting repeated on TV.'

He laughed. 'Sometimes that's exactly how I feel.' He stood up, went over and took her in his arms. She was soft and warm, and a tiny carrot scraping stuck to her chin. He brushed it off. 'Sure I can't help you a bit?'

She looked at him. Almost in the old way. *Almost*, because instead of kissing him, or just letting him kiss her, she put the knife into his hand and pushed the carrots over to him. 'Into nice little batons for the salad. Do you think you can do that?'

'That's right, go ahead and laugh at me.' He was glad to have something to do. He'd been brooding over the case for too long. After supper he'd play with the children and then try to read for a little. And for a while, perhaps, he might even forget that he was a police officer.

5

When the telephone rang Imke Thalheim's mouth twisted in annoyance. This was a very bad moment for a conversation. But she couldn't bring herself to ignore the call. Now that Jenna didn't live with her any more, she was obsessed by the idea that her daughter might not be able to reach her in an emergency.

She had often thought of employing a secretary, but always shied away from the idea because she found the mere idea of having a stranger around the house a nuisance.

She hadn't even become quite used to her cleaning lady, Mrs Bergerhausen. It distracted her when she heard her moving around the rooms. And singing. Mrs Bergerhausen loved belting out arias from operas and operettas, and knew an incredible number off by heart. After a series of conversations on the subject the cleaning lady had agreed at least to turn down the volume of her performances although, as she frequently emphasized, that took away a lot of her pleasure in singing.

Imke saved her text and picked up the phone. 'Thalheim.'

'This is Lilo Kahnweiler speaking. Good day, Mrs Thalheim. I'm the head librarian of Rellinghausen Municipal Library, and I'd like to invite you to give a reading. We hold a literary festival every year, and so this year I'd be glad to—'

'Forgive me if I interrupt you here, Mrs . . .?'

'Kahnweiler.'

'Mrs Kahnweiler, yes. I have nothing to do with the organization of my reading tours. Could you please ask my agent? She does all that.'

The librarian was persistent, and unwilling to take no for an answer. Since they were talking to each other at the moment, she said, Imke could surely give her the necessary information at once – there was no need to involve her in tedious negotiations with an agent. An unedifying exchange of words ensued. Imke ended the conversation rather brusquely, and turned back to her computer with a sigh.

Her publishers referred everyone who wanted her to do something to her agent. But there were always some people who tried to take a short cut. It was a mystery to Imke how they got hold of her number.

Fame has its price, she typed, and stared at the sentence as if it could explain what life was all about.

She had wanted to be famous for so long, and then suddenly that dream had come true. With the first book she wrote, purely for pleasure and without any literary ambitions. *The Day Will Come.* A psychological thriller that won acclaim from the critics.

Suddenly everyone was talking about her. Her engagements diary exploded. Readings. Panel discussions. Interviews. Radio programmes. Chat shows on TV.

Imke Thalheim. All at once her own name sounded to her like a stranger's. She seemed like a visitor in her own body. It wasn't all about her, it was about the person who bore her name.

About the successful author, and inside herself she couldn't keep up with that other self. For she was still the same well-disciplined Imke Thalheim who used to sit down to write a certain number of pages every morning, then cooked lunch for her daughter, dealt with office work and the gardening in the afternoon, went shopping in the evening, did the laundry and ironing, tidied the house, and maybe found time to read a few pages of a book.

All that had changed, and by now she herself had changed too.

Her agent protected her as well as she could. And Mrs Bergerhausen had become more than just a cleaning lady; she did all sorts of other work about the place when necessary: cooking, ironing, shopping, weeding.

Imke Thalheim had just one thing to do – write.

And it was getting her down. She couldn't come up with stories at the touch of a button. She needed everyday life, with all its interruptions. She needed it to refuel herself. Where was she going to get ideas if not from real life?

She could do without distracting phone calls, but not without all the rest of it. More particularly not without Jenna.

The house was so big. So empty. And quiet. The cats made no difference to that. A dog might have done the trick, but Imke was away too often. She couldn't expect a dog to put up with that.

She deleted the sentence, which was not part of her novel, shifted position in her chair and began to write.

The girl's body was found in a small wood by an elderly married couple going for a walk with their dog. The wife collapsed in tears. The husband got out his mobile, informed the police and called an ambulance at the same time.

Relieved, she let out a deep breath. The story was beginning to flow at last. Now she needed to feel her way carefully forward, and she mustn't lose the thread.

* * *

'Oh!' She looked up at him and smiled. 'Sorry.'

'That's all right.' He moved out of her way and went on along the narrow path between the rows of strawberry plants. In this cramped space, it wasn't surprising if someone bumped into him now and then. Only he sometimes had a feeling that they did it on purpose. He didn't like the way the girls looked at him. It was so . . . challenging. Shameless. Their glances were like kisses, each of them a promise.

Didn't the other men notice it? How could they laugh and joke with those girls who were only after one thing, right from the start?

Whoever you fall with, you'll be stuck with that person when you get up.

He didn't understand that. Grandmother had bowed her head and was deep in thought. She had suddenly looked very vulnerable. Nathaniel had felt for her hand under the table, but she withdrew it again. As if his light touch had given her an electric shock.

'You're not to turn out like your mother, understand?'

And he did understand, but only then. His mother had fallen. And fallen she stayed. On her own. Until Nathaniel came into the world nine months later.

He felt hot. The blood was pounding in his ears. He felt deeply ashamed, without knowing why.

What Hans doesn't learn . . .

He wanted to stop his ears. Or run out. He didn't want to hear the story. Not like this, not now.

But Grandfather took no notice. He had talked himself into a temper. Reproach followed reproach. Before long he'd be taking off his belt and making Nathaniel pay for it.

His mother had had her son, and the next day she got up and walked out.

Walked out. Without her baby. Without him.

'The slut . . . useless bitch . . . tart . . . not our daughter any more.'

Only much later, after Grandfather's death, had his mother come back, married to an ailing man who spent all day in the kitchen, drinking. He never wore anything but tracksuit bottoms and ribbed grey sleeveless T-shirts. He had a tattoo on his right upper arm, a red rose twining around a cross.

And he had bad teeth. Meat and vegetable fibres were always left between them when he ate, and then he picked them out with a matchstick or his long, nicotine-stained thumbnail.

They didn't live in Grandmother's house, but in a rented flat.

'I have my pride too,' said Mother. She worked all day in an insurance company, and did secretarial jobs for offices in the evenings.

His stepfather found a job as doorman at a factory. This post quickly went to his head. His manner of speech changed, and so did the way he moved. Suddenly he was master of the house. Suddenly he was giving orders. Suddenly he had a monopoly on wisdom.

Nathaniel had stopped listening. He had long ago learned to switch off. At first he sometimes wondered how his mother had come to marry the man, but after a while even that no longer interested him.

He was grown up now, and he had just one aim – he wanted to be independent as soon as possible.

When Nathaniel returned from his memories to the present he saw that most of the pickers had already left for lunch. He filled the crate in front of him, took it to the trailer and went to the washroom.

He had the place to himself, which seldom happened. Generally he had to listen to the other men's stupid talk, smell their sour sweat, put up with the belching and farting that they thought was a sign of masculinity.

The canteen was loud with the sound of voices. Nathaniel fetched himself a meal: spinach, mashed potato and fried eggs. The woman at the counter once again gave him an extra big helping. She pushed the plate over with a twinkle in her eye. She was around sixty, and not in the least like his grandmother.

'Thanks,' he said, smiling at her.

That was all it took to make her blush.

Women, he thought, looking for a table where he could sit alone. Never mind how old they are, they're all the same.

* * *

My mother had left the first chapter of her new novel for me to read. She had looked in briefly, as she often did when she was near us. We'd drunk coffee, and talked for a bit, and eaten some of the cake she'd picked up along the way. Then she left after less than two hours. As always, I had a feeling she wasn't happy in our flat. Not because she didn't like it, but because it was my new home.

'Would you look through that?' she'd asked, taking an orange folder out of her bag.

'Sure. This evening. I'm not doing anything else.' I took the folder and put it down on the table next to my plate. At that moment Caro came into the kitchen.

'Reading matter?' she asked. 'Can I look at it too when Jenna's finished it?' She had cut her hair even shorter than usual, and standing there in front of us, so small-boned and fragile, she looked like a child.

My mother nodded. She liked Caro a lot, even more than she liked Merle, probably because with that short, dark hair Caro looked extraordinarily like her. But perhaps she also felt an inner affinity. I'd often thought that my mother must once have been like Caro.

'But only if you'll tell me what you think of it.' She held her hand out to Caro. 'Promise?'

Caro shook hands. 'Promise.'

My mother drove home again. I took her manuscript to my room with me, switched on the radio, lay down on my bed with a ballpoint and a notepad ready to hand, and looked at the cover page.

Murder in the Silence.

That didn't really mean anything, it was just the working title, which sometimes changed several times before the book was completed.

Fine. Makes me curious, I wrote beside it. My mother was happy for me to comment on passages I liked. And she expected me to make suggestions for improvements to passages I didn't like so much.

Merle and Caro envied me for being allowed to take a hand in my mother's books, but by now that was nothing special to me. Sometimes I even had to prevent my mother from landing me with everything she'd been writing.

I recognized her behind every sentence. Her opinions. Her hopes and fears. But I recognized myself too. She'd given one of her characters part of my thoughts, had given me a twin, if only on paper.

At those times I thought it wasn't easy being a writer's daughter, and wished I had an ordinary mother like other people. One I could have talked to without fearing she might put everything I'd said into her latest novel.

I'd read somewhere that artists are unscrupulous about finding material for their work, and it was sad to think that my mother was no exception there.

There was a knock, and Caro put her head into the room. 'May I?'

I put the manuscript down and sat up. 'If you must.'

Caro didn't joke back, which was strange. She cleared the chair where I'd dumped a whole week's worth of clothes for washing, sat down opposite me and played with her fingers. 'Did you ever have a boyfriend who didn't want anything from you?' she asked.

A bell rang inside my head. She wasn't asking me a thing like that for no reason. I looked at her more closely. Even though it was so hot, she was wearing a long-sleeved T-shirt. As she always did when she wanted to hide her arms.

'How do you mean?' I asked back. 'Nothing at all?'

She nodded.

I wondered what to say, but she got in first. 'Actually he told me not to talk about him.'

'He *what*?'

She immediately began making excuses for him. 'He has his reasons, and I respect them even if I don't know what they are. I've had such a bloody time myself, how can I condemn other people?'

'Listen, Caro, it's no man's business to forbid you to do anything!'

She beat about the bush. 'Well, he didn't actually forbid me. He just *asked* me not to tell anyone about us. He said we had to be certain first.'

'Certain? Certain of what?'

'Certain we really love each other.' Suddenly she was lively. Her pale cheeks flushed and her eyes were shining. 'I think he's had as bad a time in life up to now as I have. He couldn't bear another disappointment. That's why he's trying to make sure.'

'And how is he planning to do that?'

'Well, by making us wait.'

'Wait for what?'

She bowed her head, and almost whispered. 'He doesn't touch me. He doesn't even kiss me. Not properly, I mean. He kisses me like a brother kissing his sister.'

'But he's spent the night here with you.'

Caro tugged and pulled at her fingers, making the joints creak. She seemed to be all tensed up.

'Has he or hasn't he?'

'Yes. But he didn't touch me.' She leaned forward, looking intently at my baffled face. 'Do you think he's gay?'

'How on earth would I know, Caro? I've never set eyes on him. I don't even know his name.'

'I don't either.' Her eyes filled with tears.

'You don't know his—?' I couldn't make anything of all this. What kind of relationship was it where everything was a secret? 'How about him? Doesn't he know your name either?'

'Silly question!' She passed a hand over her eyes and grinned. 'I told him my name the very first evening.'

'So what do you call him?'

She looked past me. 'I think up a different name for him every day. It's a kind of a game. Though I don't know why he likes it so much. Perhaps it's like in "Rumpelstiltskin" – as soon as I guess his real name I'll have earned his love.' She smiled, but it was a wry smile.

I stood up, crouched down beside her and took her hand. 'Do you want my advice, Caro?'

She shrugged and avoided my eyes.

'Keep away from him. I have a funny kind of feeling.'

Slowly she rose and stood there in my room looking small, thin and lost. 'It's no good now,' she whispered. 'I'm hopelessly in love.'

'For ever and ever?' I laughed to make her laugh, but she didn't.

'Till death do us part,' she said calmly. Then she did something strange. She took my face in both hands and kissed my cheeks. 'Thanks for being such a good friend, Jenna. I've always wanted to tell you that.'

In the doorway she waved to me again.

I lay back down on the bed and picked up my mother's manuscript. I'd think some more about Caro and her peculiar boyfriend after I'd phoned my mother. And I'd talk to Caro again in the evening so she wouldn't go back to building walls of inferiority complexes around herself.

I picked up the ballpoint and wrote a comment in the margin of the first page of text. One thing at a time.

* * *

Caro lit the candles she'd stood on the side of the bathtub. It was much too light still for candles, but they were a pretty sight burning. She'd spent six euros twenty on bath oil. Even though she was skint. The foam whispered as she climbed into the tub.

She'd once seen a film about Cleopatra. The bath scenes were what had stuck in her mind most. Sheer luxury. And a maidservant for every move she made. Cleopatra was washed, oiled, perfumed and dressed. The ingredients for her bath were mixed according to her mood.

Was it really true that she bathed in asses' milk?

The foam tingled on her skin and felt cool. The water under it was blue, and so hot that Caro had goose pimples for a moment.

She slowly slipped in and closed her eyes. She was doing all this for him. She wanted to be beautiful for him. Especially this evening.

Hadn't they waited long enough? Wasn't it time for a real kiss at last? Real touching?

She could imagine how his hands would feel on her skin. Better than anything she'd ever experienced before.

She had cut her hair for him. After her bath she was going to varnish her nails for him, although they were too short really. She still hadn't quite given up biting her nails.

'For you,' she whispered. 'For you. For you. For you.'

What would she call him this evening? She hadn't thought up a name yet.

'Darling,' she whispered. 'Beloved. My one and only love.'

She smiled to herself. Once she used to think those words were ridiculously sloppy. That was how the old poets wrote, but who said anything like that today?

Once. In the past. But all that was far, far behind her.

Now she was just going to look to the future.

And be happy, thinking of their life together.

Which was going to begin this evening.

6

When I opened the door Merle came to meet me. I could see at first glance that something was wrong.

'What's the matter?' I asked, slinging my bag into the corner. I was back from being in a TV interview with my mother. It had been a long evening, and then I had stayed the night and had breakfast at the mill. After that just two hours of maths, because I'd missed the first four lessons.

The television channel had been shooting a programme on star author Imke Thalheim and was keen to include her private life. Which meant mainly her boyfriend, Tilo, and me.

I don't like these occasions, when I appear as just a kind of decorative object attached to my famous mother, but the younger of the two cameramen was so sensational that I'd happily have gone on an hour or two longer, just to have him looking at me through the lens. His outrageous smile, rather arrogant but still very attractive, had bowled me right over.

Because it was late when we finished, my mother had persuaded me to spend the night with her and bring the whole thing to an end with a comfortable breakfast, just the three of us.

Not that breakfast had been all that comfortable. My mother and Tilo are morning people. They leap out of bed at the most ungodly hour and are ready for the day. I'm an owl, not a lark, and every morning that I have to get up before ten is a severe trial.

Tilo was reading the paper and my mother wanted to talk to me, while all I wanted was to be left in peace to wake up properly. If there's one thing I can't stand in the morning, it's discussing her manuscripts, but that was exactly what she had in mind.

When I finally left we were both fed up to the teeth with our comfortable breakfast twosome or maybe threesome. And at school I found a bad mark for maths waiting. I consoled myself with the thought that things couldn't get any worse.

'Caro isn't here,' said Merle.

I kicked off my shoes and went into the kitchen to get myself something to drink. 'So?'

'She was out all last night. Her bed hasn't been slept in.'

'You ought to be a detective, Merle. You don't even need to have passed any final school exams for that.'

'Very funny!' Merle lowered her voice as if there were a stranger in the hall trying to eavesdrop. 'No, seriously – did she tell you she was planning to stay out last night?'

'No. Must just have turned out that way.' I thought of our last conversation. Perhaps Caro had finally got past her hesitant boyfriend's reserve?

'She didn't have any of her school things with her when she left.'

'Oh, do shut up about it, Merle! You know she almost never sees the inside of school.' I switched on the coffee machine. 'Want a cappuccino?'

'I'd rather an espresso, please.' She sat down at the table, put her feet up on the chair and laid her chin on her knees. She liked wearing socks about the flat, winter and summer alike. She'd knitted them herself. They made her look like a practical, sensible person.

'Want to come to see a film with me this evening?' I asked.

She shook her head. 'Can't afford to any more this month.'

'Suppose I invite you?'

'Oh well, fine!' You never knew how Merle would react. Normally she was rather touchy about money. She'd rather take it from Caro than from me. Caro's money was clean. Mine, which was really my mother's money, stank of social injustice.

In Merle's view wealth ought not to exist. Unless everyone was rich. Socialist system after socialist system might collapse, but Merle was still a convinced anti-capitalist.

I admired her for it. She was consistent, not just in her opinions but in practice too. As a radical animal rights campaigner she always had one foot hovering on the threshold of jail. She kept bringing home people who hid out with us until they found a safer place to stay. Down in the cellar there were stacks of leaflets waiting to be distributed, and before demos Merle and her like-minded friends sat on the kitchen floor for nights on end writing slogans on banners.

In the morning there were often people Caro and I had never seen before sharing our breakfast. They were left over from some group meeting or other, and they ate our bread and cheese and helped themselves to coffee from our espresso machine.

And now Merle, of all people, was fussing like a mother hen because Caro's bed hadn't been slept in.

'I don't know what it is,' she said. 'But I've got a funny feeling.'

That was Merle all over too. She often had funny feelings which turned out to have been right afterwards. And sometimes she had dreams that came true. She could terrify Caro and me that way. As soon as she looked at us with that special, thoughtful expression we were afraid she was going to tell us about another of those dreams.

I pushed her cup over to her and sat down. I'd been through a difficult breakfast with my mother and a horrible morning at school. Just at the moment nothing else could bother me much.

'What kind of funny feeling?' I asked.

'As if . . . well, anyway, I'd feel a lot better if Caro walked in through that door now.' She drank her espresso and abruptly stood up. 'Don't worry about it. Perhaps I'm just a bit stressed out.' She looked at her watch. 'I'd better go. I promised Claudio I'd do an extra shift today.'

Recently Merle had been agreeing to do so many extra shifts that Caro and I suspected she and Claudio were officially an item. Claudio this, Claudio that. She positively twittered his name, and when she was sent a bunch of flowers the other day she'd quickly fished the card out of it so that we couldn't read what it said.

The problem was that Claudio already had a fiancée at home in Sicily, and Merle was old-fashioned in her love affairs.

A few minutes later the door of the flat closed behind Merle, and I heard her run downstairs. Then it was quiet. Uncomfortably quiet.

I turned up the volume of the CD player in my room. Then I took *The Importance of Being Earnest* out of the bookshelf, sat down at my desk and began preparing for the English exam. Quite soon I was immersed in the world of Oscar Wilde and had forgotten Merle and her funny feelings.

* * *

'Thank you for finding time for me and my questions. I don't take it for granted – you're a very busy man.' Imke Thalheim sat down. He made himself comfortable in the other chair and examined his visitor, who was taking a notebook out of her bag and a small pen case from which she took what was obviously a wickedly expensive silver ballpoint pen.

A woman who was good with words, as he'd expected. What surprised him was her beauty. He had seen photographs of her in magazines, but none of them did her justice. He had to force himself not to stare at her.

She was researching the novel she was working on, although she hadn't told him that. He had it from the boss.

'The Thalheim woman has friends in very high places, Melzig. I'm sure I need say no more. Do what she wants, turn on the charm, put on a bit of a show for her, you know what I mean . . .'

Bert would have preferred Imke Thalheim to come straight to him, not through the boss in this devious way. He hated the golf-club mentality: you scratch my back, I'll scratch yours.

'Coffee? Or would you rather have tea?' He wanted to get to the point quickly. The hell with turning on the charm, the hell with giving her a bit of a show. It was bad enough for him to have to kowtow to her just because she was rich and had friends in high places.

'A coffee would be wonderful.'

'Milk? Sugar?' Sweeteners probably, he thought. He'd bet she used sweeteners, with a figure like that.

'Sugar, please.'

He fetched two coffees from the machine in the hall, one with sugar and one with milk. Usually his guesses worked out ninety per cent correct. As a police officer you got used to sizing people up at first glance. A good, trustworthy eye was immensely valuable. Sometimes you didn't get the chance of a second glance.

For a while they drank their coffee in silence and looked at each other over the rims of the plastic mugs. She's sizing me up too, thought Bert. Wondering if I'd do as a character in a novel, maybe. This idea made him feel uncomfortable. Suppose she had the ability to read his thoughts?

'Right,' he said, leaning back and crossing his legs. 'What did you want to know?

She was working on a novel about a sex murderer. Of all things. She had a lot of questions about the murder of Simone Redleff, and made the connection with the north German murders as if it were the most natural thing in the world.

'I can't say anything about investigations still in progress,' he said. 'I hope you understand that.'

She nodded. 'But information about earlier cases, cases that are closed now, would help me a great deal,' she said. 'What particularly interests me is the profile of a sex murderer, though of course I realize that no one can make sweeping statements. However . . .' A smile passed over her face. 'You've probably guessed already that I'd really like to hear *everything* you can tell me.'

Her frankness was disarming. He thought that the most sensible thing was probably just to talk away, tell her the inside story of a few cases. So he began, and she made notes. Now and then she interrupted him to ask a question or make something clearer. Her questions were shrewd and clever, and showed that she'd understood what he was talking about. Her curiosity was impersonal and unobtrusive.

He liked watching her face, which reflected all her feelings. He'd seldom seen such a lively play of expression. He wondered if she guessed how much she herself gave away to an observer.

After two hours and two more cups of coffee, she rose and offered him her hand. 'Thank you very much indeed, Superintendent Melzig. Not just because your information has got me considerably further – I've really enjoyed talking to you.'

'I've enjoyed it too,' he said, and took her hand. It lay in his, slim and cool, and he held it just a little too long. 'If any more questions come up you're welcome to call me any time.'

That seemed to please her. She smiled at him, also a little too long, it seemed to him, and then went out, stepping lightly.

He stood in the middle of the room for a few seconds, then sat down at his desk and called home. Not that there was any real reason for it, but he felt he had to hear Margot's voice.

*   *   *

Imke took the lift down to the ground floor, crossed the reception area with its reflective black tiles, went through the revolving door and out into the sunshine.

That man wasn't like the police officers she had met before. His face was open and sensitive. His eyes showed that they had seen many terrible things. Above all, she had been struck by his hands: a pianist's hands, long and bony with very flexible fingers. Well-tended nails, which she liked in a man. A plain wedding ring on his hand. A strong growth of beard; already, early in the afternoon, he could have done with a second shave. Brown cotton trousers and a white linen jacket, under it a natural-coloured open-necked cotton shirt. He was slightly tanned. His hair was dark and curly and fell over his forehead. Every time he'd smiled it had been as if the room was suddenly a little brighter. And almost attractive. Although it was a bleak, impersonal office.

There hadn't been any photographs on the desk. He wasn't the kind to surround himself with pictures of his wife and children. He didn't need the illusion of home comforts to be able to work – quite the contrary, he—

Stop that. She concentrated on finding her car again in the overcrowded car park where she'd carelessly left it somewhere or other when she arrived. It was an occupational hazard of her profession that she immediately saw a story behind everyone.

Recently Jenna had told her critically that she was even grading feelings according to their usefulness in books – other people's feelings and her own. 'Be honest,' she'd said, 'you pin people down like insects and put them under the microscope, so you can study them and see what you can make of them.'

Jenna could be cruel. She didn't try to understand how hard it could be to get through life without the relief of writing. Fears could lose their terrors in the course of a story, pain could lose its torment.

In addition, authors were chroniclers. They had not just a right but even a duty to take note of what they observed. Of course there were limits. You couldn't just turn people inside out and serve them up to the world on a silver platter. But Imke had always respected those limits.

Bert Melzig, she thought, where's your limit? How far into you would you let me see? When would you begin to put up the defences?

He had been quite buttoned-up at first, and hadn't let out any information about his latest murder case. When he finally did get around to talking he had concentrated exclusively on cases that were history now. Bruno Pupecka, nicknamed the Beast of Altona. Adolf Seefeldt and Jürgen Bartsch, the murderers of those boys. Adolf Seefeldt executed, Jürgen Bartsch dead in the course of the operation to castrate him that he had apparently requested himself.

Every story brings other stories with it. Bert Melzig probably knew that, because he kept bringing new names and incidents out of his conjuror's hat, holding her entire attention, and so diverting her from the present case, which was what had really interested her most.

A clever man, she thought, smiling. Obviously she wasn't the only person able to manipulate others with words. Bert Melzig ought to be a lecturer. He could easily keep a crowded hall hanging on his lips. Would he enjoy that? Or would it scare him?

She had experienced both. Knowing that she could arouse the most contradictory feelings in perfect strangers with nothing but a few words gave her a sensation of power. At the same time, deep down inside, she felt afraid. If she was capable of it – how might the power affect her?

She finally found her car, got into it, put her head back and looked up at the sky. It was blue, but half covered by a delicate layer of grey cloud. Being alone so much wasn't good for her. She was losing contact with reality.

The reading tours didn't make much difference. She was constantly surrounded by other people on them, yet alone, because she'd hardly arrived in one city before she had to set off for the next.

Jenna had been her prop and stay. But Jenna wasn't around any more. She was living her own life.

Perhaps that was why Imke had started her affair with Tilo. He was intelligent, he was independent. He didn't cling, but when he was with her he gave her all his attention. Tilo was a psychologist. She'd been dubious about that at first. Even now she sometimes felt he was watching and analysing her – mostly when they quarrelled.

Jenna wasn't there; Tilo wasn't there much. Imke decided not to go back to the silence of the mill. She started the car and drove towards the motorway. A shopping trip would be just the thing now. Stroll around, have a coffee or a tea, watch people passing by, relax. And perhaps buy something pretty.

She still wasn't used to being rich. Shopping was as much fun as it used to be, lightened her mood when she was feeling low. Once on the motorway she stepped on the gas. She was free. It was about time she began enjoying her freedom.

* * *

He was surprised to feel the tears running over his face. It was a long time since he'd shed tears. It was a long time since anything had hurt like this.

To think he'd been so wrong!

Her face had been the face of a Madonna. Her hair like a child's hair. And he had seen innocence in her eyes.

Had she been deceiving him all along? Or had he just been blind? Had there been signs that he ought to have recognized?

Yet everything had been all right. It had been perfect. Perhaps he'd even loved her.

Why couldn't she have been patient? And trusting?

He pressed his face into his pillow so that no one would hear him. His dry, hard sobs hurt his chest.

They had been just at the beginning. And hadn't known that the end was already so close.

7

She lay there like the other girls. Her body, like theirs, had seven stab wounds. Her hair was cut short, but she appeared to have worn it short anyway, and there were no loose strands lying around. Her eyes, wide open, seemed to be staring at the sky. Such a surprised look. In all four victims. It was the hardest thing of all to take.

Victims. Bert often stumbled over the word, although he'd spoken it quite naturally thousands of times. Victims. As if there'd been a human sacrifice to the gods.

We need different words, he thought. A language leaving no room for confusion and uncertainty. He turned away and went back to the car. They'd have to wait for the results of the autopsy. Meanwhile there was plenty to do. The machinery of a police investigation was going into action again.

He found telling the families worst of all. You couldn't prepare yourself for that – it always caught you off balance; you were swimming in unknown waters with nothing to hold on to.

The brutality of the first words you spoke. The incomprehension in their faces. The sudden pallor. Then the reaction. Some wept and wailed, collapsed. Others stood frozen to the spot.

Those were times when he wished he was more hardboiled. Or should he say more professional? Many of his colleagues had grown protective armour like a second skin. He wondered how they'd done it. He envied them.

At the early morning meeting the boss had spoken of *our murderer* several times. Bert knew this was just a cliché automatically used by many police officers. All the same, he felt like jumping up and shaking the man.

Our murderer. It sounded like taking horrible, insincere liberties. They wouldn't say *our dead girl.* Whose side were they on?

They still didn't know who the girl was. She was young, like the first victims, perhaps even younger. She still had the face of a child.

What a waste, thought Bert. What a waste of beauty, youth and strength. He felt that with every murder. Something was always taken away and couldn't be given back. How much hope was lost to the world through violence, how much love, how much happiness!

Someone like Imke Thalheim ought to write about that, he thought. People ought to be told. So that they never forget again.

The dead girl had very short fingernails. She obviously bit them; he'd noticed that at once. It had been particularly touching. He himself had bitten his nails as a boy. He'd been weaned off it. Spreading mustard on his fingertips had been one of the methods used. And his father had tried sticky tape and glue. His hands had been tied to the bed at night. When he relapsed and started biting his nails again his father had punished him by putting him under a cold shower.

And by beating him. Frequently.

Even today his father still called it no more than rigorous discipline. Even today he was sure he had meant it only for the best.

Spare the rod and spoil the child.

Did this girl have a similar story behind her? Bert suspected that she did. Over his years in the police force he'd developed a sixth sense for the victims of physical abuse. This girl was one of them.

As he drove back to the office he was wondering what link there could be between the four dead girls. There was a link, he was sure of that. He just had to find it.

* * *

After long discussion Merle and I decided to go to the police. We'd tried in vain to reach Caro's parents, but we didn't really think Caro was there.

In the end Merle's anxiety had infected me too. It was an unwritten rule in our flat that you told the others if you were going to stay out overnight. And if you forgot you called. Caro hadn't been home for two nights now, and she still hadn't phoned. Her mobile was switched off, so we couldn't reach her.

We went to the police to report Caro missing. And then, suddenly, the ball started rolling of its own accord.

The officer who'd been talking to us phoned someone, and then asked us to wait for a colleague of his from the CID who wanted to ask us a few questions. He took us into a small room containing nothing but a table and chairs and offered us something to drink. But we were too churned up inside. We said no.

'CID?' asked Merle. 'Why the CID?'

'The superintendent will explain,' said the officer, and disappeared.

We sat in that bleak room looking at the yellow-painted walls. Nothing hung on them except a calendar without any entries written on it.

'Why the CID?' Merle asked again. Her eyes looked frightened. She was breathing faster than usual and rather loud, as if she had asthma. All I could hear was her breathing, the faint murmur of voices on the other side of the door and a phone ringing now and then.

I don't remember how long we sat there in silence before a man came into the room. He was wearing plain clothes, not police uniform. He shook hands with us and introduced himself. He was the superintendent we were waiting for, and his name was Bert Melzig.

He asked us all kinds of questions, and watched with his eyes narrowed as we answered them. It was just like a film.

Maybe that's why I had a premonition. Because I've seen quite enough films of that kind. I felt cramps in my stomach. For a moment I couldn't breathe.

Merle seemed to be feeling the same way. Her face was getting thinner by the minute, or that was how it looked to me. Her eyes were darker too. And huge. She reached for my hand with clammy fingers.

The superintendent was nice. He got them to bring us something to drink after all, weak, grey tea, lukewarm. It tasted horrible, with far too much sugar in it. Still, it did me good. There was something comforting about it, like the hot cocoa I was given as a child when I came in from playing outside on winter afternoons.

But he had to prepare us for something too. He had to prepare us for the film to be real and my premonition to come true. The superintendent asked if we thought we could try to identify a girl they'd found that morning.

'A dead girl?' asked Merle nonsensically. She drank all her tea in a single gulp. The fear in her eyes had turned to panic.

It wasn't particularly warm in that room, but all the same I was sweating, and I saw beads of perspiration on Merle's upper lip too. Her question echoed around the room.

'Yes,' said the superintendent, looking at us expectantly. I was grateful to him for not saying we *must* do it.

Merle's wide eyes said no. Her head nodded yes.

I sat there as if transfixed. I let Merle pull me up from the chair. Weak at the knees. Stomach lurching. The floor beneath my feet felt like cotton wool. Either all sound had stopped or I wasn't registering it.

We drove a little way in a car. No one said a word. I was glad of that too. Then we stopped. Walked through a car park. A drill was whining some-where. Somewhere else a dog barked. A door slammed.

I took Merle's hand. It was icy cold in spite of the heat, colder than mine.

'Oh, shit,' whispered Merle, her tongue colliding clumsily with her teeth.

I pressed her hand. I couldn't think of anything to say. I was trembling so hard that I had to grit my teeth to stop them chattering.

We went into an old brick building. Down an endless corridor with grubby walls. Neon tubes cast a sickly light. Our shoes squeaked on the floor, a sound that didn't seem right here. Much too loud.

The body of the girl we were to identify was lying under a green sheet. I thought how odd that was. Shouldn't it be white? Didn't old stories always say snow lay over the countryside like a white shroud?

I felt a throbbing in my ears and throat. My feet didn't want to move. Except in the opposite direction. My body felt heavy. My legs could hardly carry it.

Merle's fingers tensed in my hand. It was a horrible feeling, but I couldn't bring myself to let go of them. What would happen if I had nothing at all to hold on to?

No one had prepared me for anything like this. I just wasn't up to deal-ing with what was coming. For the first time in ages I missed my mother. Soldiers dying in war are said to call out for their mothers. I read that some-where. It upset me. It didn't seem right to think about that now.

But what was the right thing to think about? The situation itself wasn't right. We hadn't gone to the police meaning to end up in this horrible building.

We were moving in slow motion. But too fast all the same. We stopped.

The superintendent looked at us. As if wondering how much he could expect of us.

Nothing, I thought. Let us go. We were too hasty. Caro's sure to be home by now, keen to tell us what she's been doing. You don't have to show us this dead girl under the sheet. I've never seen a dead person. I don't want to.

'Are you ready?' he asked.

Merle clutched my hand and nodded. I wanted to shake my head, but I couldn't. My 'No' stuck fast in me somewhere, without a sound. Was it possible to be struck mute all of a sudden? For ever and ever? *Until . . .*

A man in a green coat, appearing as if out of nowhere, put out his hands and pulled the sheet a little way down.

There was a rushing in my ears. Merle let go of me, retched and ran to one side of the room. I heard her throwing up.

Caro had closed her eyes. She was white and still as a marble statue. The expression on her face frightened me. Her mouth looked larger than usual. Her lips were cracked and dry. The corners of her mouth turned down slightly, as if she was in pain. Or despised the whole world.

Her dark hair shone. It was still so full of life that it made her pale face look like a doll's.

Something about Caro was totally strange, though. It kept me from touching her. Something that had been quite a large part of her was missing. I couldn't pin it down at first, but then I knew what it was.

Caro wasn't clowning; she wasn't a funny lady any more.

A profound gravity had settled on her face. Final and irrevocable.

She wasn't breathing, wasn't laughing, didn't suddenly, unexpectedly jump up crying: 'Fooled you!' Her shoulders seemed even more angular. Her slight body hardly lifted the sheet.

Tears came into my eyes. I leaned down and kissed her forehead. The superintendent gently raised me by the shoulder. I laid my head on his chest. He put his arms around me and let me cry.

The man in the green coat had been looking after Merle. She was almost as pale as Caro, but pale in a different way. Merle would get over it. Caro wouldn't. Caro was dead.

Dead. Until now it had been just a word like any other to me.

I turned round once more. The sheet was spread over Caro's naked, defenceless body again.

'Please put something on her,' I said to the man in the green coat. 'She gets cold so easily.'

He nodded.

Didn't tell me that dead people don't feel the cold any more.

I thought it myself, and that was much worse.

* * *

A remarkable person, that girl Jenna, clear and direct and very strong when it mattered. Only in the course of their conversation at the police station had Bert realized that she was Imke Thalheim's daughter; her mother had gone back to her maiden name, and Jenna's surname was Weingärtner, like her father's.

Jenna didn't resemble her mother. She did not have the same beauty and assurance. None the less Bert had found her fascinating in quite a different way from Imke. Jenna seemed reserved, almost shy. Her thin face hid her feelings rather than showing them. When she looked at you, you felt she was looking right through you.

But you felt she understood you too. Something about Jenna undoubtedly made everyone want to confide in her. She had a kind of maturity unusual in a girl of her age.

Bert was on his way to see Caro's parents. His car inched along the motorway in the traffic jam. The sky was overcast. The heat of the past few days had given way to a cooler temperature that Bert found very welcome.

Other drivers seemed to be reacting to this change in the weather with road rage. There was much hooting and shaking of fists. Violence was in the air.

A police officer develops a sixth sense for such things as the years pass by, and Bert was particularly sensitive to changes of atmosphere. He had come to rely on his instincts at work. He was careful not to say so in the canteen or over a beer with his colleagues, but his instincts had often shown him the way to go when reason alone would have taken him much longer.

The new murder had been reported soon after the morning meeting, as if to lend emphasis to the boss's angry outburst, and Bert had gone to the scene.

A jogger's dog had found the body. Yet again the murder scene was a wood, yet again the dead girl had been lying in the undergrowth. The jogger, a student spending a few days with her parents, was sitting pale and motionless on a fallen tree trunk. She was still in shock, and answered Bert's questions in a thread of a voice which kept threatening tears.

She had covered Caro's naked body with her jacket. 'I know I shouldn't really have touched anything,' she said, 'but I couldn't just leave her lying like that.'

Bert had her taken home. She had walked unsteadily to the police car, her dog on its leash, with a police officer supporting her on her other side. The murderer had struck at her life too; the girl would remember this morning for ever.

Back at the office, Bert had reported to the boss and listened to yet another outburst. The murder squad had been summoned, the new situation discussed, and then they all went back to work.

Bert had taken a deep breath and sat down at his desk. Next came the usual laborious follow-up procedures: phone calls, conversations, enquiries. Beginning when he had to ask the two girls to face the shock of their friend's death.

At least he knew who the dead girl was now. Carola Steiger. Her friends had called her Caro. A pretty, pert name. Had it suited the girl whose name had been Caro – no, whose name *still* was Caro?

Bert had tried to phone her family, but there was no answer.

'You won't have much luck trying to get hold of them,' Jenna had warned him in advance. 'They don't lead a normal sort of life. It sometimes took Caro weeks to contact her family.'

Caro's parents lived in a dilapidated part of town where Bert's colleagues on the beat were frequent visitors. Six families per building, eighteen buildings on the estate in all, in groups of three. Grey plaster covered with graffiti, the bases of the buildings dark with patches of moisture and cat piss.

There was a disgusting smell, but all the same a woman on the ground floor was busy hanging out washing on her balcony. She was around sixty, with hair dyed orange and a bad case of smoker's cough.

Bert glanced at his notebook to make sure this was the right building and went to the entrance. The stink was overpowering here. He tried to take shallow breaths as he glanced at the names beside the door.

The Steigers' bell had a note hanging askew beside it and stuck in place with parcel tape, their name handwritten in clumsy capitals. Bert pushed the button. Nothing stirred.

He decided to ask the woman on the balcony for information. 'Hello?' She turned.

'Good afternoon. I'm looking for the Steigers.'

She gave him an appraising glance. 'You'll be lucky!' This was evidently meant to be answer enough. With an air of grim industry she went on hanging out her washing. Cheap red and black lace underwear coming apart at the seams. A man's underpants, baggy and grey from too much washing. Polyester tops with busy patterns, short-sleeved Hawaiian shirts.

'Do you know when I can contact them?'

Reluctantly she let her strong arms drop, still holding a shapeless bra. She looked suspiciously at Bert. 'Who wants to know?'

He went up to the balcony, took his ID out of his wallet and showed it to her.

She read slowly and with concentration, her lips silently forming the syllables. A bubble of saliva burst on her lips. Then she folded her arms. 'So who says this is genuine?'

Bert sighed. 'I only want to know when I can find the Steiger family.'

She hung the bra up, adjusted the clothes dryer and fished another item out of her laundry basket. 'Wouldn't call 'em a family. Bunch of nutcases, more like. That Caro's the only one as is any good. Haven't seen her around for ages, though.'

She shook out a shirt with two or three quick movements. 'She's right to get out too. She won't come to no good here. I mean, look at it!' She stopped in mid movement and turned to Bert again. 'Something happen to her?'

Bert was used to taking refuge in vague remarks when necessary. 'This is purely a routine inquiry,' he said evasively.

She felt his withdrawal at once, and distanced herself again. 'Both parents out of work, brother at a difficult age. I don't know no more. If I did I wouldn't tell you.'

Bert believed her. 'Well, thank you very much,' he said, and took a closer look at the building. Junk mail was spilling out of the letterboxes. Two of them had been half wrenched off the wall and were hanging at an angle; the others were battered, as if someone had been letting off steam by taking a hammer to them.

A plate with the dried remains of some cat food lay in the grass beside the steps. Half a metre away was an empty schnapps bottle. Flies buzzed around a black heap of dog dirt. A windowpane on the second floor was broken and had a piece of cardboard in it. Someone had scrawled FUCKING AWFUL WORLD in red on the pane next to it.

Caro, thought Bert. How did you ever manage to cope here?

But he knew the answer. She hadn't coped here. She had made a break and run for it. She'd run for her life.

And then lost it in a wood.

A young man came out on the balcony of the first-floor flat on the right and lit a cigarette. Late twenties, Bert guessed, body-builder's figure shown off to good effect in a sleeveless black shirt. Both his upper arms were heavily tattooed. He leaned on the balustrade and looked down at Bert with a bored expression.

'Maybe you can help me,' said Bert. 'I'm looking for the Steigers.'

'Next door.' The young man pointed to the other flat on the same floor. 'Almost never home, though. Kalle in trouble again, is he?'

'Kalle?'

'The lad.'

'Not that I know of.'

Caro and Kalle, thought Bert. He saw dead Caro's thin body before him, remembered her pointed face. He wondered what her brother, Kalle, looked like. Somehow he felt sure he would be tall, broad and burly. Had the frail Caro loved her thick-set brother?

Nonsense. Bert dismissed his reflections. For all he knew Kalle was much younger than his sister. Maybe a lanky, freckled boy with arms and legs too long for him, a lad who missed his sister, resented his background and was always getting into mischief.

Bert nodded to the young man and returned to his car. A reprieve for the family, but in the end they'd have to face Caro's death. With their pain, their grief, their guilty feelings. Whatever their way of life, it would fall apart and leave them unprotected.

They had to come to terms with not just a death, but a murder. There was a world of difference.

* * *

She was absorbed in her work when the phone rang. Reluctantly she picked up the receiver and looked at the display. It was Jenna.

'Darling, this isn't a terribly good moment. I've just reached the place where in defiance of all common sense Justin decides to— What's the matter? Why are you crying? Calm down, darling.'

Tears always alarmed her, especially her daughter's. Jenna was an intelligent, self-controlled young woman. She was not inclined to be sentimental and certainly not given to self-pity. Imke had seldom seen her cry. In fact she couldn't even remember the last time.

'Dear, if you don't stop sobbing like that I can't understand a word.'

It wasn't weeping. It was pure despair. There was more than man trouble behind this. It suggested something beyond words. Jenna was beside herself.

'Jenna! Darling! Please, please calm down!'

Only once before had Jenna been in a state like this, when she was eight and her cat was run over. Jenna had cried and cried, and finally ran such a high temperature that Imke had called the doctor. He had given Jenna a tranquillizer and prescribed a new kitten. The kitten didn't stop her grieving, but it made the grief easier to bear.

'Caro . . .'

Well, at least she knew it was something to do with Caro now.

'What about her, darling?'

'She's . . . she's . . .'

'Come on, it can't be that bad. What about Caro?'

You could solve any problem if you really put your mind to it. Perhaps Caro was pregnant. Something could be done about that. On the other hand, if Caro was pregnant Jenna wouldn't be as upset as all this. Imke began to feel afraid.

'Jenna, tell me! Tell me what's happened!'

Sobs. They sounded hoarse and convulsive, as if Jenna's tears had all run dry. Imke wanted to shout at her. That sometimes helped when people were hysterical. But was Jenna being hysterical?

'Caro. She's . . . dead, Mama.'

Imke felt two things simultaneously: great shock and immense love for her daughter.

'Dead? But how . . . ? Was it an accident?'

When people died so young they died in accidents. No other idea even occurred to Imke. Caro was never ill.

Jenna started sobbing again. When she could speak her voice grew both softer and more high-pitched with every word. 'She . . . she . . . was murdered.'

Imke almost dropped the receiver. Incredulously she stared out of the window. It was as if someone out there had suddenly turned off the sound. Her mind was blank. And I'm a crime writer, she thought. I write about murder every day. But when it actually happens to someone I know I can't take it in.

Stammering and faltering, Jenna told her how she had found out.

'Stay where you are,' said Imke. 'Don't move. I'll be with you right away.'

She switched off the computer, put her shoes on and left the house five minutes later.

* * *

He missed her. She had left such a gap in his life.

He saw her in his mind's eye. He heard her laughter.

Caro . . .

She'd invented lovely names for him. Romeo. Lionheart. Darling. Jorian. And she'd given them to him like flowers, or the poems she wrote herself.

Her childlike hands.

And then, suddenly, he hadn't recognized her. Red lips, red nails, blusher on her cheeks. Made up like a woman.

He'd accepted that. If she fancies it, he had thought, well, I don't mind. It was wrong. It wasn't what he liked. But he believed love made you magnanimous and tolerant.

But then . . .

But then she'd kissed him. In a disgusting way. Had climbed on his lap, shameless as a cat, gasping and moaning and whispering to him that she'd waited long enough.

In a moment she'd become just one among many. The sort of girl he could have found on any street corner in this town.

Red lips. Red nails. Skirt pulled up.

Her passion had overwhelmed him. Afterwards they lay side by side, breathing hard.

'And now,' she had whispered in his ear, her voice drunk with pleasure, 'now you must tell me your name.'

He did that too.

She'd said it aloud to herself, again and again, and every time it had felt as if she were driving a knife into him.

Defiled. Defiled. Defiled.

She hadn't been his girl any more. She'd dragged everything down into the dirt.

8

The superintendent had driven us home. Merle hadn't said another word. She was still white as a sheet. I tried to get her to go and lie down for a bit in her room, but she shook her head. 'I'd go crazy,' she said. 'Don't leave me alone, Jenna. I'll go out of my mind on my own.'

I finally managed to persuade her to lie down on the sofa in the kitchen. She let me cover her up, and like a good girl she drank the herb-flavoured spirits I gave her. Someone or other had brought the liqueur to the flat as a present once; it was home-made.

Merle swallowed it and shook herself. 'Yuk,' she said, like a small child.

I drank some too, straight from the bottle, but it didn't make me feel any warmer, and my sick feeling didn't go away.

'Will you sit with me?' asked Merle, with a desolation in her voice that left me helpless. I pulled up a chair and sat down.

'That wasn't Caro.' Merle took my hand and squeezed my fingers. 'I don't want to remember her like that. It wasn't Caro, it was just her shadow. Do you see what I mean?'

I thought shadow was the wrong word.

'Or more like her husk,' said Merle. 'Caro herself had left her body long before.'

Merle read everything she could lay hands on about life after death. She was an expert on the subject, and her eerie stories had often given me and Caro sleepless nights.

'Moving into the world beyond,' she said, and paused meaningfully as she always did when she was on that subject, 'is particularly difficult after a violent death.' She looked at me, and I could see in her eyes the pain I felt churning around in myself. 'She wasn't prepared for it, Jenna.'

'What do you mean?'

'She was snatched away from life so suddenly. Now her soul is bewildered. She doesn't know where she belongs.'

'Oh, stop that!' Wasn't it bad enough that Caro had been murdered? Did I have to think of her still suffering in the next world? 'I don't want to listen to this.'

Merle began crying again. I patted her arm. That was all I was capable of doing. As soon as the shock wore off I knew I'd be collapsing myself.

'Shall I phone my mother?' I asked.

Merle liked my mother better than her own – that was no secret. Her parents lived in a boringly neat and tidy house in a boringly neat and tidy village, with boringly neat and tidy gardens like graveyards.

They'd set foot in our flat just once, and stood in the hall looking like shop-window dummies and searching for words. Which they didn't find. Not even when we were all sitting comfortably having coffee in the kitchen, with a cake that we'd baked specially.

Apparently they let off steam afterwards. The flat wasn't clean enough for their liking. They didn't think Caro was the right sort of friend for Merle. And they regarded me as a spoiled brat. Merle never invited them again.

'Yes.' She nodded. 'Phone her, please. Now.'

We were about to offload a whole lot of responsibility on my mother. But isn't that what mothers are for? I thought about that as I dialled the number. When I heard my mother's voice, however, I suddenly felt like I was four or five again. Something horrible had happened to me, and I needed comfort.

I could hardly get it out.

Caro. Is. Dead.

It sounded as if someone else had said that. As if I were just quoting. It had nothing to do with me. Nothing to do with Caro and Merle.

But we'd been in that dreadful building. I'd seen that Caro was dead. I still just couldn't get my head around it.

It wasn't half an hour before the bell rang. We both ran to let her in. As if simply pressing the buzzer would make us feel better.

My mother put her arms round us, her right arm round Merle, her left arm round me. She wept with us. Her mascara left streaks down her cheeks. She looked like a clown.

Then she let go of us, dried her tears and marched into the kitchen. 'What you two need now is an espresso,' she said. 'And then something to eat. What about a pizza?'

We couldn't even imagine eating.

'Merle, what's the number of the pizza parlour where you work? You'll find it does you good to get something warm inside you.'

Her forthright manner couldn't hide the fact that she was anxious about us. I could see it in her eyes. They went from Merle to me and back again, examining us.

A little later (Claudio always gave our orders precedence) there were three pizzas on the table in front of us, filling the kitchen with their aroma. Merle and I realized that we were actually starving.

We ate in silence. My mother, well aware that we usually just had cheap plonk in the place, had conjured up two bottles of Bordeaux out of her bag. She insisted that we both had some, but she herself stopped after one glass, because she'd be driving home.

The wine quickly went to my head, but it didn't make me feel any better.

After eating half her pizza Merle pushed the plate away, took a large gulp of wine and stared into her glass. 'Like blood,' she said, and her lips began to quiver.

From now on there'd be a whole series of terms we couldn't use without feeling a shock.

Blood. Death. Pale as a corpse.

Perhaps we'd never be able to drink red wine again either.

'Is there anyone you suspect?' asked my mother cautiously when Merle and I were almost tipsy.

'Suspect?' Merle looked blankly at my mother. I didn't understand the question at once either. But then it wiped all other ideas out of my head.

My mother was asking about Caro's murderer.

He was out there somewhere. And maybe we knew him.

Imke didn't wait until she was home. She got into her car, fished her mobile out of her bag and called him. Sometimes her habit of storing every new phone number at once paid off.

'Melzig here.'

He positively barked his name down the phone. Probably – no, certainly – she was disturbing him. It was just after midnight. Normal people weren't sitting at their desks expecting phone calls at this hour.

'It's Imke Thalheim.'

He drew in his breath sharply. As if her name came as a shock to him.

She didn't waste time skirmishing politely, but gave vent to her indignation briefly and succinctly. 'How could you do it? Putting the girls through that cruel procedure.'

He didn't apologize or look for excuses. 'I was very sorry to do so,' he said. 'How are they both?'

'How do you *think*?' Imke was beside herself with fury. Her voice quivered treacherously. 'I've just come from their flat. They were shattered, knocked right backwards.'

'They're young. They'll get over it.'

He was right, and she knew it. It infuriated her to hear him reacting so calmly and thoughtfully, while she was spitting like an angry cat.

'Your daughter is a remarkable young woman,' he said. 'Don't worry about her. She's strong.'

Why did she react so indignantly to what he said? Because he wasn't giving her any real excuse to attack him? 'It's all very well for you to talk,' she spat. 'Your children, if you have any, haven't been expected to identify their murdered friend. Your children won't be having nightmares about it. And your children,' she added as a chill of horror seized her at the mere idea, 'your children aren't in danger.'

'What do you mean?'

'I mean Caro's murderer could have been going in and out of the girls' flat. Is that so unlikely?'

'It's not to be ruled out.'

'Not to be ruled out! Oh, wonderful! And what are you thinking of doing now? How are you going to protect the girls?'

'I said it couldn't be ruled out. But I don't think it's very likely. Trust me, Mrs Thalheim. The moment it's necessary to give the girls protection, that's what we'll do.'

She ended the call and put the mobile back in her bag. Tears rose to her eyes. She'd been trying to hold them back all evening, and now she couldn't control herself any longer. In the dark shelter of her car she wept until she felt better.

Then, after blowing her nose hard, she thought about it. Had she been right to leave the girls alone in their flat?

'You go home, Mama,' Jenna had said, her words slightly slurred by the wine, positively pushing her to the front door. 'Thank you very much for your help. But now we can manage on our own, Merle and me.'

Should Imke invite them to come and stay with her at the mill until the case had been solved?

No, the mill was too far out in the country. The danger would be more rather than less for the girls in that isolated place. If the murderer knew them. Which wasn't certain.

Imke leaned forward so that she could look up at the windows of the flat. All dark. So they'd gone straight to bed. And they would sleep soundly – the wine they'd drunk would ensure that. A deep, sound sleep. In a flat in the middle of the town. In a building with ten tenants. What could happen to them there?

She blew her nose again, started the engine, switched on her headlights and drove away. The streets were deserted. As if fear were keeping everyone at home.

Nonsense. It was nearly one in the morning now. The beer gardens and bars had closed. A slight rain was falling. It was cool. Much too cool for a night in July.

The darkness on the country road was black and dense. For safety's sake, Imke switched on her central locking. You never knew. Only recently she'd read about a woman who was attacked by a man at a red light. He had simply opened the passenger door and got into the car.

She switched the radio on. The music distracted her from her thoughts and the horrible feeling that she couldn't cope.

As she turned into her drive the car's headlights fell on the walls. The watermill emerged from the darkness so suddenly that Imke held her breath in alarm. Her nerves were overstrained. She needed rest. And sleep.

She put the car away in the barn and went up the gravel path. Every step she took crunched and echoed through the night. Imke made herself walk slowly. She didn't want to look frightened, just in case someone was watching her in the darkness.

That was her way of protecting herself. No one had ever seen her afraid of anything.

Imke had reached the steps up to the front door when a shadow whisked towards her. Her heart missed a beat. She put her hand to her mouth so as not to cry out.

The shadow mewed plaintively and rubbed round her legs.

'Edgar!' Relieved, she bent down and picked him up. 'You frightened me!' She carried him indoors, put him down, bolted the door, lowered all the roller blinds and switched lights on everywhere.

Home. And safe.

She thought of Caro. And this time her tears were solely for the girl who had been her daughter's best friend.

NECKLACE MURDERER'S NEW VICTIM

18-year-old Simone Redleff's murderer seems to have struck again. His latest victim is 18-year-old school student Carola Steiger from Bröhl. She was studying at the Erich Kästner Grammar School, where the teachers and pupils are deeply upset by the girl's death.

Chief Superintendent Bert Melzig confirmed the similarities

between these two terrible crimes: in both cases the victim was killed in a wood, both victims were stabbed seven times, and both girls had necklaces removed.

A special inquiry has been set up to investigate these murders and the two in north Germany (see our earlier reports). It is headed by Bert Melzig. The reward for information providing clues that lead to the arrest of the criminal has been increased to 7500 euros. That may account for the many calls being received by the police daily, but none has produced a hot lead so far.

Fear is at large, stalking our towns and villages, and it will continue to do so until the police finally act.

* * *

It was horrible reading that newspaper story. Knowing that other people seeing it would shiver in that half-horrified, half-gleeful way you do when you come upon accounts of macabre deaths: it wasn't you, you were only reading about it. As if you had a front-row seat. In safety. You didn't see any danger from where you were. Everything was just in general terms.

Caro's full name brought me up short, as it always had when I met with it before. Carola just didn't suit her; it was much too ordinary, too much of a good girl's name. But I didn't stop to think why, because the news story had infuriated me. It was full of commonplaces. The piece went from cliché to cliché.

Clues. Reward. Criminal. Murderer. Victim. Arrest. Hot lead. Terms I'd read or heard a hundred times. I couldn't make any sense of them now. This was about Caro, and none of those words really sounded like her.

The headline was so tasteless. NECKLACE MURDERER'S NEW VICTIM. As if the whole world were one big cinema, and we were all characters in a plot thought up by someone with a sick mind. It was nothing to do with good reporting, it was pure sensationalism.

The one phrase that did let a bit of humanity show through was *terrible crimes*. For a moment the reporter had put down his cliché stencil and felt something for Caro's death.

I noted his name. Hajo Geerts. I'd call him or write to him. Later. Perhaps. Sometime.

Merle was at school. She couldn't stand being in the flat any more. It was the other way round with me. Like a sick cat, I was hiding away and licking my wounds.

I missed Caro everywhere. I kept seeing her. In the kitchen, in the bathroom, in the hall. I saw her sitting in my chair. Heard her laughter. Smelled her perfume.

Her things were still all over the flat: her comb; her toothbrush and her dressing gown; her shoes, which she was always taking off and carelessly kicking aside; her magazines scattered everywhere; her yoghurts were still in the fridge.

Neither Merle nor I had yet plucked up the courage to go into Caro's room. We had even locked the door. We'd left the key in the lock, and it was as if someone had written on that door, in invisible ink: CARO IS DEAD.

Again and again, almost obsessively, I had to imagine how Caro had died.

All alone. And afraid.

I reproached myself. Wondered feverishly what I was doing at the exact moment when my friend was murdered. I'd been at the mill that evening, being in that TV profile of my mother. I'd acted the part of celebrity's daughter to the best of my ability, smiled obediently at the camera, answered all the questions patiently. And then there was that cameraman. His nickname was Lucky. I thought that was silly but fascinating. I avoided looking at him, but I followed all his movements out of the corner of my eye. Felt his glance, his attention on me.

So had Caro died while I was flirting? Or not until later that night, when I was lying in my old bed at the mill, thinking up stories in which Lucky and I played the leading parts?

How can someone you love die, and you don't even notice at the time?

I left the newspaper on the kitchen table, went to my room and threw myself on the bed. I felt like someone realizing in the middle of a dream that they're in the middle of a dream. But I didn't wake up. A dullness had spread through my mind, and it seemed to filter all my thoughts.

Caro is dead, I thought. She was murdered.

They were only thoughts. Just words. I didn't let them get close to me. Perhaps the shock was still protecting me. But for how much longer?

* * *

Bert had opened the paper with reluctance. Why did he read these reports at all? They were always the same. As if every case wasn't about someone unique.

He thought the emotional bit about fear at large stalking our towns and villages was downright embarrassing, and the suggestion that the police had been asleep on the job instead of doing their duty outrageous.

He'd tangled with that reporter a couple of times before. One face among many. Nothing to imprint itself on Bert's mind apart from the north German name that reminded him of his childhood. This Hajo Geerts had asked the usual questions and drawn the usual conclusions.

Not a spark of creativity, thought Bert. And no feeling for language. Although a newspaper, even a little local rag, could be so lively.

It didn't really matter to him what the press wrote. But it did matter to the boss. Bert sometimes suspected that the boss assessed his officers' success solely from what the papers said. He wasn't just vain, he was extremely ambitious.

Bert drank his coffee, kissed Margot and went to the garage. The children had already left for school. After working into the night, Bert had got up an hour later than usual this morning.

'You have to conserve your strength,' Elias had told him again only the other day. 'I'm not joking, Bert. You're the perfect candidate for a heart attack.'

After painfully weaning himself off smoking on Elias's orders, he was now carrying seven kilos of extra weight around with him. No wonder, in his job. Sitting around all day. Seldom or never walking anywhere. Hardly even time to eat a proper lunch. Usually he just managed to snatch a quick bite in a snack bar or a roll in a café, with mayonnaise dripping out from under the cheese and ham. Empty calories. Too much fat, not enough fibre.

Not that he would have stopped to think about his lifestyle much, but Elias was always on at him about it. So was Margot, who had been following a balanced diet for years.

The car didn't start until the third attempt. Probably the ignition needed attention. Or it was the first sign of something more serious. They'd had trouble with this car from the outset; it was costing them a small fortune.

Driving to the motorway, Bert tried to prepare for his meeting with the boss. He'd be waving the newspaper about again, banging it down on the table and staring at Bert with his face unhealthily flushed. He was another candidate for a heart attack. Bert felt sure his blood pressure frequently reached record heights.

But Bert wouldn't have to listen to his strictures for long. He had an appointment to see Caro's parents at ten. They had preferred to visit his office, which he could well understand, for when he drove out to see them a second time and break the news of their daughter's death he had seen inside their flat, and it was a sight he wouldn't forget in a hurry.

All the surfaces in the small kitchen were covered with dirty dishes. The wallpaper and curtains were yellow with nicotine. Blue clouds of smoke rose from the coffee table in the living room.

Bert had counted six cats there, sleeping in spaces inside the oak wall unit or curled up in armchairs. One was sitting motionless, watching the illuminated aquarium with its slimy green sides.

Caro's mother, a plump, unkempt woman, was chain-smoking as she stroked the black cat on the sofa beside her. Her husband paced up and down the living room.

'I knew something like this would happen sometime.' He kept repeating it like a mantra.

Bert's questions were getting him nowhere. They either couldn't or wouldn't provide any answers. He didn't press them, and offered them another appointment.

'But not here,' Caro's mother had said, and then lapsed into silence again.

On the way back to his car Bert had thought of Caro. What an achievement, getting away from this nightmarish background. He had a very good idea of the part played in Caro's life by guilt and atonement. You didn't survive the kind of childhood she must have endured without scars. Brave girl, he had thought.

He was thinking the same thing now, caught up in the slow-flowing traffic on the motorway. If you allowed yourself the luxury of living in the country and working in town, this was the price you had to pay. He turned on the radio.

One of those new pop groups. He could never remember their names.

They sprang up out of the ground and disappeared from the scene again just as quickly. Had Caro liked this kind of music? Had she liked going to night-clubs? He decided to visit her friends again and look at Caro's room.

Everything took time. Although he knew that, it sometimes depressed him, because the murderer could find another victim any day.

'*Let me tell you something*,' sang a soft male voice.

There were moments when the different levels of reality didn't fit together. This was one of them. Murder and music. Could there be greater opposites?

* * *

He'd seen her in a dream.

She had still been alive, and so incredibly young.

She'd laughed. Had put back her head and laughed.

He had particularly loved her laughter.

And her high spirits. They bubbled over. That was the way she'd lived too.

She'd reminded him what it could be like to be happy. There had been moments when he'd felt happiness.

String the moments together into a necklace and hang them around your neck, he thought in his dream. So you'll never forget her.

He had almost succeeded. But then he woke up, and there were tears running down his cheeks.

He missed her. Oh God, he missed her so much.

9

He didn't seem like a CID man, or at least not the way I'd imagined one. Although he observed things very closely. He had a watchful, attentive face with watchful, sensitive eyes.

Merle offered him a coffee, and he stood up and went to stand behind her because he was fascinated by our espresso machine. Having him around made Merle feel awkward. With her being a militant animal rights supporter, there were worlds between them.

All the same, she explained the functions of the machine when he asked about it. Her voice sounded different from usual, and she paused after almost everything she said. When Merle talked like that she was on her guard.

'A marvel of technology,' he said, impressed, took the first cup from Merle, carried it to the table, put it down in front of me and sat on the chair beside me, on my left.

Merle's movements had changed too. They were rapid and jerky. Coffee slopped over. When she went to mop it up she dropped the dishcloth.

That's the way you get to look suspicious, I thought. He must have noticed there's something wrong with her. But he probably assumed that Merle was still in shock, and perhaps she was too. Neither of us knew how we were going to get through the day.

He didn't try small talk. 'How are you two managing?' he asked.

There was no answer to that question. Because there were no words to describe our state of mind.

Merle, who had sat down too now, shrugged.

He nodded. 'I can imagine how you feel.'

'Oh, have you lost someone too?' asked Merle. She looked straight at him. I knew that look of hers. It was pure provocation. Was she about to pick a quarrel with him?

'No.' He returned her gaze steadily. 'But I have a great deal to do with people in your situation.'

Merle raised her cup to her mouth. Her hand was shaking, and she put the cup down again.

'I'm here to ask you a few questions,' he said. 'And then I'd like to have another look at Caro's room.'

His officers had done that very thoroughly already. And he'd been with them. They'd touched everything, moved every piece of furniture, opened every book. The superintendent had spent a lot of time with Caro's photograph album in particular.

In her photos Caro looked so alive and so familiar. As if the door might open any moment and she'd come in, saying, 'Guess who I just ran into!'

'You know where her room is.' I didn't want to go with him, and nor did Merle.

'Snooping,' she said with dislike when he'd disappeared into Caro's room. 'They even took her diary away. Come to think of it, are they allowed to do that?'

'No idea. But if it helps them . . . I mean, you want them to catch the man too, don't you?'

Merle looked at me with a fierce expression in her eyes. 'I'd like to shoot the bastard.'

'Wouldn't you prefer to leave that to us?' We hadn't heard the superintendent coming back. He sat down at the table with us again.

'You're thinking of shooting Caro's murderer?' asked Merle. She seemed absolutely set on having a fight with him.

'Not shoot him,' he said calmly. 'But we'll make sure he's punished.'

'Fifteen years in a nice cell all to himself, with books and TV, a balanced diet, medical care and everything else he needs? And then early release for good behaviour? Or maybe just three years of psychiatric treatment on account of diminished responsibility?'

'His life in jail won't be as pleasant as that,' said the superintendent. 'The mere fact of a locked door and a barred window can send people out of their minds.'

'And when he comes out he'll write his memoirs and turn up as surprise guest on all the chat shows?' Merle pushed back her chair violently and stood up. 'I could tell you what to do with your idea of punishment.' And with that she left the kitchen. I watched her go, wondering what to do. Go after her? Stay here?

'Give her time,' he said.

'She's not really like that,' I explained. 'She hates violence, she's totally opposed to the death penalty. She even thinks ordinary prison sentences are too cruel. I don't know what's got into her.'

Even as I said it I realized I wasn't telling the truth. Merle did accept violence if it was in a good cause. She'd changed a lot since she joined the militant animal rights group. They set laboratory animals free in crazy undercover operations, and if someone crossed their path while they were doing it they had no scruples about simply putting him out of action. But I could hardly say so to this man, who was on the other side.

'I'm happy to try answering your questions,' I suggested. 'And if we need Merle, then I'll go and get her.'

We agreed on that. He wanted to know just about everything. What had

Caro's attitude to her family been like? Who were her friends at school? Did she do a job in her spare time? Did she lead a well-regulated kind of life? What about her relationships? Was there a steady boyfriend? And had we noticed anything different about Caro recently? 'Maybe small details that could seem to you quite unimportant.'

'She wasn't happy,' I said. 'Although she'd just fallen in love. There was some kind of problem there.'

His eyes were watchful, and I told him about Caro's peculiar boyfriend. How she was afraid he might be gay, and she hadn't known his name.

That sounded weird, but then it *was* weird.

I told him that Caro kept thinking up new names for him. And he had forbidden her to talk about their relationship. And he'd asked her to wait.

'Wait? What for?'

I was embarrassed, talking to a strange man about that kind of thing. I hummed and hawed a bit. 'He didn't . . . didn't touch her,' I said, feeling that I was blushing.

'I see.' The superintendent looked around the kitchen, giving me a chance to get my self-control back. 'How long had they known each other, Caro and this young man?'

'A few weeks – I don't know exactly. I don't even know if he's young.' The fact was, I knew terribly little about him, and I bitterly regretted not urging Caro to tell me more.

The superintendent was watching me. I could imagine what he was thinking. 'It's not that we kept ourselves to ourselves,' I tried to explain. 'We talked about everything. But only when we felt we needed to. I think that's the difference between living here and when we used to live with our parents – no one makes us do anything.'

'How often did Caro meet this man?' asked the superintendent.

I shrugged. 'This was the first time she ever made a mystery out of a boyfriend.'

'You said you didn't know if the man was young. Do you mean it's difficult to assess his age?'

'No, I mean Merle and I never saw him.'

'He never came to the flat here?'

'Yes, he spent the night now and then. But we didn't meet him.'

'Why do you think Caro wanted to hide him from you?'

'Well, he'd forbidden her to talk about him.'

'Did she tell you why?'

'He wanted to be sure first. To know for certain that it was real love for both of them.'

The superintendent thought about that for a while. Somewhere outside a police car or an ambulance drove by with its siren howling. Too late, I thought. No one can help Caro any more.

'Did your friend often have such complicated relationships?'

'She did have trouble with her boyfriends. Most of her relationships didn't last long.' He might take that the wrong way. As if Caro would go with anyone. 'She was desperately looking for the love of her life.'

'Is that the way she put it?'

I smiled when I remembered Caro talking about love. 'Yes, just like that. And she felt sure she'd found it in this man.'

'So *she* was sure? *He* was the one who wasn't?'

I nodded. And I wondered why he'd doubted it. Caro's boyfriend had as tough a life behind him as she did, she'd told me that. Understandably, you wouldn't want to commit yourself to someone else straight away.

But if the someone else was Caro? Caro who'd fall flat on her face for the hundredth time sooner than do anything by halves?

'Where can I find this man?'

Good question. If only I'd known I'd have been to see him long before now. To talk to him about Caro. To ask questions.

'I don't know,' I said. 'I just wish I did.'

The superintendent asked me more questions. He wanted to know when I last saw Caro. When Merle had last seen her. Whether we were in touch with Caro's family. Whether we'd had any odd phone calls in the last few weeks. If we'd noticed any strangers outside the block.

I answered as well as I could. Then I saw my hands beginning to shake with sheer exhaustion. He noticed too, and left. The wooden steps creaked as he went downstairs.

I knocked on Merle's door. She was lying on her bed listening to music, hugging her pillow in her arms. 'Has he gone?' she asked in a voice full of tears.

'Yes, just this minute.'

'Good.' She relaxed a bit. 'Sorry I left you on your own, Jenna.'

'That's OK.'

'Did you find out anything new?'

I had. Roughly the time of Caro's death. She had died between midnight and three in the morning. I told Merle in a whisper. I couldn't bear to hear it out loud.

And the superintendent had told me something else.

'She's being buried on Monday,' I said quietly.

Merle pressed her face into the pillow and burst into tears. I lay down beside her and held her close. We stayed like that.

'Do you know the last thing Caro ever said to me?' Merle asked after a while. 'She said I was a total idiot.' She laughed and sniffed and laughed again. 'Because of Claudio, of course. Same old subject.' Her laughter turned into sobs. 'Though Caro wasn't one to talk, was she?'

'No. Not Caro of all people.' I wished I could burst into tears like Merle. I got a headache instead of crying. Or stomach cramps. Sometimes every bone in my body ached.

'What was the last thing she said to you? Can you remember?'

'She . . . she said thanks to me for being friends.'

Merle stared at me. 'But that sounds like saying goodbye, Jenna!'

'No, it was simply the right moment for it. She'd been talking about this boyfriend of hers. She said she'd fallen hopelessly in love with him.'

Till death do us part.

'Jenna! What is it?'

'Till death do us part, Merle.'

'What?'

'That's what Caro said. When she was talking about the way she loved him. Till death do us part.'

Merle started crying again. 'Do you think she had some kind of presentiment?'

I didn't. But perhaps her subconscious had picked up something that she'd been closing her eyes to.

Till death do us part.

'Listen, Merle,' I said. 'We must try to find this man.'

She went tense with horror. 'Do you think he did it?'

At last, when I thought of that idea, my tears came. Merle put her arm round me and hugged me.

'I hope not,' I said when I'd calmed down a bit. 'But I'm sure he can cast some light on the darkness.'

Light on the darkness. I was getting to talk like the characters in my mother's novels.

* * *

When Bert drove home that evening the motorway was closed because of an accident, and heavy traffic was slowly making its way along the country roads, through little villages that weren't made for it. Bert had a headache and a pounding in his stomach. He turned off the radio and felt his tense nerves relax at once.

Sometimes he wished he was in a job where he never had to speak to a human soul. His throat was sore with all the talking. His eyes were tired. And he felt stressed by the sheer concentration of listening.

His conversation with Mrs Thalheim's daughter had been the pleasantest part of it. It was her friend Merle's behaviour that had given him something to think about. She'd acted as if she had a guilty conscience. Why would that be? He didn't believe it was anything to do with Caro's death. But he'd keep an eye on the girl in any case.

What had really shaken him was the interview with Caro's parents. Cold as a dog's nose. Unfeeling. The woman had filled his office with cigarette smoke, her husband had wandered restlessly up and down as he did at the first interview, hands behind his back.

They had both talked in short, abrupt sentences, not because they were grieving but apparently out of habit. Their attitude had been aggressive, and they complained of anything and everything, including their dead daughter.

'Nobody bothers about us,' Mrs Steiger had said. She didn't explain what she meant by that, just threw the remark out.

As her parents saw it, Caro had let them down. Just made off, wriggled out of her responsibilities. And threw herself at that rich cow, the daughter of that bestselling writer – what was her name again?

'. . . ashamed of us, that's what it was.'

Their daughter had been stuck-up, they said. Always thought herself special. Making trouble the whole time.

'. . . turned Kalle against us too, she did.'

The brother couldn't be found at the moment. Gone to ground. Somewhere. It didn't bother them where he was, how he was living, whether he might be in difficulties.

'. . . old enough to look out for himself.'

The social services were to blame for everything. The youth welfare office. The probation officer who didn't make sure Kalle stopped breaking and entering. Maybe they'd try to get on a chat show. Just so as to let off steam for once.

What about Caro's boyfriends?

'No idea. She was already a tart at twelve.'

For a moment Bert thought he'd misheard. But her father really had said it. A tart. At twelve.

Bert could have hit the man. His professionalism stopped him. He sealed his feelings off. He had practice in that. Once he'd closed his feelings down, the words he heard didn't reach any deeper level in him. That kind of thing was necessary for survival. He'd learned it as a child.

He even managed to smile at Caro's parents. An entirely automatic gesture, and very helpful when he wanted to get someone to talk.

They fell for it. Just as he'd expected.

He listened attentively, noting undertones. The Steigers drew a picture of their daughter marked by a lack of parental love and years of distrust, by outright violence and the anger that they were still expressing. Bert understood why Caro had left home.

He knew how much courage that took. He knew because he himself hadn't managed to do it. He'd suffered day after day from his father's aggressive behaviour. Had lived in constant fear of him. What should he have done? He couldn't leave his mother alone.

His father had seen his wife and son as his property. Their wings had to be clipped, he'd shouted. To stop them getting above themselves. But he hadn't just clipped their wings, he'd broken them.

It takes broken wings a long time to mend. Sometimes it still hurt today, many years later.

Caro seemed to have a similar odyssey behind her. Bert remembered the sight of her bare arms, and his throat constricted. 'Had she been self-harming for long?' he asked.

Mrs Steiger looked at him sullenly. 'Putting on a show again.'

'And?' Bert controlled himself, with difficulty. 'Did your daughter get any help?'

'One of them trick-cyclists, you mean?' Her father laughed. 'That'd have been all we needed!'

The air in the office was suddenly stuffy, and not just because of all the cigarette smoke. Bert opened the window. He was beginning to lose his temper. Time to end the interview.

He did that, briefly and conclusively. Held the door open for them, nodded goodbye. He wouldn't have shaken hands with them now for the world.

* * *

He did his work and tried to feel nothing.

Easier said than done. He only had his emotions under control when he was feeling good. Feeling good. That didn't happen often.

Caro had managed to make him forget. Caro and her cloud-cuckoo-land.

Because of course it had never been anything more. He realized that now.

She didn't live in the real world. That had fascinated him. She'd taken him with her on outings to a world of her own making. There wasn't any violence in that world, there was no hunger, there were no wars. It was a world of complete harmony.

At first he'd suspected she was on drugs. But she wasn't. She didn't need that stuff. She was just naturally crazy. In an attractive way that enchanted and disarmed him.

His mother wouldn't have liked Caro. She wouldn't have been able to relate to her. She liked girls to be quiet, modest, inconspicuous. As she'd tried to be herself all her life.

Unsuccessfully. Glimpses of the girl she'd once been kept flashing out from under that bland façade. A girl who fell head over heels in love. With consequences that had determined her whole future.

To Nathaniel, Caro had been a revelation. She'd been the image of everything he looked for in a girl. She'd been young, beautiful, child-like and pure. There'd been something amazingly touching about her faith in the good in human nature when you thought of her loveless childhood.

'With you,' she'd said, nestling close to him, 'with you I could do anything. Maybe even make it up with my parents.'

He'd liked to listen to her, liked the sound of her voice, which was more grown up than she was. And when she was silent and thoughtful he'd liked that about her too. He'd been able to be silent with Caro.

Strawberries. Endless, perfectly straight rows of plants. Among them hands, arms, bent backs, hair, sunlight, heat, sweat, sounds, words and laughter. And over it all the intense fragrance of the ripe fruit.

Nathaniel worked in silence. He had no one to share the silence with now, so he kept silent by himself.

10

It wasn't the day for a funeral. The sun was shining. The birds were singing their heads off. I felt as if I'd never seen the sky look so blue before.

Everything smelled of summer. Even the old cemetery wall with moss and lichen growing in the cracks seemed fragrant. It was just before eleven, but already so hot that the asphalt on the roads seemed to be steaming.

Merle and I walked there. We felt somehow as if that was the right thing to do. We wanted to be as keenly aware as possible of being with Caro on her last journey.

Her last journey. I'd never really been able to make much of that expression before. Early in the morning, when I was lying in bed and couldn't sleep, it had made me cry.

'We ought to have kept watch over Caro last night,' said Merle. She'd gone to sleep with those words on her lips and got up saying the same thing. In between she had guilty feelings. 'We didn't even ask for a wake.' She blinked at the sun. 'And now there's nothing we can do about it.'

I linked arms with her. 'Stop tormenting yourself, Merle. We wanted to remember Caro the way she was, right?'

Merle nodded vigorously. She was desperately grasping at every straw I held out to her.

'Anyway, we'd have been too late.' Dead people, Merle had once assured me, can still hear and feel for several hours after they die. In those hours, she said, it was important to be with them, talk to them, touch them.

'Caro had been dead too long. She wouldn't have known we were there.'

We were both fighting back tears. We walked the rest of the way in silence.

If we'd thought we'd be the first we were wrong. The car park was crowded with cars gleaming in the sun. Outside the chapel of rest, people were standing about in small groups. Most of them wore black. Here and there you saw a dab of white or a bright colour shining like a flower.

Almost our whole school year was there. And Mellenböck, the teacher who was in charge of our year.

'Him, of all people,' whispered Merle. 'Hasn't he done enough to Caro already?'

Mellenböck taught physics. That is, if he got around to it, because mostly we spent his lessons eating the cakes we had to bring if we'd forgotten our homework or our books.

To Mellenböck, someone like Caro was a second-class citizen, and he let her know it. Every time it was Caro's turn to bring a cake she used to cut a special slice for Mellenböck and spit on it.

We took no notice of him. We went into the chapel of rest and sat down in the second row.

The coffin was surrounded by a sea of flowers and wreaths. It was made of oak, and it looked stern and cruel with its cold metal hinges. The arrangement of white roses on it made no difference. There were candlesticks among the sheaves of flowers and the wreaths. The candle-flames flickered in the draught.

They'd dimmed the lights in the chapel, and it was as if life had been shut out along with the sunlight.

Caro was dead. But she'd been a sun-worshipper when she was alive. Darkness made her feel sad. She'd always driven it away by lighting candles.

She wouldn't have liked it in here, in spite of the candles. The flowers smelled of death. The candlelight wasn't the comfortable kind. The whole arrangement was devout and chilly in a way that really got to me.

'I'm not going to be able to stand this,' Merle whispered.

'Yes, you are.' Even I could hear that what I'd said didn't sound encouraging but abrupt, almost like an order.

The rows filled up. I thought how odd it was that Caro, who had always felt uncomfortable in crowds of people, should bring such a crowd here after her death.

The front row stayed empty for a long time. Then Caro's parents and her brother, Kalle, arrived. Stony expressions. Fixed, pale faces. Kalle looked round for us and smiled uncertainly. You could see he'd been crying.

A little later more relations came in. They sat down, making a lot of noise, looked around without embarrassment, whispered to each other, disturbed the silence.

The pastor took his place at the lectern and leafed through a thick book in front of him. Merle and I had discussed the funeral with him and fixed it that we could say something at the end. I felt my stomach lurch when I thought of standing up, going to the front of the chapel with everyone watching, and then having to speak in public too. Merle obviously felt the same. Her hand was damp and sweaty. I held it tight, though.

Words. Prayers. Music. Caro had liked gospel singing, and there was a local gospel group that had offered to sing today. Their lovely voices filled the room, and I hoped Caro could hear them from somewhere.

Then the pastor nodded to us, and we went up to the front.

'You do it,' Merle whispered. She pressed the notes we'd made in advance into my hand.

I felt weak at the knees. I looked at the expectant faces. They were a bit blurred, like faces in a dream. I was terribly afraid of bursting into tears.

But suddenly I was quite calm. Suddenly I knew what I wanted to say. I crumpled up the notes.

'Caro,' I said, and listened to my own voice for a moment, 'I don't know if you can see me and hear me. I do hope you can. Because I have something to say to you.'

I hadn't thought all this out. Even so, I wasn't afraid I might get stuck. This was something between Caro and me, and I wanted to bring it to a proper end.

'You didn't just die. You were murdered.'

Whispering passed through the rows, rustling. People sat up straight. But I wasn't going to be stopped now.

'I wish I knew what kind of explanation God would give for that. But he doesn't talk to us human beings. And being God, he doesn't have to give reasons for what he allows to happen.'

Out of the corner of my eye I saw the pastor putting his hand over his face, a helpless gesture, because he could hardly stop me in front of all these people.

'There was still so much you were going to do in your life. Most of all, you wanted to be happy.'

Merle reached for my hand. I could tell that she was crying.

'They haven't found your murderer yet. Perhaps he thinks he'll get away with it. I'm not prepared to forgive him. I hate and detest him. He hurt you. He stole your life from you.'

Merle wiped her eyes. I suddenly saw a number of handkerchiefs being taken out, and I met my mother's anxious eyes. But I hadn't finished yet.

People were whispering. I didn't mind.

'I won't give up until he's been arrested. So that he can pay for what he did to you. That's a promise, Caro, and you know we've always kept our promises to each other. I'll find that man.'

After those last words my calm deserted me, and I began shaking all over.

FAREWELL TO CAROLA – AMAZING SCENES

Yesterday Carola Steiger, the Necklace Murderer's youngest victim, was buried at the Forest Cemetery. The chapel of rest could not hold the crowd of mourners who had come to say goodbye to the girl who was so brutally murdered, and some were forced to stay outside.

The mourners included bestselling author Imke Thalheim. Her daughter, Jenna Weingärtner, a close friend of the murder victim, made a moving but sensational farewell address in which she threatened the murderer, saying she would find him and bring him to justice.

Later, Pastor Friedhelm Offtermatt made it clear that he deplored any ideas of revenge and retribution. He asked the mourners to pray for Carola and also for her murderer, a man who had 'gone astray'.

Amidst the commotion that then broke out, Jenna Weingärtner and her friend stood up and left the chapel. Many of the mourners followed them and waited outside to accompany the coffin to its grave.

Bert spared himself the rest. He'd read the report so many times already that he knew it by heart. For once, Hajo Geerts had not exaggerated. And for some reason, Bert didn't know why, he'd even refrained from making a meal of what happened.

Sensational and *commotion* were mild terms for the turmoil that had broken out after the pastor's closing words. 'Please!' the pastor had called. 'Please, I beg you, calm down. This is a funeral!'

'Exactly!' Bert had heard a man at the back shout. 'A funeral! Remember that, will you?'

Bert had hoped Caro would have a dignified and appropriate funeral service. But while he was sorry things had got out of control, it had crossed his mind that the conflicting emotions expressed here were not at all inappropriate.

A young girl had been murdered. That was monstrous. It called for a more meaningful response than a few biblical platitudes.

Bert suspected that the journalist's restraint had something to do with Jenna. She had been impressive. Her clear voice filled every corner of the chapel of rest, and the urgency of her words had reached everyone there.

Including Bert. He had admired Jenna's courage. And Merle's endurance, for although she couldn't stop crying she had not left her friend's side. But in spite of the respect Bert felt for both girls he was extremely annoyed by their conduct. Jenna had unmistakably threatened Caro's murderer. That's the last thing I need just now, thought Bert, a couple of avenging angels getting under my feet.

Something told him that Jenna's vow was not to be dismissed lightly. That girl meant what she said. Which didn't just mean she could make life difficult for the police; she might possibly put herself in danger too.

He stood up and went to the large pinboard that covered almost the entire surface of the wall between the door and window of his office. Bert used it to sort out his ideas.

He had pinned all sorts of things to it. Photographs of the murder victims and the places where their bodies had been found. Newspaper cuttings. Notes on which he had scribbled down his thoughts. Drawings of the necklaces the victims had been wearing. A map of the local areas where the crimes had been committed, with crosses marking the spots. A similar map from north Germany.

Sometimes Bert shifted one of his notes. There was constant movement on that wall. Each incident kept taking new shape.

A policewoman on Bert's team who had gone to Caro's funeral too had unobtrusively taken photographs of the mourners. Bert had printed out some of them and pinned them up on the board.

It was extremely unlikely that the murderer had been among the crowd. On the other hand, such things had been known to happen. Many murderers acted like artists standing back to look at their completed work and present it to the public.

Usually Bert had no difficulty in slipping into a murderer's skin. He didn't find it too hard to understand such a person's motives and follow their thought processes. Because there's a potential murderer in every one of us, he thought. Only most people don't like to admit it.

He looked at the photos of the funeral. Upright, decent citizens come to mourn together. So many that a strange face wouldn't have attracted attention.

And suppose the murderer was mourning Caro himself? What had been his connection to the dead girl? Was she a victim chosen at random? Or had the murderer known her?

Perhaps even loved her, thought Bert. Possibly loved her too much. Or too little. He sat down at his desk again and drew Caro's diary towards him.

Her handwriting was familiar to him by now, hastily scribbled and clumsy, leaning slightly to the left as if about to fall on its back any moment. Typical diary handwriting, plain and honest. Caro had been sure that no one would ever read her most secret thoughts.

She used straightforward language without flourishes or roundabout phrases. Sometimes she was angry with life, letting off steam about her disgust with other people. And her self-hatred.

Caro had not been kind to herself. She hadn't liked herself much. And she hadn't expected life to be good to her.

Until she met this man. Then her emotions had leaped and danced.

2 July

All my thoughts are full of him. I'm flying, I'm floating, I have butterfly wings. I feel as if I've known him for ever. Then again he seems like a stranger. Perhaps that's how it is when you're really in love.

All the other boys and men I've ever known pale beside him. What on earth did I see in them?

He looks at me, and the look in his eyes silences me. I'd do anything for him, anything.

3 July

He doesn't have much spare time. I long for the hours when I can see him. I'm hungry for the sound of his voice, the smell of his skin, the few touches he'll allow.

I don't understand why he's so odd about that. As if he were afraid of my hands and my lips. He seems to like just looking at me best. Looking and looking. Until I feel embarrassed and start to laugh.

4 July

Didn't see him again today.

A lost day. Black. Black. Black.

Where are you, dearest?

I don't even know his name.

5 July
He kissed me! At last!
His breath smelled of summer and sun.

Love made her almost lyrical. Bert carefully turned the next page. Everything she said was so much alive, so hopeful, so exuberantly happy. Although doubts gradually crept in.

6 July
Why can't I tell the others? For the first time ever I'm lying to Jenna and Merle. But he wants to keep it a secret. He says he's had bad experiences.

Bad experiences! Is that meant to be a joke? My life is a patchwork quilt made of nothing but bad experiences.

7 July
As if we were just acting out our love. For an invisible audience. As if someone had written the screenplay in advance.

Never mind what I say, he just doesn't listen. 'It's still too soon.' That's what he says, every time.

He can be very affectionate. But sometimes he's cold and abrupt. Then he looks at me in a way that scares me. I haven't found out yet why his moods change so suddenly. There must be something that triggers them.

8 July
I love him, love him, love him!

9 July
He doesn't like me to wear make-up. Or sexy clothes. He doesn't know the first thing about fashion, and he's more antiquated than the Pope. But I love even that about him.

He hates it when I talk or laugh too loud. He thinks it's vulgar. I didn't know there were men who still used that word. Sometimes he talks like a character in a Rosamunde Pilcher novel.

In fact there are a lot of things he doesn't like. But I'm glad he tells me what they are. That way I can make sure I don't annoy him.

10 July
I don't think he'd like it if he knew I write a diary either. So I must never tell him! Because I can't do without my diary even for love of him. It's helped me to stay alive all these years.

Stay alive. Bert went to the coffee machine in the passage, put in fifty cents and watched the brown plastic cup drop out. The machine made a couple of noises that sounded as if it were giving up the ghost, and then dribbled out the coffee in a thin stream.

Perhaps, thought Bert, sipping his hot coffee and slowly returning to his office, perhaps I'm on quite the wrong track following this trail. But it's all I've got.

His feelings told him he must find the man Caro had written about in her diary, the man who seemed to have occupied all her thoughts. It hadn't been a normal relationship.

Bert remembered those first weeks with Margot. When he had finally conquered her he'd been beside himself. He had gone through the days in a dazed state of happiness, getting on everyone's nerves with his talk of love. It would have been unthinkable for him not to tell anyone about it. It would have torn him apart.

11 July

I'd like to write sonnets. About him. About me. About us. And scatter them all over town from a plane. So everyone can read them. So everyone will know - this is the man I love.

But I'm not even allowed to talk about it.

'What about Jenna and Merle?' I asked him. 'We've always told each other everything.'

'It's only for a short time,' he said, and he looked at me in a way that made my heart begin to flutter like a captured bird. 'After that you can print it in the newspaper if you like!'

He took me in his arms, and I wanted to unbutton his shirt. But he held my hands tight and kissed me. And then he began to talk about something or other, and the mood was broken.

Thoughtfully Bert drank his coffee. It tasted remarkably good for coffee out of a machine. Perhaps the caffeine would get his brain moving. He felt slow and lethargic.

An hour later he closed Caro's diary and pushed it to one side. He must try to stay objective. This girl and her story were getting too close to him. That wasn't a good idea. He must keep a cool view of the case. That was the only way to succeed. The fate of a victim ought never to touch him too much personally.

He thought of Caro's thin little face. Her slight body. Her sharp shoulders. Her bitten fingernails, and the scars on her arms and legs.

Sighing, he drew all the documents on the case towards him. There were quite a number of them by now. He would have loved to immerse himself in something else, just to take his mind off the case, but everything on his desk revolved around Caro.

When his policewoman partner came into the room to discuss something with him, he snapped at her for no reason. She just raised her eyebrows. They'd been working together as a team for years, and knew each other's strengths and weaknesses as if they were an old married couple.

'Sorry,' he said. 'I don't know why this case is getting under my skin so badly.'

It was because Caro had been very like him. Because she had suffered, as he had. But that was no one else's business.

* * *

Imke Thalheim was anxious about her daughter. She tried to suppress her anxiety, just as she tried to suppress all feelings that threatened her peace of mind. Writing normally helped her.

So she had gone back to the watermill after the funeral, fed the cats, made a cup of tea – Winter Magic blend, even though winter was very far away – and took it out on the terrace with her to get into the writing mood.

It didn't work. She'd been unable to do anything but worry all day. She had phoned first her mother and then Tilo, who was at a congress in Amsterdam. Even talking to them hadn't been any help.

After a sleepless night she was sitting on the terrace again now, with another cup of Winter Magic. Perhaps she'd manage to write a few lines today.

High summer had come very early this year. The sun was blazing down on the meadows. Imke looked at the sheep grazing peacefully. The cats lying about lazily in the shade of the barn. Perching on a fence post, a buzzard returned her gaze, unmoving.

These familiar sights were a slight comfort, but they couldn't dispel the anxiety that had Imke in its clutches. How could Jenna put herself in such danger? Had she gone out of her mind?

Speaking directly to the murderer. Even threatening him!

She felt chilled to the bone. Perhaps the murderer had been among the mourners in the chapel. Perhaps he had heard Jenna, had even decided to take her up on her challenge!

Imke's hands were numb. She put her cup back on the table and massaged her fingers. How was she going to write a single line if she was in such a state?

The doorbell rang. Imke got up and went indoors to answer it.

Tilo was standing outside smiling his own special smile. 'I felt I wanted to see you,' he said, pulling her close.

'Why aren't you in Amsterdam?' Imke kissed the place on his throat that was so delightfully sensitive. She could smell the perspiration under his arms, and somehow it did her good. 'The congress can't be over yet.'

'I took the last day off.' He held her a little way away from him and looked searchingly at her. 'You're looking good. Just a little pale around the nose. Tired?'

She shook her head and went into the kitchen ahead of him. Took a cup out of the cupboard. 'I'm just having tea. Would you like some?'

An unnecessary question. He was a tea addict, and never turned a cup down. Winter Magic was not one of his favourite blends, but he wasn't complaining. He looked concerned about something.

'Is there some problem?' asked Imke when they were out on the terrace.

'That's what I'd like you to tell me.' He leaned back in his chair, waiting for her answer.

'Thinking of anything in particular?' He looked marvellous. Lightly tanned, fair hair now going grey, but even the fact that it was receding slightly at the temples suited him.

'To tell you the truth, it's Jenna and her dangerous game with this so-called Necklace Murderer.'

Imke looked at him in surprise. 'But how did you know about—?'

'I read the paper.'

'Yes, but the newspapers in Amsterdam . . .'

'They have German papers there too, and it was in all of them. GIRL THREATENS FRIEND'S KILLER. GIRL ON THE TRAIL OF NECKLACE MURDERER. The press isn't going to miss a gift like that. Particularly when the girl concerned is the daughter of bestseller Imke Thalheim.'

'Those wretched muck-rakers!'

'They live by their sensational stories. You know that better than anyone, Ike.'

He was the only person who called her Ike. Hearing her pet name moved her so much that she felt like crying her heart out on his shoulder. 'Is that why you came back early?' she asked.

'I guessed you'd be beside yourself with worry.'

'Then help me,' she said, and tried to breathe deeply and calm the trembling of her hands.

The shakes had taken over from her numbness and were gradually spreading to her whole body. Breathe in, she thought. And out. And in. And out. 'Tell me what we can do.'

11

He would really have liked to pack his things and move on. The area, his colleagues at work, the heat – it all sickened him. It was like that every time, afterwards. Everything was intensified. His dislike for human company got out of all proportion.

He needed distance. So that he could breathe again.

He still missed Caro, but there was anger in him as well as grief. Anger with her for disappointing him.

He clung to that. Anger was a good feeling. It made him strong. Unlike grief. Grief ate him away.

What about love?

Two parts coming together. The way things ought to be. Two parts joining into a single whole. Round. Beautiful. Perfect.

Then the unified whole broke. Not just into two parts; it splintered into a thousand fragments.

Leaving him lying there. Destroyed. Blown up. Exploded.

Even if he laboriously put himself together again, the cracks would never go away. He'd always be able to feel them. Like scars.

And whose fault was that?

It was always women who set off the destruction.

He couldn't put up with that. He couldn't come to terms with it. He was a man with a dream. He dreamed of a perfect life. A life with a wife and children. In a clean little house in a clean little town.

He dreamed of Sunday afternoons in a garden full of flowers, with coffee and cake served under a sunshade with blue or green stripes.

Now and then friends would come to visit, not too often. They'd all eat together when the children had gone to bed. Out in the garden in summer. At a well-scoured old wooden table in front of the fire in winter.

The meal, the surroundings – it would all be perfect. The table decorations. The lighting. The music. They'd drink wine from expensive, heavy glasses, and eat cheese and fruit for dessert.

All memories of an earlier life would be extinguished. There'd be no more waking from nightmares, no unexpected flashes illuminating dark moments in the past, not even the trace of any regret. Everything would be all right.

He'd have a proper career. One to be proud of. And education. Conversation would hold no terrors for him. His tongue wouldn't stumble.

'Nate! Your turn!'

He came out of his thoughts with a start. Malle was holding his weekly wage packet in one hand and holding the door to the office open for Nathaniel with the other. Dangerous, thought Nathaniel, drifting away like that. I must keep better control of myself.

Their wages were paid every Thursday afternoon. Mostly by the farmer's wife. She did that kind of thing, but Nathaniel couldn't imagine her doing any of the work on the farm herself. Her fingernails were too long and red for that.

She sat at the shabby black desk with a lot of papers and the box with the wage packets in front of her. Looking at him, she smiled. 'Hello, Nathaniel.'

He just nodded. He didn't like her calling him by his first name (as she did with everyone), and he avoided using hers, although she wanted him to. It was Vivian, although as far as he knew she wasn't British or American.

When he didn't return her smile she handed him the envelope with his wages and pushed the receipt pad his way. It seemed as if the air around her was cooler than anywhere else. 'You'd better count it,' she said.

He'd have done that anyway. He trusted no one but himself.

'The fattest wage packet again,' she said.

In her mouth, he thought, it sounded like an obscene remark. Everything about her seemed suggestive. He felt uneasy around her, hated being alone with her. He quickly signed the receipt for his wages, managed to sketch a smile and got out fast.

'Coming for a drink this evening?' asked Malle, who had been waiting for him.

Nathaniel nodded. You had to run with the pack now and then. If you didn't want them tearing you to pieces later. He gave Malle a friendly slap on the back and went to his lodgings to shower and rest for a while before going out to the pub.

Malle was a walking newspaper. And sometimes it was a good idea to hear some of the local gossip. There'd been a lot of it since the two murders.

It was like a party in the kitchen. Merle had invited the hard core of the animal rights group to our flat. They met by turn at the various members' homes, and the meetings were sometimes explosive.

I'd long ago given up arguing with them. Basically we felt the same, but I didn't always agree with their choice of methods. They showed no consideration for anyone or anything when they were going to break into a laboratory or search the offices of firms and organizations they disliked.

Caro, Merle and I had often taken in some of the animals they liberated from experimental laboratories: frightened, anxious dogs; suspicious and aggressive cats; apathetic rabbits. We kept them for a while and fed them up.

Those had been the times when Caro was particularly likely to harm herself. As if the sight of the poor animals was like seeing her own reflection in the mirror.

Merle had made tea and put rolls, cheese and fruit on the table. As a meeting, it was a terrible muddle. Members of the group kept jumping up and rudely interrupting whoever happened to be speaking at that moment.

'That's how it is with people who are really committed,' Merle claimed. 'They don't sit about on their fat behinds letting life pass them by – they really care about something.'

Bastian, Matze, Kika, Dorit, Uwe, Judith, Lizzie and Bob were the core of the group, along with Merle herself. They worked out plans for their operations. Then they got in touch with other supporters, who came from all spheres of society and were of all ages, but had some important points in common: they loved animals, they were aggressive, brave and dependable.

I wasn't one of them, though I did sometimes work with them. They thought of my sort as casual labour, people who could be used now and then but weren't really part of the group.

Caro had been casual labour too, but her reservations about many of their operations were even stronger than mine. Once, during a meeting at our flat, she'd hung a banner on the wall on which she'd written, in pink, SO WHO'S GOING TO PROTECT HUMAN BEINGS FROM OTHER HUMAN BEINGS?

My eyes were streaming with the cigarette smoke, and the noise was almost unbearable. I picked up a roll, fled to my room and sat down at my desk. As I ate I let my thoughts wander.

That superintendent didn't want a joint operation with Merle and me. He'd made it very clear that he wanted us to keep well out of the police investigations. So we'd have to do it on our own.

I put the last piece of the roll in my mouth and wiped my hands on my trousers. Then I went into the hall and stood outside Caro's room for a moment. It still cost me an effort to go in.

Merle and I hadn't changed anything. We'd just tidied it up after the police had touched everything in the room, even the things Caro wouldn't have wanted anyone in the world to see.

After they'd gone again we had opened the window to get rid of the policemen's presence. Until it smelled of Caro again – her face creams, her perfume.

Hesitantly I opened the door. Whenever I went into that room I felt Caro's absence so strongly that my heart beat faster. All the noise in the kitchen helped me not to turn back and give up my plan.

I sat down at Caro's desk and switched her computer on. The police hadn't taken it with them; perhaps they'd copied the contents onto disks, or got access to Caro's data some other way.

My idea was very simple. I didn't understand much about computers, but Caro had been an expert. Never mind what technical problem you were battling with, she could solve it. The computer had been so much a part of her life that I could well imagine finding an answer to our questions on it: a clue, something.

All the letters she'd ever written were neatly saved, and so were her emails. I didn't like poking around in Caro's private things, but I saw nothing else for it. Caro was dead and couldn't tell us anything about her murderer. Where else could we look for a lead except in her room?

I spent more than an hour sitting at her desk; I'd killed three midges, and I was getting so tired that I could hardly prop my eyes open. And then I found them. Caro's poems.

I'd never known that Caro wrote poetry. The find was so sudden that I wasn't ready for it. Tears rose to my eyes. I read the first poem, and it was like hearing Caro say the words.

EVENING
darkness outside
the window
my face on
black glass
pale
far away
another woman's
skin.

A cold shudder ran down my back. That was good! Really good! And Caro never got high marks for her essays in school exams.

GIRLFRIEND
facing me
quiet
beside me
close
no words needed
maybe hands.

I rushed into the kitchen. Everyone turned to look at me. They didn't like being disturbed. Judith was just reading out some statistics. She stopped for a moment, looked hard at me, and then, with some hesitation, went on reading. I signalled to Merle.

She got up at once and came over to me. 'What's the matter?'

Did I look so upset? Of course – I'd been crying, I probably still had tearstained cheeks. I wiped the back of my hand over my face. 'There's something I have to show you.'

I took her into Caro's room and pointed to the computer. Merle stared blankly at the screen.

PAIN
and sometimes
I need more than
this little bit
of life
sometimes I need
fire under
the skin
to know
that I'm
still here.

Merle had turned pale. 'Is that . . . ?'

I nodded. 'Caro's poems.'

'She never mentioned them to me,' said Merle.

'Or me.'

'How many are there?'

'No idea. I've only just found them.'

'*To know that I'm still here.*' Merle rubbed her arms. 'And now she's . . .' Her lips quivered. She blinked her eyes fast to keep from crying.

'I'll print them out,' I said. 'And when you're finished in the kitchen we'll sit down together and look at them, OK?'

* * *

'Think of that, will you?' said Malle, who was already having difficulty speaking clearly. 'Actually challenges the murderer!'

Nathaniel turned the beer glass in his fingers. He knew exactly how much he could take. He was never going to turn into one of those stupid drunks propping up the bar evening after evening. Turning loud and aggressive or quiet and morose. He couldn't stand either sort. There was nothing more repulsive than a boozer's glazed, dog-like eyes.

His grandfather had often looked like that. Nathaniel had soon learned that it was a mistake to underestimate a drunk. One moment his grandfather might have that dog-like look, the next he'd be swinging back his arm to hit the boy.

'Brave girl, that.' Malle clicked his tongue. 'But dead stupid, if you ask me. She'd better watch out or she'll be the next victim.'

Whenever people talked about the Necklace Murderer it took Nathaniel some time to realize that they meant him. The term simply didn't fit.

He didn't feel like a murderer. It wasn't that he had wicked, evil instincts. Quite the contrary. He had high expectations of life and of women. Did that make him a criminal? Just because he had those expectations and couldn't bear to have them disappointed?

Malle's information came from one of the girl strawberry pickers. She liked funerals and had gone to Caro's. But it had been in the papers too, he said. Even the regional TV had transmitted a short report. Though only because the girl was a famous writer's daughter.

Nathaniel hadn't been at the funeral. He couldn't have borne it, and it would have been too dangerous. He mustn't challenge Fate. And he very seldom read newspapers, so this was the first time he had heard the story.

The girl's name was Jenna. Caro had told him a lot about her. The first time he heard it he'd thought what a pretty name it was, and he'd asked what she looked like.

'She's pretty too,' Caro had said, nestling close to him. 'You'll like her.'

He'd put his arm round her, and they had looked for a place for their picnic. Finally they'd found a patch of bright sunlight falling through the trees and giving a little warmth. He liked being with Caro best in the woods, in the almost solemn silence that was broken only by the birdsong. It was still rather cool, but that hadn't bothered either of them.

Nathaniel used to take refuge in the woods as a boy too. Only there could his soul heal after Grandfather had beaten him yet again. How much damage had been done to it? How many cracks were there in it?

'You'd never know Jenna had a mother who's simply rolling in money,' Caro had said. 'I think she sometimes even feels embarrassed about it.'

She had aroused his curiosity. All the same, he always blocked off conversations like this at once. He didn't want to be drawn into Caro's life. Not before he was sure of himself. Getting too close to someone too soon had wounded him before. His body was covered with the scars of those wounds.

'And they say she looks like an angel,' said Malle, ordering another beer. His glance slipped sideways, and Nathaniel knew he was giving himself up to his drunken dreams. Evenings with Malle always ended that way. And with Nathaniel getting him back to his room because Malle was in no state to find it on his own.

First, however, he wanted to finish his beer, and he was glad that Malle would leave him in peace to do so.

Jenna. The name went around and around in his head.

Like an angel, Malle had said.

Who are you, thought Nathaniel, you with the courage to pick a quarrel with me?

Beside him, Malle started singing. Some stupid hit song. The landlord was already giving them a black look.

'Come on,' said Nathaniel. 'I'll take you home.'

'Home, home, ho-ome sweet home,' babbled Malle. 'Home sweet home sweet . . .'

Nathaniel paid and got Malle out of the pub. Malle stopped singing. He started wailing about his screwed-up life. His failed marriage. His kids growing up without him. Hardly even knew him. He swore at Nathaniel for not letting him have another little drink. Just so as to forget.

Nathaniel wasn't listening. Jenna's name had lodged itself in his head. And what Malle had told him. Something had just begun. A game of some kind?

The girl had challenged him.

'OK,' he murmured when he had seen Malle home and was on his way to his lodgings. 'If that's the way you want it, girlie.'

His footsteps echoed in the moonless night. He suddenly felt light-hearted. As if that was just what he'd wanted – a purpose.

* * *

Early-morning meetings were torture to Bert. Particularly since he'd stopped smoking. He seldom slept for more than four or five hours a night, and he felt absolutely exhausted.

Once he'd been able to sleep whenever, wherever and for however long he liked. Now it took him at least an hour to fall asleep. He woke up several times in the night, staggered out to the bathroom and then lay in bed wide awake. Listened to Margot's deep, regular breathing, or even worse her quiet

141

snoring. Towards morning he finally fell into a deep sleep, only to be mercilessly woken from it by the alarm.

Bert spent his mornings in a state of dull, dragging weariness. Doing anything, even thinking, was too much for him. Sometimes his head dropped on his chest as he sat at his desk, and then he woke with a guilty start.

Recently there'd been early-morning meetings every day. Ever since the second murder the media had been cranking things up. The public was hysterical. The Necklace Murderer could strike again any day. No one felt safe. It all put the police under pressure.

Everything felt very sensitive so early in the morning. As if the gods hadn't yet decided which way they would make the day go.

His colleagues pooled their results. Only to discover that there were no results worth speaking of. House-to-house enquiries were still in full swing. People called in with scraps of information every day, and they all had to be dutifully followed up.

Dutifully. Bert stumbled over the word. These days, who still thought about terms like duty, decency, industry, order? They were values of the past, long forgotten and gathering dust.

We'll soon get to the point, thought Bert, where kids have to look up words like that in the dictionary because they don't know what they mean. The next moment he was wondering since when he had started sounding like his father, who was always going on about the evils of modern society.

* * *

Supper was ready; the table was laid in the conservatory. It had been Tilo's idea to invite Jenna and Merle over. 'We ought to create the right conditions for a conversation,' he had said, 'without putting the pair of them under pressure. What could be better than a meal?'

Imke heartily distrusted psychologists. She didn't trust even Tilo when he said things like that. How, she still sometimes wondered, could she have fallen in love with someone who did nothing all day but worm people's most secret thoughts and feelings out of them?

They had agreed on eight o'clock. A good time. They would all have the working day behind them and be ready to relax. Even Tilo, who didn't have a spare moment in his diary, had promised to be there on time. They were having tomato soup with prawns, hot garlic bread, salmon salad with fresh fruit, and strawberries and cream. Then espresso to finish.

Imke didn't very often cook. Perhaps that was why she'd enjoyed it so much. It was pleasant to give herself up for a few hours to the illusion that everything was the way it used to be again: Jenna was still at home, and life wasn't so complicated. In addition she was stuck at a difficult place in her novel, and glad of any distraction.

I always did like running away from problems, she thought as she inspected the table again to see if she'd forgotten anything. She adjusted the position of a glass, moved a knife, straightened a napkin.

Sometimes she wished life was like her books. Wished she could take responsibility for everything in reality too. Create the characters. Go with them on their way. If she had that power she'd make sure that Jenna never had to suffer.

And Caro, she thought, wouldn't have died.

She heard the sound of tyres on the gravel and went to open the front door. Lovingly she hugged first her daughter and then Merle. Recently she'd often felt as if she had three daughters, and now it was a little as if with Caro's death she had lost one of them.

Don't get all emotional, she told herself. And stop making all misfortunes your own.

The girls were looking pale, and far too thin. They probably weren't eating much. Imke couldn't blame them. She thought it must be dreadful to be living in the flat where Caro's room was still left as it had been. As if their friend might come back any minute.

Tilo's car drew up just as they had sat down in the living room. He hugged the girls too.

They moved into the conservatory. Imke had opened both sliding doors so that a breath of cool, refreshing air came in. The heat of the day was taking a long time to wear off. Soon she wouldn't be able to keep it out of the house at all.

'Caro wrote poems,' said Jenna, coming straight to the point. She had filled a plate to the brim with soup, and was now stirring it hesitantly as if she'd taken on too much. 'We found them on her PC.'

'Incredible poems,' said Merle. 'I've never seen anything that good before.'

'Do you by any chance have them with you?' asked Imke, her hunting instinct immediately aroused.

'Not just by any chance,' said Jenna. 'On purpose. We'd like to know what you think of them.'

'What I think of them?' Imke was pleased to see Merle helping herself to a generous plateful. 'I'm not sure if I'm any judge of poetry. I'm not a poet myself.'

'It's not about the quality,' said Merle. 'It's about what they say.'

'Didn't the police take her computer?' asked Tilo. 'I'm surprised. I thought they'd be looking for clues everywhere.'

'They only had to copy the data,' said Jenna, and smiled when Tilo struck his forehead with the flat of his hand. She reached into her backpack, which was beside her chair, took out a blue folder and handed it to her mother.

'That was a mistake,' said Tilo. 'Now all she'll do is read. So much for our nice cosy meal together.'

Sure enough, Imke had already put her reading glasses on, opened the folder and skimmed the first sheet of paper. Concentration was writ large on her face.

'How are you two managing?' asked Tilo. The wine in his glass sparkled like liquid rubies.

'Only just under a week of school to go,' said Merle, 'and then it's the holidays at last and we can get down to work.'

'Work?' asked Tilo, although he immediately knew what she was talking about. 'What are you planning to do?'

'Find Caro's murderer.' Jenna spoke in a tone of surprise. As if she hadn't expected him to be so slow on the uptake.

Tilo had not intended to lecture them, but that was exactly what he now did. A mistake, he thought. A bad mistake. Breaks every rule. But he went on talking, couldn't stop himself.

Jenna and Merle took second helpings of salad and plenty of garlic bread. Politely let him unburden himself. Ate in silence.

Imke, who had noticed none of it, closed the folder and put it on the floor beside her chair. 'Amazing,' she said. 'Such talent.'

'But what else do you think?' asked Jenna.

'What about?' Imke asked in return.

'About the imagery,' said Merle. 'We've spent hours trying to work out what some of them are meant to be saying.'

'A metaphor can mean different things to different people,' Imke said. 'It's never completely clear. Interpretation is bound to be subjective.'

'Well, for instance, who would *the black man* be?' asked Jenna. 'And what did she mean by *lord of pain*?'

'Do the poems connect up?' asked Merle. 'Do they tell Caro's own story?'

'What if they did?' asked Tilo.

'Then,' said Jenna, giving Merle a meaningful look, 'we'd be quite a lot further on.'

'I can only warn you not to take them literally,' said Imke. 'Caro coded what she was saying in those poems. Otherwise she might as well have written them straight into a diary.'

'That makes sense.' Jenna pushed her plate away. 'But codes can be cracked, can't they?'

'Without Caro's help?' Imke thoughtfully shook her head. 'Very problematic, I'd say.'

'But it's all there.' Jenna picked Caro's poems up from the floor. 'Her childhood. Her relationship with her parents. Her self-harming. Our flat. Merle and me.'

Imke saw how eager her daughter was, and felt afraid. The girls won't rest, she thought, until they've set something in motion. Fear reached out and took hold of her. And suddenly she realized that she would never stop worrying about Jenna. A mother's fate, she thought. Sounds like the title of one of those American movies they're always showing on TV these days.

'Here.' Jenna had been looking for one poem in particular. 'Listen to this:

'*QUESTIONS*
you promise me
your life
yet you give
nothing away
while you

know all
about me.

'That *you* – couldn't it be her last boyfriend?'

'Not necessarily,' said Tilo. 'It could just as well be someone she was going out with earlier.'

'Or pure imagination,' said Imke. 'Not all works of literature are auto-biographical – you know that, Jenna. Think of my books.'

Jenna nodded. 'All the same, everything about your real life, our life, is there in your books. If anyone looks for it carefully.'

'Why shouldn't it be a poem about an earlier boyfriend?' Tilo insisted.

'Because Caro dated her poems,' said Merle. 'So we know that she wrote them at the time she was going out with this man we never got to meet.'

'She told me a bit about him. Just before her . . . before she . . .' Jenna cleared her throat. 'Before she was murdered. He made himself very mysterious. Caro didn't even know his name.'

'How long had they been going out together?' Tilo's own hunting instincts were aroused now. He couldn't ignore unusual modes of behaviour. He automatically jumped at them.

'We don't know exactly. A few weeks.'

'And she didn't mind when he wouldn't tell her his name?'

'It was a kind of game – a game she didn't understand. She thought up a new name for him every day.'

'Fascinating,' said Tilo.

Imke glanced at him disapprovingly.

'Caro had this weird idea that she'd have earned his love on the day she guessed his real name.'

'Rumpelstiltskin.' Tilo ignored Imke's silent reproof. He lived on stories like this.

'Caro thought of that too,' said Jenna. 'She laughed at it, but she really did believe it would all work out. A happy ending, like in the fairy tale.'

'Fairy tales are cruel,' said Tilo. 'Did she forget that?'

There was an uncomfortable silence. Imke went into the kitchen to make espresso. Jenna went with her.

'Whoever heard of such a thing?' Imke was angrily clattering the coffee cups. 'A love that has to be earned.'

'A special aspect of love,' said Jenna.

Imke took her reference. 'But that's sick.' She shook her head and started the espresso machine.

'This *you* in the poems,' said Jenna when they were all sitting around the table again, 'there's something rather dark about him. I wonder why he fascinated Caro so much.'

'We'll know once we find him,' said Merle.

'It's not your job to do the police's work for them. And it's dangerous.' Imke looked at Tilo for support. 'Very dangerous.'

'Have you stopped to think that this man may be Caro's murderer?' asked Tilo.

'If he is,' said Jenna, 'then we want to find him all the more.'

Imke knew how obstinate her daughter was. She knew it was pointless trying to make her change her mind if she was set on something. She had never done it in the past. But perhaps there was another way. 'I'd like to give you girls a present,' she said. 'Three weeks' holiday, somewhere of your own choice. How about that?'

Jenna put a hand on her arm. 'Not so long ago we'd have jumped at it, Mama. But this isn't the time for a holiday. We owe Caro that.'

'Yes, it would have been great.' Merle smiled at Imke. There were tears in her eyes. 'But it wouldn't work, not without Caro.'

'I know, I know,' Imke said, sighing, when she and Tilo were alone again just after midnight. 'Nothing works without Caro. It's going to be like that for a long time.'

Tilo kissed her and gently stroked the nape of her neck. But she pushed his hand away. 'Not now, Tilo,' she said. 'Don't be cross, but I have to study Caro's poems. I owe her something too.'

12

The murderer had raped his first three victims. But he used a condom each time, and he had left no traces behind. Caro hadn't been raped. However, she had had sexual intercourse shortly before her death.

They had found a dark hair at the scene of the first crime. It had caught in a strand of the victim's own hair that had been cut off. All the same, it could just as well have come from someone who was not the murderer. The police had drawn a blank at the other crime scenes.

Murders in the provinces were provincial by their very nature. Any traces left by the murderer were often carelessly trampled underfoot. By whoever found the victim, by police officers arriving at the scene ahead of the forensic unit, by reporters who, especially in small country places, picked up the scent of a story from afar.

No definite leads. Nothing you could build on.

Bert had conducted countless interviews. But he still hadn't found that mysterious boyfriend of Caro's. No one had seen him, not even Jenna and Merle. Although he had spent the night in their flat. How was that possible? For someone to enter other people's lives and leave no trace apart from a few diary entries and a handful of poems?

After the diary, most of Bert's hopes had been pinned on the disk with the poems. But he hadn't been able to find any clues in them.

He had distributed print-outs to his colleagues, hoping one of them might have a feeling for poetry. No luck. All he had discovered was that he was the only one who ever read a book.

His colleagues in north Germany were marking time too. And the press there were being as poisonous as the press here. The silly season, thought Bert. The papers are glad of anything that means they don't have to dig out old Nessie stories again.

A special unit had now been set up consisting of the leading investigators here and their north German colleagues. They were working closely together and sharing all their information. No luck so far. It was infuriating.

The local police psychologist, appointed to the special unit by the boss, had drawn up a profile of the murderer. She presented it at one of those early-morning meetings. Their man was unmarried. Inhibited (or possibly the opposite). Son of a dominant mother. Only child. Childhood marked by violence. Strong religious convictions. Poor social skills. Intelligent. Cautious. Low threshold of aggression. Sexually inexperienced.

'Why don't you say *perverted* or *pervert* anywhere?' Bert had asked the psychologist.

'We don't think in categories like that,' she had replied. 'It's not a case of value judgements. It's a case of assessment.'

'No,' Bert had contradicted her. 'It's a case of hand-picking your words. If these murders aren't perverted, what is?'

They didn't get on with each other, that was an open secret.

But Bert would rather rely on his feelings than a psychological profile. And his feelings told him to concentrate on Caro's unknown boyfriend. The girl had not been raped. Perhaps because the murderer was in love with her?

Bert opened the window of his office, took off his jacket and got out the diary and the poems again. The truth lay before him on his desk. He just had to recognize it.

* * *

She was different from Caro. More serious. More reserved. Rather prickly. Kept an observer at a distance. It wouldn't be easy for young men to approach her.

Nathaniel had known which of them was Jenna and which was Merle at once. He didn't have much time for the animal rights movement, or at least not when it went too far. He'd heard on the radio recently that a German Shepherd dog was legally entitled to more square metres of living space than a child. What crazy kind of world was this?

He'd parked outside their block of flats and waited. He'd get to see them sometime, he thought. It was evening and he was in no hurry.

When they came out he got out of his car and followed them. The thought of Caro briefly flashed through his mind. He didn't have the pain under control yet.

'Time heals all wounds,' his grandmother was always saying. He'd have liked to believe her. But even as a little boy he'd known the saying was just a kindly lie. There were wounds that nothing and no one could heal.

Jenna and Merle had linked arms. They were talking to each other, but not laughing the way girls usually did. Their mourning period too would be a long one.

They stopped outside the Odeon and studied the posters. A cinema. That was good. Dark and anonymous enough for him to get closer to them.

They decided on a comedy feature film. He was glad of that too. You learned much more about someone who was laughing than someone in tears.

And then he was sitting behind them in the dark, so close that he had only to put his hand out and he'd have touched Jenna.

* * *

She wrote and wrote. The words were flowing out of her. Caro had done that, with her poems. Imke felt like a parasite. But what was she supposed to do – deliberately interrupt the flow?

The love story in her new novel had gained in colour, honesty and poetry. She owed it to Caro and her feelings for this man who was such a mystery to everyone.

Imke salved her conscience by telling herself that she was creating something like a memorial to Caro with this book. But a persistent voice inside her kept saying that she was exploiting Caro in a mean, miserable way.

Edgar and Molly lay on the rug by the window asleep. They liked the muted typing sounds and the quiet hum of the computer. The landscape outside shone as if it had been polished. There had been a shower that afternoon, doing the plants good.

An idyll. And the land around her was hers as far as she could see.

She'd never get used to being rich. She'd always go around with the secret fear that she might wake up one day and find it had all been a dream.

The telephone rang.

She didn't pick it up. When she was writing almost breathlessly, as she was just now, she let nothing disturb her. Her ideas might suddenly stop flowing, just like that.

Suppose she published Caro's poems, as their editor? Posthumously? As a real memorial to her?

No time to think about that. Not now.

She didn't want to think about Caro's murder any more either. She'd thought about it too long already. It had dried up all the words inside her. In particular she didn't want to think of the murderer. She was afraid to do that. As if she would be challenging Fate and putting Jenna and Merle in danger.

A few more pages and then she'd call Jenna and make sure the girls were all right. Just a few more pages. She'd waited so long to be able to write again.

* * *

We'd really earned that film.

We had spent all afternoon searching Caro's room yet again. The police had been thorough, but they hadn't known Caro. It was possible that things we might immediately notice hadn't meant anything to them at all.

'Every reasonable person gets love letters,' Merle had groaned, closing the desk drawer again. 'So why not Caro?'

'Because she was anything but reasonable,' I said. Although Merle knew that as well as I did.

Caro had been a collector, a magpie. She'd made little nests everywhere to keep her finds in. Buttons. Postcards. Stones. Birds' feathers. Glass beads. Was something here a present from the unknown boyfriend? Or a memento of him? Or would something like that be in a special place of its own?

There was still a Phil Collins CD in the CD player. The last CD Caro had ever played. We looked through the songs. 'Come With Me'. 'Driving Me Crazy'. 'Can't Stop Loving You'. 'You Touch My Heart'. As if all of it had some special meaning during the last days of Caro's life.

But Caro had simply liked Phil Collins. Perhaps one of his songs had been *their* song. Caro's and the unknown man's. Every love story had its song, after all.

YOU
who are you?
all those
unasked questions
all those

songs not sung
nine lives
unlived
and on your mouth
a terrible red
sweet smile.

From the first that poem had scared me. Every time I read it or even just thought about it, something inside me shrivelled up into a small, hard kernel.

Lives unlived. Caro had wanted to stop wasting her life. And she was well on the way to doing just that. Living all the lives she'd longed for.

All those songs not sung. What had Caro meant by that? That she'd missed out on something? Something lovely? That he had missed out on something?

And then that *terrible red sweet smile.* I couldn't make much of that. *Terrible* and *red* – was he a transvestite or something? With brightly painted lips? Did this connect up with her fears that he might be gay?

Our last conversation. It had been about him. I ought to have listened more carefully. I ought to have picked up alarm signals. Surely there'd been some. I just hadn't noticed them.

I'd noticed that Caro was self-harming again, yes. But that was nothing new. Caro had always had phases when she hurt herself, and phases when she was in control.

Merle and I were used to it. We'd stopped bombarding Caro with questions. Trust breeds trust, that's what we'd believed. And it had worked too.

'Why didn't Caro talk about this man, though?'

'She was afraid to,' said Merle, still holding the Phil Collins CD. 'Because he'd forbidden her to say anything about him.'

Forbidden her! Caro!

For the hundredth time I thought about my last conversation with her. Generous, affectionate Caro had fallen in love with a man who didn't touch her. Who was carrying a whole load of problems around with him, and that's why he was waiting to be sure their love was exactly what he wanted.

'Can you love someone you're afraid of?' I asked.

'You can be afraid of someone you love,' said Merle.

We went on searching in silence. By the time we'd finished we had found two things we hadn't seen before: a black cotton scarf about sixty centimetres square, and a pressed flower. A white flower with three green leaves.

I'd found the scarf under Caro's underwear, and Merle had discovered the flower and leaves in Caro's favourite book, a second-hand edition of Rabindranath Tagore's poems. We didn't know whether these things had any significance, but we put them to one side with the feeling that we'd taken a small step forward.

So we really had earned that film. And laughter – we'd have to get used to that again. I thought of what everyone had kept saying to us lately: life goes on. Dreadful as it was, yes, we were finding out that it was true.

What had I expected? Did I think the world would stop going round? 'We're like ants,' I whispered to Merle. 'Scurrying busily around, and it makes no difference whether we get trodden on or not, because the scurrying will still go on without us.'

'Shush!' Merle stuffed some popcorn into my mouth.

She was right. Nothing in life was certain. We all ought to laugh and eat popcorn while we still could.

* * *

He couldn't hear what they were whispering. Yet he was so close that he could feel the warmth of their bodies when he leaned forward.

'Jenna is like a gift from God,' Caro had once told him. 'But for her I probably wouldn't still be alive.' She'd smiled at him and wrinkled her nose, a gesture that always moved him. 'Or I'd be in the nuthouse by now.'

She certainly hadn't been trying to make herself interesting. It wasn't just talk, it wasn't exaggeration. Caro said what she felt, and expressed it in a perfectly truthful, natural way.

What you must have gone through, he'd thought, and loved her all the more for it. He had noticed some time ago that her arms were covered with scars, even though she tried to hide them.

Later she had let him stroke her arms. He'd known that she couldn't have given him any greater proof of love. All the same, he had still wanted to wait. He hadn't been sure yet. Because his soul looked like Caro's arms. Covered with scars. But his weren't self-inflicted. They had been made by other people.

What Caro liked most about Merle had been her fighting spirit. She had admired her political commitment. 'I think it's very political, campaigning for animal rights and the prevention of cruelty to animals.'

He had learned a lot about Caro's flatmates. Far more than he wanted to know. Everything he heard had spun threads linking him to Caro and Caro to him.

He had spent the night at the flat a couple of times, throwing caution overboard. At first it alarmed him but he got a kind of kick out of it. Then he calmed down. He'd let Caro's room and Caro's presence work on him.

She had read him poems by Rabindranath Tagore, and they moved him deeply, though he couldn't usually make much of poetry. The language had been simple and easy to take in, colourful and close to reality. It had created images in his head and revived long-buried memories.

There'd been no sound from the other rooms. It had been late; the town was deep in slumber. Later he had crept into the bathroom and looked around it, marvelling at all the tiny bottles, jars, pots and tubes covering every available surface.

And he had looked into the kitchen, where pure chaos reigned. Crockery from the last meal still stood on the table. The sink was full of stacks of dirty pans and dishes. Cooking ingredients were scattered about the work surfaces.

He thought the room was comfortable all the same. The pot plants on the windowsill were bursting with health. The pictures on the wall were warm and cheerful.

Several collages hung in the hall, with pictures of the three girls. Perhaps, he had thought as he stood looking at the photos, perhaps we can be friends some day. He had never had a real friend in his whole life.

Caro would have liked that too. 'I want to show you off, that's what it is,' she had said. 'Do you mind?'

To think she was so proud of him had overwhelmed him.

The whole affair with Caro, she herself and everything to do with her, had been overwhelming. It had made him throw caution to the winds; it had lulled his natural suspicions.

He'd really thought he had found his love.

In the dark cinema no one could see the tears running down his cheeks. He suppressed the sobs that rose to his throat, went on weeping silently for himself, for Caro, and for a love that had been only a craving after all.

* * *

Margot punished him with contempt. The children were already in bed. This was the second day running when they hadn't set eyes on him.

She hadn't even made him a sandwich. Bert sat in the kitchen and drank a beer, although he didn't really enjoy it. He'd eaten almost nothing all day, he felt queasy and he was frustrated.

He heard voices on TV in the living room. A thriller. As if Margot wanted to demonstrate how to solve a case. Bert grinned mirthlessly. The people who wrote the screenplays worked out their cases on paper. Unfortunately it didn't turn out that way in real life. You could have brilliant intuitions, you could work with an experienced team and put all you had into it – but without that little bit of luck you wouldn't succeed.

He'd been thinking over the possible leads all day, yet again. He had spent over an hour in front of his pinboard wall staring at the photographs, maps and notes. He had read Caro's diary and her poems again. He had phoned north Germany and drunk six mugs of coffee as he sat and thought and thought. Reaching no conclusions.

That's how it is, Margot, he thought; that's how it is in real life. My job consists mainly of tedious, unspectacular, painstaking work on details, and plain old thinking. And your TV thriller is a long way from the reality of police work.

Bert finished his beer and stood up. Every bone in his body ached. He felt like an old man. He dragged himself upstairs and quietly went into his son's room. He straightened the quilt, which had slipped, covered the boy up and stood there for a while looking at the relaxed, childish face.

But for you, he thought, and your sister, I'd pack a bag and look for a room somewhere. I feel empty, worn out and misunderstood.

He didn't have to cover up his daughter in the other room; he just stroked her hair gently. She was sleeping so soundly that she didn't even move.

Bert sat down at the end of her bed, leaned back against the wall, drew up his knees and put his arms round them. He heard the sleeping girl's regular breathing, and closed his eyes in relief. She was alive. Healthy and happy. No one had done her any harm yet. At the age of eight she was still cared for, protected from the world.

So far, thought Bert. His eyes were burning with weariness. He really ought to go to the optician and get glasses. Only when? He never had time.

So far, he thought again. I ought to know that you can't protect anyone from the world.

As if in answer to his thoughts, his daughter moaned slightly in her sleep.

'It's all right,' murmured Bert reassuringly. 'Go back to sleep.'

Sometimes he felt as if being a parent consisted mainly of such phrases, uttered like magic incantations. *Everything will be all right. Nothing will happen to you. Don't be afraid.* Had he ever believed his own words?

Every time he found himself looking at the body of a child or a young person yet again, Bert phoned home to make sure his own children were all right. At the sight of the dead body, a pang of pain that left him breathless always went through him.

What would he feel like if someone had done to his little daughter what the Necklace Murderer had done to those four girls?

I'd kill him, thought Bert coldly. Track him down and kill him.

But he wasn't going to burden himself with those thoughts now. He just wanted to sit here and watch his daughter sleeping. To make up for not spending time with her today.

Another half an hour, perhaps, and then he'd go down and try to talk to Margot. A marriage wasn't over until you'd both run out of words. And feelings. Where there were still quarrels, there was hope.

He didn't notice when his chin sank on his chest and he fell asleep. Still half asleep, he felt Margot waking him up. He stumbled into the bedroom, undressed and fell on the bed. He felt Margot covering him up, breathed deeply in and out, and slept through until morning.

* * *

He couldn't sleep. It was oppressively close in his room. The air was still and heavy as if there were a thunderstorm coming.

He had taken in almost nothing of the film. For one thing he didn't like comedies; for another he wasn't much good at spying. He was far from having the qualities of a good detective.

He would have liked to introduce himself to the girls. Tell them how much he missed her. How badly she had disappointed him. And how, in the end, her love hadn't been true love after all.

Caro had got under his skin, and now he couldn't get rid of her. As if she had dug herself into him. Like the prickles of the sea-urchin he'd trodden on once when he was on holiday. But a doctor had been able to take those out.

In the dark cinema, memories of his time with Caro had attacked him like a swarm of gnats. They left him bathed in sweat.

Perhaps, he had thought as he clung to hope, perhaps pain and grief are like the crisis in a fever, and when they've passed off I'll be free. Free of Caro. Free of love. Free of remorse.

Free of any feelings at all.

If a miracle could bring Caro back to life, would he pray for that miracle?

Yes. Yes. Yes! He almost screamed it out loud. He put his hand over his mouth. He mustn't lose control.

To distract himself he had concentrated on the girls in front of him. Had reminded himself why he had followed them here. And that worked. His sadness died down and gave way to curiosity – curiosity about this girl who had ventured to challenge him.

Perhaps the onslaught of his feelings a moment ago really had been a kind of baptism of fire. Perhaps he was capable of looking to the future again now.

He needed all his strength, for he must go carefully. It was inexcusable to assume that the police were a bunch of fools. If you underestimated your enemies you strengthened them.

That applied to Jenna and her friend too. Their grief and anger made them unpredictable.

He sat upright and tensed all his muscles. Like a panther, he thought, smiling in the darkness; a panther about to spring. A black shadow, lithe and silent. Dangerous.

Did this girl Jenna know that?

13

It was two in the morning by the time Imke switched off her computer. She felt empty and exhausted. The sense of elation that she had been expecting didn't come. She felt more like crying.

She went to the bathroom and then downstairs to the kitchen. She hadn't eaten anything since the late afternoon. Edgar and Molly were standing outside the door to the terrace, mewing. She'd completely forgotten them. Feeling guilty, Imke let them in and put food down for them. When her writing was in full flow she couldn't think of anything else.

She put the dirty crockery that had accumulated in the dishwasher, wiped over the work surfaces with a damp cloth and put the kettle on. The kitchen was a pigsty. The floor badly needed cleaning. You could see every mark on the black and white tiles.

She was missing Mrs Bergerhausen at the moment. Even her singing. The school holidays began this week, and she was taking the whole six weeks off to look after her various grandchildren. She invited them to stay with her in turn during the holidays and spoiled them rotten.

Imke made herself a cheese sandwich and brewed a pot of black tea. She would have liked to eat in the conservatory, but she felt as if she were exposed on a platter there for anyone to see. Since the murders, and Caro's murder in particular, she found the isolation of her house rather threatening. Especially at night.

'So why do I write psychological crime novels?' she asked the cats, who just flicked their ears briefly at her and went on eating greedily. 'I suppose one's imagination is bound to get the better of one sometime.'

She let the tea draw, put her teacup and plate on a tray and took it into the living room. Perhaps there'd be a good late-night film on TV. The scene that she switched on to was a conversation between a mother and her daughter.

Jenna! She'd forgotten to call her. There was a murderer on the loose around here, and she was writing so hard that she forgot her own daughter. Although the murderer had already killed Caro.

Imke zapped through the programmes, looked with distaste at young women tarting around in sexist advertising spots, and at the same time was aware of the absolute stillness out there in the dark.

She didn't like the atmosphere between two and five in the morning. She'd once read somewhere that most people die during those hours. She felt thin-skinned and vulnerable, and closer to death than life.

Later, she thought. Straight after breakfast she'd call Jenna. And try dangling the idea of a holiday in front of her again. The girls would be safer travelling than anywhere else, no matter where they went.

Perhaps she should ask Bert Melzig for help. He could have a serious talk to Jenna and Merle. Point out what danger they were in, particularly after Jenna's thoughtless threat. Perhaps the girls knew something about the murderer without realizing it. Or the murderer thought they did.

And suppose he had a key to their flat? Imke bit the ball of her hand to keep herself from crying out. Suppose Tilo was right and Caro's unknown boyfriend was the murderer? She must make sure that Jenna got the lock changed. Or even better, she'd call a locksmith herself in the morning and present the girls with a *fait accompli*.

Edgar and Molly wanted to go out. Imke opened the terrace door for them and closed it again quickly. She didn't have to worry about the cats, anyway. They had no murderer to fear; only at worst the martens who roamed in these parts.

The world, thought Imke, is a very cold and hostile place. She switched the television set off, left her tray in the living room and went upstairs. She lay down in bed with a book, her eyes heavy with weariness. But she was in too emotional a state to sleep, and so just lay there, deep in thought.

* * *

Halfway up the stairs I met Mrs Mertens from the flat below us, with two-year-old Carolin balanced on her hip. She smiled at me shyly and went on downstairs. Carolin called something after me in her bird-like little voice, but I didn't catch what she was saying.

The other people in the building were reacting rather awkwardly to Caro's death. They had all told us how sorry they were, sounding embarrassed about it, and after that they avoided talking to us. Perhaps they had been to the funeral, but Merle and I hadn't noticed any of them at the time.

At the time. Goodness, what did that sound like? As if it were years ago. I'd lost all sense of time since Caro died.

I opened the door of the flat and waved the bag of rolls. Merle was up now too. She'd laid the table and cleaned out the espresso machine. We'd resolved not to wallow in our grief for Caro so much that we let ourselves go.

The holidays had begun and we planned to make good use of them. Get dressed, have breakfast and put our plan into practice – that was our programme for the next few weeks. Our plan was to find Caro's murderer.

As we sat eating breakfast the doorbell rang. Dorit and Bob, bringing us two cats they'd rescued from an experimental lab in their latest operation.

The cats were lying apathetically in their containers, pumped full of medicinal drugs.

I put a tray of cat litter in the bathroom for them. Merle spread a blanket under the wash-basin. They needed to be in a small enclosed space where we could easily keep an eye on them at first. Later, when they felt more confident, they would gradually explore the rest of the flat. That was how it always worked out.

After Dorit and Bob had gone again my mother rang. She told me she'd arranged for a locksmith to change our lock. As she was talking all my old annoyance surfaced again. How much longer was she going to interfere with my life, unasked?

'We have a clear agreement,' I said. 'You live your life and I live mine. Can't you stick to it for once?'

I could hear her drawing in her breath sharply. Perhaps her writing wasn't going well and she was edgy. 'Please, Jenna,' she said. 'You have to look after yourselves. Murder isn't just a word on the news any more.'

Half an hour later my father was on the phone. He seldom rang – only when it was something important, really. I didn't hold things against him any more, but the small amount of closeness between us was close enough for me.

This time he was inviting me to go on holiday with him and Angie and my little half-brother.

'Was that Mama's idea?' I asked.

He denied it so indignantly that I was sure I'd guessed the truth.

'The invitation's for your friend too,' said my father. We weren't so close that he could be expected to remember Merle's name.

I said no thank you. 'Nice of you, Daddy, but you don't have to protect us. We can do that for ourselves.'

'Princess,' he said, so quietly that I could hardly hear him, 'I need you. Look after yourself.'

He hadn't called me 'Princess' for ages. 'I will. Don't worry.'

There was a click as he hung up. I went on holding the receiver for a while. A holiday with Angie was about the last thing I could imagine. My mother must be desperate to come up with ideas like that.

I went into Caro's room, took a photograph album off the shelf and chose a photo of her. Then I looked in on the cats again. They were fast asleep. I closed the bathroom door and went to Merle's room.

'Can we go now?'

Merle folded up the map of the town she'd been studying and nodded.

'Where shall we start?' I asked when we were outside by my car.

'In The Candle,' said Merle. 'Caro often went there.'

The Candle was a bar where the local punks often met. Caro had drifted about in that scene for a while herself, and after she moved on she'd stayed faithful to the bar. She'd kept some of her old friends from then too.

There wasn't much going on in the place so early in the morning. Stale, cold cigarette smoke mingled with the fresh variety. Two guys I'd never seen before were sitting at a table at the back smoking a joint. I kept my breathing as shallow as I could. I'd always disliked that sweetish smell. I'd regularly smelled it in Caro's room.

'No one else here?' Merle asked the waitress, who seemed to be new.

The girl shrugged. She was chewing gum. Her hair was shaved except for a bright red strip running from her forehead to the nape of her neck.

I showed her the photo. 'Have you ever seen this girl here?'

The waitress looked suspiciously at the photo and then took a slow step back. 'Nope. And even if I had, what's it got to do with you?'

'Her name was Caro,' I said, 'and she was our friend. She was murdered.'

The suspicion in the girl's face disappeared. 'Oh, the Necklace Murderer?' she asked.

I nodded.

'I'm really sorry. But I can't help you. I've only been here a week.'

The guys at the table at the back hadn't seen Caro either. We left The Candle and went back to my car.

'We'd better leave it here,' said Merle.

She was right. We'd be quicker on foot in the alleys of the Old Town, which were very short of parking spaces. We could take the car later when we went out to the suburbs. We were planning to visit all the cafés and bistros where Caro had ever been, and all the bars and clubs too.

The police had probably done the same themselves, but perhaps they'd overlooked something. And people who'd never open their mouths to the fuzz would be ready to talk to us.

It was a good plan. One step at a time. No one could stop us now.

* * *

Bert heard the gravel crunch under his tyres. He felt like someone in a film as he went up the drive. Real flesh-and-blood people didn't live like this! But wealth probably blurred the boundaries of normality. He looked at the old building and had hard work suppressing his envy. It was as if his dream had taken shape here.

The house in a row of similar homes that was all he and Margot could afford seemed like a shoebox compared to this lovingly restored mill. You needed money, he thought, to get hold of such good things.

As he got out of the car Imke Thalheim came to meet him. She was wearing a sleeveless white dress which set off her suntan. 'It's so kind of you to find time for me.'

Somehow she always seemed to strike the right note. This remark took the wind out of his sails, because he didn't really have time for this visit at all. But the boss had preached him a sermon only that morning. Imke Thalheim was to be given preferential treatment, and so was her daughter. 'With their connections, they can make life hell for us.'

But something in Bert had been more than ready to agree to Imke Thalheim's request anyway. While they went towards the house he wondered what she wanted to talk to him about. She hadn't given any hint of it over the phone.

They went into a beautiful hall where it was pleasantly cool. Two cats were lying curled up together in one of the rattan armchairs, right in the sunlight falling through the high windows. The smaller cat got up, stretched, jumped down to the floor, came over to Bert and rubbed round his ankles.

Imke Thalheim looked at him in surprise.

'Most cats do that,' he said, embarrassed. 'Must be something about me they like.' Only now did he notice the water running through a channel in the floor.

'The architect thought it would be a good idea to divert part of the mill-stream to run through the house,' said Imke Thalheim, with the easy self-assurance of a prosperous woman. 'But he didn't stop to think that my cats like to play at catching fish. We're always having little floods in here.'

'What about when it's high water in the millstream?'

'That doesn't affect this channel. It's all been carefully planned.'

She led him out onto the terrace and invited him to sit down at a table laid for two people. Then she left him alone to fetch the coffee.

Bert looked around. The landscape reminded him of north Germany. The wide open spaces, the bleating of sheep, the splashing of the stream nearby immediately made him feel pleasantly drowsy. What wouldn't he give to be able to live like this.

He thought of the housing estate where he and his family lived. Wall to wall, door by door, window by window with the other houses. Gardens so tiny that they didn't deserve the name, with hardly room for a few shrubs and plants, perhaps a tiny pond.

Imke Thalheim brought the coffee and put a Swedish almond tart, already sliced, on the table.

'Would you like some?'

'Yes, thank you.'

He held out his plate, and she put a slice of the tart on it. 'It's delicious,' she said, 'but death to the figure.' Then she flushed slightly, immediately hearing what she had said.

Bert was used to it. Most people confronted with violent death reacted with great sensitivity to associated words. He tried the tart. 'It's really good,' he said. 'But you didn't ask me here for a cosy chat over coffee.'

'Well, no.' She had recovered herself, and was eating with a good appetite. 'I wanted to talk to you. And since I hadn't got around to having any breakfast I thought something to eat might be a good idea. Before you ask – no, the tart isn't home-made. I bought it.'

'I wouldn't have asked.'

'Of course not. How silly of me.'

Bert felt as if he'd known this woman all his life. The to and fro of their conversation seemed like an old, familiar game between them. At the same time everything she did and said was excitingly new.

'I want to talk to you about my daughter,' she said.

He nodded. He might have known it.

'I'm worried about Jenna and Merle. Can you reassure me? Have you got anywhere with the investigation? Do you have any suspects?'

Bert put his plate down. 'You know I can't discuss that.' He should have been angry. Had she asked him here for this? But he wasn't angry. He was glad she'd called him.

'Nothing you say will leave this house.' She gave him an ingenuous look.

And it's a writer talking to me, thought Bert. A woman who probably can't help exploiting everything anyone tells her. But she wasn't just a writer. She was also the mother of a girl who might be in danger.

'We've had a great deal of information from the public,' he said cautiously, 'and we're following up every lead.' He shrugged. 'So far, however, none of them has proved hopeful.'

'I've read Caro's poems,' said Imke Thalheim.

Bert wondered why that surprised him. It would be pointless to ask her how she came by the texts.

'She was an immensely gifted girl. But I don't need to tell you that. I expect you've read them too?'

Bert nodded.

'She coded what she was saying very skilfully.'

He nodded again.

'There must be clues to the identity of this last boyfriend of hers in the poems.'

'You're assuming that he's the murderer?'

'Yes. Because Caro's poems describe a very dark and dangerous love.'

Isn't that the only real kind? Bert wondered. Isn't anything else just superficial?

She looked searchingly at him, and he felt as if she had guessed his thoughts. Embarrassed, he avoided her eyes.

'That doesn't necessarily mean it ended in murder,' he said, and felt insincere. Hadn't his own thoughts been leading him in the same direction?

'I feel quite sick to think this man could be lurking somewhere near the girls unnoticed,' said Imke Thalheim. 'And until his identity *is* known he can't be ruled out as the murderer.'

'He's like a phantom,' said Bert. 'I've studied Caro's diary too, but there are no useful clues to the man there. Nothing. Nothing at all. It's infuriating. One human being surely can't enter the life of another without leaving any trace.'

'Particularly not if the two of them are in love.' Imke Thalheim leaned back and crossed her legs. 'Do you think Jenna and Merle are in danger?'

He had already noticed that her tactics consisted of lulling him into a sense of security, and then suddenly asking an awkward question. So he was ready for it.

'Not immediately,' he said.

'That leaves my imagination plenty of scope.' She narrowed her eyes. 'Have you any idea what it's like to see your child making for an abyss and being unable to help her?'

'Send the girls away,' he said. 'It's the holidays, isn't it?'

'That's exactly what I wanted to discuss with you.'

'I'd like to know where they're staying, that's all,' said Bert. 'In case any more questions come up.'

'Yes, but they refuse to go away. That's the problem. So I thought of you. Would you talk to them again, put them under pressure a bit?'

'Under pressure? Jenna and Merle? You must be joking.'

'Oh, you're right. They're both so pig-headed. I'd like to drag them to the railway station with my own hands and put them on a train!'

'Why don't you?'

'Now you know them, can you ask me that?'

They laughed, and the awkwardness that had been hovering over their conversation was dispelled.

'All right,' Bert promised. 'I'll try. But don't expect too much.'

She went out to his car with him. As he was going to shake hands she leaned forward, stood on tiptoe and dropped a quick kiss on his cheek.

* * *

Out on the road, Bert put his John Miles CD into the player, stepped on the gas and tried to clear his head. He was not the kind of man who had affairs. He loved his wife. He was fond of his children. He liked his life the way it was, and he didn't need any complications. A police officer couldn't even think of approaching a woman who was involved in a case of his.

Impossible. A woman like Imke Thalheim. A man like him. Unthinkable. They were like fire and water. Mountain and valley. Light and shade.

'Music Was My First Love' was playing. Hearing that song, Bert always felt as if he had only to spread out his arms and he could fly. He turned up the volume. The car seemed to be positively floating along the road.

Her laugh. The way she put her head on one side when she was listening to you. The way she moved. And why had she kissed him?

There'd be no future in it, he told himself.

He realized that many passages in the song he was listening to were sentimental, but it almost knocked him flat. The little hairs on his arms stood on end and a shudder ran down his spine.

He had to force himself to hold onto the steering wheel tightly to prevent himself from turning round and making the most stupid mistake of his life.

* * *

She had just entered the house when Tilo rang. The affectionate note in his voice was exactly what she needed. She told him the facts about her meeting with Bert Melzig, leaving nothing out except the kiss. Most of her actual feelings she kept quiet.

Tilo listened. He was giving her time he didn't really have.

'Perhaps he can make the danger they're in clear to the girls,' said Imke. 'I'm at my wits' end. Oh, by the way I sent them a locksmith to change the lock on their front door.'

'Good idea,' said Tilo.

'I know. Well, it was one of mine!'

He smiled; she could sense it, and suddenly she felt very close to him.

'Thanks,' she said softly.

'Thanks for what?'

'Just for being you.'

Afterwards she sat there for some time with the receiver in her hand, angry with herself and her wretchedly impulsive nature. A kiss on the cheek didn't have to mean a thing. But did the superintendent know that too?

* * *

I'd never have guessed how many cafés and bistros Caro used to hang out in. How many people she knew. Or how many people had liked her. Some of them cried when they saw the photo.

But none of them knew anything about a boyfriend.

'Is he the one who . . . I mean, did he . . . ?'

I knew how difficult it was to say it. It was difficult enough even to think it. I was beginning to dream about it. Merle was the same. We were both afraid of going to sleep.

'Nothing there.' Groaning, Merle crossed The Cockatoo off the list. 'My feet are sore, my tummy's rumbling, I'm sweating like a pig and I feel frightful.'

I glanced at the list in her hand. Next on it was the Tower Café. 'We'll have something to eat there, OK?'

The mere idea of food gave us new energy. We walked faster; we felt hopeful again. Someone or other must have seen Caro and this man together. People couldn't make themselves invisible. You always left some kind of trace behind, no matter how tiny.

* * *

He wondered what he felt for this girl Jenna. Did he have any feeling for her at all? He couldn't say.

Curiosity about her, perhaps. Yes, a little curiosity.

Since he lost Caro something in him had been extinguished. He was tired and aimless; he felt burned out. Day after day it had been as if he were standing beside himself, feeling detached.

First Jenna's challenge, which was still the main subject of conversation locally, had roused him. She had started him thinking, set his mind going again. He had wondered if he could make a conquest of her.

A conquest. He liked those proud words. Hardly any of them were in use today. Those proud, powerful, strong words. You couldn't survive in this superficial world without them.

Getting a girl who hated him to fall in love with him. He smiled. That would please him. That was the kind of game he liked.

She didn't know him. She knew nothing about him. She had no idea that he was the man she hated.

And there was something else too: she had been Caro's best friend. So in a way that made her part of Caro. If she loved him it would be as if part of Caro still belonged to him.

He smiled again as tears rose to his eyes. Perhaps he hadn't lost Caro entirely after all.

14

At the time of the first murder Bert's mind had gone straight to the strawberry pickers. Typical. *Take your washing off the line, the circus folk are coming to town!*

Now his thoughts had gone back to the pickers again. There had been lines in one of Caro's poems that ran:

> *you stride through*
> *the world*
> *in seven-league*
> *boots*

Seasonal workers went from place to place, staying anywhere they found a job. Could that be where the idea of seven-league boots came from? Was the man Caro had loved, the man who might have been her murderer, one of the strawberry pickers?

Bert swore. He would rather have something more solid than poems to support his ideas.

The boss had warned him not to be too quick to concentrate on one person, and so perhaps not follow up other clues persistently enough. 'What kind of connection could there have been between Carola Steiger's unknown boyfriend and the first victim, Simone Redleff? There was never any talk of a strange relationship in her case.'

It was an objection that couldn't be dismissed out of hand. Simone had not had a steady boyfriend. At least, she'd never mentioned a boyfriend to her parents, or taken one home either.

Could that first murder have been at random? Had the murderer not known his victim at all? But then how did the second fit into the picture?

Bert called his colleagues in north Germany. At the time of the murders there they had taken a very close look at the seasonal workers employed over a large area. Had drawn up lists of names for the countryside around Jever and Aurich, just as Bert had done here.

Directly after the murder of Simone Redleff Bert had suggested they exchange their lists. Among the strawberry pickers near Eckersheim he had found the names of a few asparagus cutters, strawberry pickers and itinerants working in orchards who had also done casual jobs last year in north Germany. But they all had alibis.

Nothing new from north Germany itself. They were working in the dark there, like Bert and his colleagues here, except that the force in the north had been at it considerably longer.

Bert looked through his interview notes again. Most of the strawberry pickers had been taciturn, some of them hot-tempered and aggressive. They had all stonewalled. If they couldn't get out of being questioned by the police, at least they wanted to make it as difficult as possible for them.

The notes were little snapshots of the people Bert had spoken to. For him, they said much more than a tape-recorded interview because he had to choose between his impressions and what he was told. It usually turned out later that he had in fact noted down the really essential points.

Margot described his methods of investigation as hand-knitted. When she was in a good mood she said it affectionately; when she wasn't she made it sound cutting. But it was true. Bert had developed his own methods over the course of the years. He had spent a long time trying out the different ways of combining what you knew with your intuition.

And his methods were old-fashioned. When it came to the crunch he trusted his head more than the most sophisticated police technology. And his feelings. But he hardly ever said so. A lot of his colleagues regarded him as an oddball anyway.

Even when he re-read them, the notes suggested nothing suspicious. Perhaps he ought to question the strawberry pickers again.

There was no obvious connection between the first and second murders, the boss was right about that. Nothing. Nowhere. Except for the fact that the girls had been killed in the same way, and had both lived not too far from Eckersheim.

And the strawberry fields belonged to an Eckersheim farmer.

Bert shut his notebook and put it back in his jacket pocket. He left the office, got into his car and set off to see the strawberry farmer. He still didn't know exactly what he was going to do when he got there.

After that he'd try to reach Jenna and Merle. Apart from the fact that he had promised to do so, he felt nervous at the mere idea that they might already have started going around the neighbourhood in search of the murderer.

* * *

The Tower Café really was a café in a tower. A tower dating back to the fifteenth or sixteenth century. When I was still at primary school we'd once gone on a sightseeing expedition to the Old Town of Bröhl, where we were made to listen to a lecture on every bit of old historic wall from our teacher Mrs Laubsam.

I fell in love for the first time on that expedition. He had wonderful red hair, his name was Justin, his father was German and his mother was English, and when he got excited he mixed up the two languages.

The tower was round, as a tower ought to be; the chairs and tables were antiques or at least looked the part; the guests were a mixed bunch. The pictures on the walls were originals. They were for sale, but the prices were far from affordable. I'd never seen anyone leave that café carrying pictures.

Merle and I had summer salad with garlic bread, and avoided talking about Caro at first, because we were both missing her terribly. The three of us had been here together a lot.

'Enjoy your meal?' asked the waitress. She was in her late twenties, very tall, very slim and very pretty. She'd been working here for a long time. A name badge pinned to her white blouse said ANITA.

'As usual,' said Merle.

'Yes, it was really good,' I agreed.

'Your friend not with you today?' she asked as she stacked Merle's plate on top of mine.

'Caro's dead,' said Merle. She sounded kind of defiant. As if Anita had been going to deny it.

Anita turned pale. She stared at us without a word.

'She was murdered,' I said.

Anita let go of the plates and clapped her hand over her mouth. She supported herself on the table with her other hand.

'When was she last here, do you know?' asked Merle.

We ought to give her a little time, I thought. So that she can get control of herself. She's had the wind taken right out of her sails.

Anita shook her head. She was fighting with tears. 'You don't notice that sort of thing. I mean, you don't expect someone ... someone to be murdered.' Her voice had grown quieter and risen higher with every word she said. The last word was just a breath.

'Do you remember if she was on her own?' I asked. 'The last few times she was here, I mean.'

She thought about it, her hand passing mechanically over the top of the table. It made a dry sound. 'She brought a friend sometimes, a man. Not often – perhaps twice or three times.'

My heart beat faster. 'Did you know him?'

She shook her head again. 'Never saw him before. Or afterwards either.'

'What did he look like?' asked Merle. She seemed to be holding her breath in suspense.

'Tall. Strong, but slim. Fit. About thirty, dark-haired. Good kind of face.'

Whatever that might mean.

'Anything special about him?' I asked.

'He was very tanned,' she said hesitantly. 'I mean, genuinely tanned, not a sun-lamp job. I thought at first he must come from the Mediterranean. But then I noticed that he didn't have any accent.' She smiled. 'They were very much in love. Real lovey-dovey stuff. I remember thinking: I could fancy him too. But he had eyes only for her.'

'Did you notice anything else?' I asked.

'He didn't do much talking. He just listened to your friend as if he was afraid of missing a word she said.' She nodded thoughtfully. 'That's all. I don't have time to stand around watching the customers and wondering what they're like.'

Someone called to her, and she picked up the plates again and took them into the kitchen. Then she saw to her other customers. After about ten minutes she came back to our table. 'Why do you want to know all this?'

'We're trying to piece Caro's last few days together,' said Merle.

'As a kind of farewell,' I added.

'Yes, I see.'

'Could we have a couple of cappuccinos?' I asked.

'Of course,' she said. 'What are your names, by the way?'

I smiled at her. 'I'm Jenna, my friend is Merle.'

We watched her as she went into the kitchen.

Merle leaned over to me. 'Perhaps she knows more, Jenna. Perhaps she'll remember it bit by bit.'

I reached for her hand and held it tight. I felt quite dizzy with excitement.

* * *

Arno Kalmer had a nose for police officers. Just the way the dark Peugeot drove into the yard told him the car belonged to a cop.

That superintendent got out. He closed the door but didn't lock it. Did he seriously think thieves would give his car a wide berth just because he was a CID man?

Arno Kalmer spat. He'd known it wasn't over yet. The lull had been deceptive. Whenever something happened anywhere, his people were always the first to come under suspicion.

Not that he couldn't understand why – these seasonal workers were odd folk; you didn't judge them by ordinary standards. They were very different from each other, except in one way: being their own masters mattered more to them than anything else.

Some of them had scarpered after the first round of questioning. They didn't like people looking at their papers. Not even when they had nothing to hide.

This worker or that was always disappearing overnight. You had to reckon on it from the start if you didn't want the whole harvesting campaign to be wrecked.

Arno Kalmer was not fond of his workers, but he was dependent on them, and he respected their hard work. The only farm labourer he employed all the year round was lazy and work-shy. He could learn a thing or two from the seasonal workers.

Sighing, he went to meet the superintendent. He didn't have to ask what he was here for.

'Let's sit down somewhere and talk,' said the superintendent.

They went into the house.

'My wife has gone shopping,' said Arno Kalmer. 'But I can make us a coffee. Would you like one?'

Bert Melzig asked for a glass of water instead. He sat down on the bench in the kitchen and took his notebook out of his pocket.

* * *

He'd seen the superintendent's car drive past. At least, he assumed it was the superintendent's car, though he hadn't been able to recognize the driver from a distance.

It was only to be expected. He mustn't get upset. That was the game as he'd played it several times before, and he would win yet again. Smiling, he bent over the plants and went on working.

'Feeling cheerful today?' asked Malle, balancing a full crate on his paunch.

'No more than usual,' grunted Nathaniel. He would rather have told him to mind his own business, but only one of his fellow workers liked Nathaniel, and that was Malle. Now and then you might need an ally.

Some of them had made off in a hurry. The superintendent would look hard at them first. That gave Nathaniel time.

He clicked his tongue. Time? What did he need time for?

The fragrance of the fruits was breathtaking. They were dark red and warm from the sun. Almost all the pickers had eaten too many of them by this time, but Nathaniel still thought they were delicious.

If he was honest with himself, he could feel a nagging uneasiness. The superintendent had come back. The hunt had begun. It was important not to make any mistakes now.

He rose effortlessly to his feet, picked up his crate and went over to the trailer to deliver his fruit. No one would be able to tell that he was at all nervous. He'd have made a good actor. Grandmother had always said so.

But she hadn't meant it as praise. And when she said so Grandfather had promptly hauled him off to the barn again.

Nathaniel straightened his back. No one was going to beat him any more. Ever.

Grandfather had finally got the point too.

Some day, thought Nathaniel, everyone will get it.

* * *

Anita couldn't remember any more. She helped herself to a coffee and a cheese roll and sat down with us for a while. The place wasn't very busy just at the moment, and she hadn't had any breakfast yet.

She was the kind of person who always looks good, even chewing and with crumbs in the corners of her mouth. She could probably even cry without getting swollen eyes.

'You don't by any chance know his name?' I asked, not very hopefully.

She shook her head. 'I didn't even know your friend's name till now.' She bent forward and spoke very quietly. 'Tell me – why are you *really* asking about him? I don't believe you about the goodbye bit.'

Hesitantly I looked at Merle. After all, it was no big secret that we were looking for Caro's murderer. I'd announced it to all and sundry. It had even been in the paper.

'You think he's the murderer.' She put the roll back on her plate and brushed the crumbs off her fingers. 'I knew it. So I've served the man who murdered your friend. And three other girls too. Oh, God!'

Merle wrote our home phone number and our mobile numbers on a beer mat and handed it to Anita.

'OK,' said Anita, who was taking a little while to steady herself. 'I'll call you if I think of anything. I promise.'

'Well, we know a little more now,' said Merle when we were outside, counting the information off on her fingers. 'He's around thirty, he's tall and dark-haired, and he's sexy-looking. That Anita was crazy about him.'

'And we know he's a good listener,' I said.

'And he was very much in love with Caro.' Merle shook her head. 'You don't kill someone if you're in love with them.'

'Who says so?' Merle jumped to conclusions quickly. It gave her nothing but trouble in maths lessons. 'What about crimes of passion?'

'He cut off the girls' hair. He only couldn't do that with Caro because she'd got in first, so to speak. So the pattern is the same in all the murders.'

'Couldn't they have been pure crimes of passion?' I so much wanted Caro to have been loved. To have had that at least.

'How many passionate loves do you think you have in a single life?' asked Merle ironically.

She was right. 'But suppose he isn't Caro's murderer at all?' It just wasn't possible that Caro had loved someone who would murder her!

'That's exactly what we're trying to find out, Jenna.' Merle was speaking like a mother to her child: patiently, slowly, and only a tiny little bit annoyed.

'You don't want him to be the murderer either,' I said.

'Of course not.' Merle took the list out of her bag. 'But what confuses me is that he doesn't get in touch with us. He ought to be very upset, he ought to want to talk, perhaps have something from Caro's room. In memory of her.'

'He didn't even want her to tell us about him.'

'That's right,' said Merle grimly. 'I have a whole lot of questions to ask him. That's why I want to find him.'

* * *

How often had she tried reaching Jenna or Merle now? Ten times? More than that? She told herself it was the holidays, and the girls had better things to do than sit around at home. But it was no good. She worried.

The manuscript was growing, chapter by chapter. It was flowing freely now. She had never before written any of her novels in such almost feverish haste. Each book had its own character. Each book was another part of her life.

Half an hour ago, when she had stopped for coffee on the terrace, two things had entered her mind: first, she didn't have enough firewood for the coming winter stored in the woodshed, and second, she had grown fond of the murderer in her novel. The firewood order could wait, but she must distance herself from the murderer as quickly as possible.

The thought had occurred to her a couple of times in the last few days that her own writing might have prepared the ground for those terrible murders. Her brain had immediately dismissed this as a fantasy, but the feeling wouldn't go away.

She made herself another coffee and took her cup out into the garden. The sight of the unspoiled landscape, with the sky stretched over it like a blue cloth with a few white patches, calmed her.

If it were really the case, she thought, that my invented crimes spun invisible threads reaching into the real world, and real crimes were committed along the way, I'd stop writing at once. Or write only love stories.

The phone rang. Imke had used a cordless phone since she came to live in this big house in the middle of the country, so she always had it close to her. She answered after it had rung twice.

'How would you like to invite me to tea?'

Her mother. And Imke immediately realized that she was just the person she needed now. Her mother had all kinds of faults, and could be infuriating, but she was to be relied on in difficult situations. She was like a rock among the breakers then.

'When can you be here?'

A short silence. 'Is it that urgent?'

Yes, dammit. It was. They had to talk. Her mother had plenty of sound common sense. She somehow always managed to put things on an even keel again. Wasn't that what mothers were for?

'I'll have the kettle boiling.'

Like a child, she clung to the expectation that a talk with her mother would dispose of all the threats. And she began humming, very quietly.

* * *

'Can I vouch for my workers?' Arno Kalmer laughed. His laughter was mirthless and too loud. 'Look, I hardly know 'em. Of course there's some come back every year, but only for a few weeks.'

'So the answer is no?' asked Bert.

Kalmer leaned forward. His dark eyes were glowing feverishly. Bert had noticed that on his first visit. The man seemed to be under pressure the whole time.

'Yes. No.' He raised his hands. 'Don't you see anything but black and white? Nothing in between?'

186

If he hadn't made Bert dislike him from the first, this remark would have done it. 'Like maybe?'

'You're laughing at me.' Kalmer leaned back and folded his powerful arms. They were very hairy. There was a broad scar over his right wrist.

'Nothing is further from my mind. I'm just trying to be precise.'

Now he had set Kalmer against him. He watched the farmer's composure turn to rage. 'So do you think it's right for every crime committed in these parts to bring the police to my farm first?'

Bert did not reply. That was the only way to loosen the man's tongue.

'The people that work for me work hard and they have stamina, which is more than you can always say for the folks around here. They're reliable. Their private life is none of my business.'

Bert still said nothing.

'There's trouble among them sometimes, sure. But you get that behind every darn door in this darn village, understand? My workers may not fit the picture of the settled life. They're travellers. Some of 'em would rather sleep in the barn than a bed.' He looked challengingly at Bert. 'So does that automatically make them criminals?'

Why, Bert wondered, don't I like this man? Because he's saying just what I think myself.

'Of course not,' he agreed.

'Then what do you want here? You questioned them all way back. Found out anything new that brings you to me?'

'I'm sure you'll understand that I can't say anything about that.'

Bert himself realized how smooth he sounded. Sometimes he hated the face he presented to strangers. Sometimes he wished he could shed his police officer's skin in such interviews and just be himself.

And what would appear once the police officer had shed his skin? he wondered.

He took down the names of the men who had left earlier than expected. In something of a hurry, as the farmer had reluctantly admitted. Then he finished his glass of water and rose to his feet.

Kalmer went out to his car with him and watched as he drove out of the yard.

He's glad to see the back of me, thought Bert. He asked himself when he'd last pleased anyone by turning up as a cop.

When he went to see Imke Thalheim.

He felt better at once. He turned up the radio and drove towards Bröhl to talk to the girls. Not just because he'd promised Imke Thalheim he would, but because he must not, whatever happened, fail to keep an eye on them.

* * *

The dark car was driving away again. Relief spread through Nathaniel's body like a wave.

I must watch out, he thought. If I get worked up about something it makes me vulnerable.

He never wanted to be vulnerable again.

Nathaniel the dragon-killer.

His hands were shaking. Only very slightly, but they were shaking.

He breathed in deeply and breathed slowly out again.

That always helped.

In. Out. In. Out.

He could almost have started to pray.

15

Everyone recognized Caro, but no one except Anita had ever seen her with anyone but Gil or her earlier boyfriends. Some weren't sure. They wavered, and then wouldn't commit themselves.

If only we'd had a photo of the funeral – then perhaps someone would have recognized the man. I didn't for a moment doubt that he'd been there with Caro on her last journey. If he was innocent.

I hoped so. I had to meet him. Because he'd loved Caro. Had been close to her, like Merle and me.

hello
black man
you belong
to darkness
not to me
hello
beloved
come up
with me
into the light

What was his secret? Why was he lying low? What had made him keep Caro in that cage of silence like a bird forbidden to sing?

Late in the afternoon we'd almost worked our way right through our list. We decided to go home, feed the cats and have a bit of a rest before setting out again in the evening to visit a few jazz clubs and bars.

We weren't confining our search to Bröhl, because the town had always felt too cramped and constricted for Caro. She moved in wider circles. Not for the first time I was grateful I had my Renault. Even without air conditioning it got us where we were going more comfortably than a bus or train.

The cats were awake. They'd finished the food in their bowl. One had made a little puddle beside the litter tray. They were huddling anxiously in the space between the bathtub and the shower cubicle.

I cleaned up and put down canned food and dry food for them. They watched me closely, but shrank back every time I put a hand out to them.

'They're disturbed,' said Merle, putting two pizza baguettes in the oven. 'No wonder after what they've been through. Why don't we keep them?'

I'd been thinking that myself. It was getting harder and harder to find homes for all the cats, dogs, guinea pigs, rats and mice that Merle and her group rescued.

'I think a cat adds a certain something to everyday life.' Merle poured milk into a small bowl and took it into the bathroom. I followed her and looked over her shoulder. The cats would let her touch them; they were still very suspicious and shy, but they didn't flinch away.

'I wouldn't mind,' I said.

The doorbell rang downstairs, and I pushed the button to open it. I knew him by the sound of his footsteps. He always took two steps at a time. He arrived at the top out of breath.

'Stairs like that are quite a fitness challenge,' he said.

I took him into the kitchen. We offered him a coffee, but he said no. 'I just wanted to find out how you were doing,' he said.

'No ulterior motives?' asked Merle suspiciously.

'Of course not,' I said. 'Want to bet?' I was exhausted and irritable, and there was something I didn't like about the way the superintendent was looking at us, because it made me feel guilty.

'I hope you've given up the idea of looking for Caro's murderer,' he said straight out.

'No,' said Merle. 'We haven't.'

'And? Any news that you're keeping from us?' he asked.

'Not so far,' I said. What we'd learned from Anita was still so vague that there was no real reason to tell the police.

'Is there any point in telling you once again that you're in danger if the murderer heard your threat and took it seriously?'

We shook our heads.

'I could have you put under observation,' he said. 'To prevent you from interfering with police inquiries.'

He might do it too. From now on we'd keep an eye open for anyone following us.

'It's not by any chance my mother behind this visit, is it?' I asked.

His silence, and the fact that he avoided my eyes, spoke volumes. But before I could give him a piece of my mind, the baguettes were ready. Merle took them out of the oven. 'Like to eat with us?' she asked.

'No, but thanks for the invitation all the same.'

I went to the door with him. On the landing he turned once more.

'Please look after yourselves! And don't make the mistake of underestimating the murderer. I've left my card on your table. You can call me any time if you need me. Any time, do you hear?'

I heard his footsteps die away and disappear. The superintendent was very nice really. I closed the door and went back into the kitchen.

'His card.' I picked it up.

'The hell with it,' said Merle.

But I didn't throw it away. I propped it beside the phone. You never knew.

* * *

Imke welcomed her mother's visit. For the first time in ages not a sharp word was spoken between them, which was so unusual and unexpected that Imke's eyes were moist with emotion. 'You've been a great help to me,' she said. 'Thank you.'

'Stop thanking me all the time.' Her mother waved her plump, bejewelled hand in the air. 'You'd do the same for me.'

I hope so, thought Imke. The role of comforter isn't exactly tailor-made for me. Not that her mother had comforted her at all. She had simply straightened things out a little. Look at the problem realistically, and it's half solved. That was her motto. And she obviously managed very well that way. At least, she'd never yet asked Imke for help.

'Send the girls to stay with me for a while, why don't you?'

'Jenna and Merle are past the age when they can be sent anywhere, Mama.'

'Can't you try?'

It wasn't a bad idea. At least then they wouldn't be on their own in the flat, where all the tenants left their front doors unlocked just as they liked.

'I'll think about it,' Imke promised.

'How's the new book going?' asked her mother, changing the subject and thereby venturing onto thin ice. Their views on literature differed widely.

'All right,' said Imke evasively.

'What subject have you picked this time?'

Was there real interest in her voice? Or was her mother just making conversation? Imke wasn't sure. 'In a way I'm coming to terms with the murders of Caro and Simone Redleff in it.'

'I don't believe it!' Her mother put her cup down. 'Have you never thought that disaster can be . . . well, invited?'

'You mean by writing about it?'

'Exactly.'

'I don't believe in such things, Mother.'

'What things?'

'All that mystical stuff. It's crazy.'

She ought not to have said that, but the words were out now, and she couldn't take them back.

'Sorry, Mama. I didn't mean . . .'

'That's all right. I know you think nothing of such ideas.'

'It does me good to write about the subject,' said Imke. 'It helps me to work out my anxieties. I simply capture them on paper.'

'On the screen, you mean.'

'Of course. On the screen.'

They laughed, and that somehow cleared the air. A glider passed overhead without a sound. Gnats danced in a dense cloud outside the kitchen window. The air smelled of summer.

Leave my child alone, thought Imke. Leave my child alone.

She realized that she was talking to the murderer in her mind. The real murderer, not his reflection, the one she imagined as she wrote. 'Come on, Mother,' she said, rubbing her arms. 'Let's go indoors. It's getting cool.'

* * *

Cool? Imke's mother looked at her daughter in surprise, but she didn't say anything. It was hotter than it had been for a long time. She got up and followed Imke into the house. In the doorway she turned again.

What had struck her first when her daughter moved into this house was the absence of any of the noises of civilization. She had liked that at the time. Now she felt differently.

Imke ought not to be living here alone. That man of hers, Tilo, should move in with her. Until they'd caught the murderer.

She didn't like her daughter's lover. His eyes were too sharp. You always felt he was finding out your secrets. But he was the only person available.

'Couldn't that Tilo come and stay for a while?' she called towards the kitchen, where she could hear Imke clattering crockery. She closed the terrace door and carefully bolted it.

'When are you going to stop calling him *that Tilo*, Mother?'

Yes. When? She sighed. It was difficult to avoid quarrels, because they both had such keen hearing. Neither of them missed the slightest nuance of a remark or a tone of voice.

A dog wouldn't be a bad idea either, she thought. A big, strong dog with paws like a beast of prey's. A dog who'd give his life to protect his mistress. 'How about getting a dog?' she called.

'A dog? Any other suggestions?'

She sighed again. Her daughter was always so fearless about herself. As if some secret magic made her immortal.

Very well, she thought. I'll go into the kitchen and break it to her gently that she's wrong. That she can't live as if she wore a cloak of invisibility. That she has very vulnerable spots.

And then we'll quarrel again. And I'll reproach myself, and she'll reproach herself too. And a little later we'll phone and apologize and resolve to treat each other more gently next time. But we won't succeed any better than today.

The telephone rang. She jumped, and was annoyed with herself. Had fear dug its claws into her too now?

* * *

It was difficult to follow them without losing them. It always looked so easy in crime stories. There was a lot of traffic today, as if everyone was out and about in this fine weather.

He was glad he drove an inconspicuous car, a Fiat, not too new, not too old, not too large, not too small, a sludgy colour – nothing to attract attention.

They drove into the car park of a nightclub and got out. He stopped by the side of the road, switched his engine off and watched them. Only when they had disappeared through the bright-green door did he follow them.

It wasn't one of those modern clubs where only the very young went. The place looked outmoded, as if time there had stopped ten years ago.

There wasn't much going on yet, and the music was playing at a volume which let customers talk without shouting at each other. He sat down at the bar and bought a Coca-Cola. On principle, he never drank alcohol when he was driving. He could do without complications.

Jenna and Merle were sitting at a table with some other young people, passing a photo round. The young people looked at it in turn and handed it on. Glanced at it. Shook their heads. Shrugged regretfully.

For a moment he felt unsure of himself. Was it by any chance a photo of him? His fingers tightened round his glass, but then he pulled himself together. Caro had never photographed him. She'd never been in the room where he was lodging. And even if she had – there were no photos of him in existence anyway. Perhaps apart from those that his mother still had.

And Caro couldn't have taken a photo of him secretly. He'd have noticed. So the girls were probably passing a photo of Caro round, hoping someone had seen her with him.

No, that's nonsense, he told himself. They couldn't know anything about him. Caro had promised to keep it a secret.

The girls stood up and moved to the next table. Nathaniel acted on impulse. He took his glass and sat at a table in a corner, right at the back of the place. Then he stayed there waiting. Watched them go from table to table.

He was perfectly calm now. He'd never been in this nightclub with Caro. He'd only very occasionally been out with her in this area anyway. Usually they'd got into his car and driven out of Bröhl. To some town or a pretty place in the country, where they got out and walked around.

Sometimes he invited her to a meal at a country pub, sometimes they drank cappuccino and ate cake in a coffee bar. They had never met anyone they knew, he made sure of that.

Most of his fellow pickers had no cars and were restricted to places near Eckersheim. Usually they were too tired for long outings anyway. All that bending and carrying tired you out, and it wasn't easy to cope with it.

However, Caro had known a lot of people. He'd always regarded it as a challenge to avoid them. And he had succeeded. No one would remember seeing them together. Someone might have caught a brief glimpse of them, but such vague memories couldn't be any danger to Nathaniel.

The girls would be coming over to him next. He had brought a book with him especially for any such contingency. He took it out of his pocket, opened it and pretended to be reading it.

'Excuse me, may we disturb you for a moment?'

He frowned, looked confused, gave just the impression he meant to give.

He had been reading, someone spoke to him, and he had a little difficulty in returning to real life.

'We'd like to ask you something,' said Jenna. 'It won't take long.'

He liked her eyes at once. The smile on her face as she looked at him filled them, made them sensuous and soft. 'By all means.' He nodded.

Merle handed him the photo. 'Do you know this girl?'

The sight of Caro was a shock. He hadn't been prepared for it. He reached into his pocket, took out a handkerchief and blew his nose to gain time. Then he shook his head. 'No, sorry.'

The way she smiled at the camera! How beautiful she was! And how familiar. She was still a part of him.

He managed to smile. 'I really wish I could have helped you.'

'Helped us with what?' asked Merle, looking at him as if she were sizing him up. He had imagined her something like this, and Caro had described her that way too: cool, logical, straightforward. 'But with such a soft, soft heart,' Caro had added.

'Finding her,' he said quickly. 'You're looking for her, aren't you? I mean, why else are you showing her photo round?'

'Well,' said Jenna, 'it's really her boyfriend we're looking for. Tall, slim, dark-haired. And very suntanned.' She smiled at him, suddenly shy. 'A bit like you.'

He felt his scalp tingling. 'I wouldn't mind being her boyfriend, but I'm afraid . . .' He raised both hands in a gesture of regret. 'A pity. Your friend's a pretty girl.'

Jenna was going to say something, but Merle got in first, thanked him and drew Jenna away with her.

Just in time. He was feeling quite ill with the strain of appearing natural. He waited until the girls had left the club, then he went out too. He was already in his car, ready to drive off, when he saw their Renault leave the car park.

* * *

Bert had come home from work early today. He had played football in the garden with the children and then cooked with them. They put chips in the oven, grilled some sausages and ate both with plenty of ketchup and much laughter.

Margot had used the time for herself. She had read, made some phone calls and tinted her hair. For some time she'd tended to keep out of joint family activities. As if the hours she had to herself were the best in the world.

In a way Bert could understand that. Everyday life was exhausting. You had to find ways of refuelling. But their most important refuelling stop had always been in their own relationship, when just the two of them were together. They'd put up with anything simply to be with each other. And that had changed.

Bert couldn't get used to it. It still hurt.

He was sitting on the patio with Margot. They both had a glass of red wine beside them. Someone was having a barbecue somewhere near. A smell of charcoal and grilled meat hung in the air. Their neighbours to the right were sitting in their garden too, talking quietly. The sound of TV came through the patio door of their neighbours to the left. They were watching a Western.

Bert thought of Imke Thalheim's property. If she was sitting out of doors at the moment she could probably hear crickets chirping. He cast a guilty glance at Margot.

She was looking at a gardening magazine. To get ideas, she said. Bert couldn't imagine Imke Thalheim doing that. He hadn't seen any *ideas* at her place when he was out there. It had all looked untouched and natural.

'How's your work going?' Margot asked, interrupting his train of thought.

Concentrate, he told himself. And he told himself something too: people started being secretive long before actually beginning an affair. 'I'm getting nowhere,' he said. 'We're marking time.'

She closed the magazine and looked at him. Tolerantly, he thought, not with real interest. Perhaps she had a clear idea of the way a policeman's wife ought to be. And suddenly he didn't want to talk about the investigation.

He went to get Caro's diary out of his case. When he came back to the patio Margot had gone indoors with the magazine and her glass of wine. Perhaps his silence had hurt her feelings.

He leafed through Caro's entries. He almost knew them off by heart, he'd read them so often. Eavesdropped so often on a girl's feelings – feelings that weren't meant for his eyes. He sometimes felt dirty.

Caro had not written at length, hadn't lined up a whole string of random events. Every entry was self-contained and carried weight. Her words were brief and carefully chosen, with nothing superfluous.

Bert spent about an hour with the diary. Then he looked at the list of strawberry pickers again. Brooded over names that meant nothing to him. He'd have someone checking up on each of those workers. Why they had left early. Why in such a hurry.

Perhaps the appearance of the police had simply made them nervous. That didn't necessarily mean anything. Many seasonal workers got involved in something that wasn't entirely legal. Bert wasn't interested in such things. He wished he'd made that clear to them during the first interviews.

He read some of Caro's poems again. Let the images work on him. Somewhere in here was the answer he must find. He felt sure of that. Sighing, he dug his hands into his hair and thought.

When he came back to himself again the wine bottle was empty and the lights in the house were switched off. It looked as if Margot had already gone to bed. All right, he thought, gathering his things together. But it wasn't all right. He would have liked to feel a little human warmth, if only for half an hour.

* * *

Nothing. No one but Anita had seen Caro with her boyfriend. It was as if we were jinxed. Tired and frustrated, Merle and I drove home and didn't say a word on the way.

The cats were waiting for us, asking for food. That was a good sign. They'd accepted us. We decided to start leaving the bathroom door open so that they could explore the flat in their own time.

We gave them fresh food and then made ourselves some tea. After that we sat in the kitchen feeling dismal.

'Perhaps the superintendent's right,' said Merle. 'Perhaps it's beyond us.'

'Nonsense. It's a very complicated case, that's all. Otherwise the police would have got somewhere too. But they haven't, have they?'

What did we have? Caro's poems, a black scarf, a pressed white flower and some leaves, and Anita's description of the man who had been in the café with Caro. Not a lot to go on. It was like relying on something as fleeting as a fragrance, a perfume, an aftershave, here one moment and gone the next.

'I don't know.' Merle's mouth twisted. 'I feel really odd. I think I'm frightened.'

'Frightened? What of?'

'Nothing definite. It's just a kind of menacing feeling. Don't you feel it too?'

'I feel dreadfully tired, that's all. You start seeing things when you're tired. I'm going to bed now.'

'Good idea.' Merle got up and took the cups over to the sink. 'Things will look quite different in the morning.' My grandmother's favourite saying. I didn't know Merle's mind worked that way too.

I fell into bed, and just managed to turn the light out before I went to sleep.

I heard noises a few times in the night. It's the cats, I thought, and turned over on my other side. We still had to get used to there being four of us in the flat.

* * *

The cats had given him a fright. He hadn't been prepared for them. At first he'd thought he heard one of the girls in the kitchen, but then that small shadow scurried past him, followed by a second one next moment.

A good thing they hadn't got a dog. That would have been a disaster.

He didn't really know what had driven him here. Caro had had the spare key made for him, and insisted that he must take it. 'Just in case,' she had said, without explaining what she meant by that.

And now here he was again.

He stood in the kitchen, drinking in the atmosphere of the room as he'd done before. Faint light from the streetlamps outside lit the room well enough for him to see outlines.

What was he doing here? This was madness!

Without a sound, he crossed the hall and carefully opened the door of Caro's room.

It looked as if they'd left everything just as it was.

He sat down on the bed and passed his hand over the sheets.

Perhaps he'd come to say goodbye. At last.

It had never seemed so hard to him before.

16

They'd sent the locksmith away again! They didn't need a new lock, they said. It must be some mistake. The locksmith had briefly reported back to Imke. As long as he was paid for turning out he wasn't worried.

Imke was stunned. The two of them couldn't be so stupid that they didn't see the danger. Or were they trying to lure the murderer? Did they want him to enter the flat?

Fantasies. She went out into the garden. She had to do something – physical work of some kind – to keep her from going crazy.

As she stood out there, looking around, she didn't know where to begin. Undecidedly she walked a little way towards the pasture where the sheep grazed, and then went back indoors.

Mrs Bergerhausen had left her with an immaculate house when she went on holiday, but there wasn't much of that left now. Everything looked somehow dulled. Not as bright, not as shiny. Even outside. But perhaps she was just imagining things here too.

She put the breakfast dishes into the dishwasher and switched it on. Wiped over the table. Put the newspaper into the basket kept for papers. Added the soiled tablecloth to the rest of the contents of the laundry basket, filled the washing machine, chose the programme and switched that on too. After a while she found she was doing all these things without thinking about them.

When the phone rang she was down in the cellar. She hurried up the steps and answered it breathlessly. Bert Melzig.

'About my visit to Jenna and Merle – I didn't make much headway. I had another serious talk with them and left them my card. I'm afraid that's as far as I got.'

'You did what you could. Thank you.' Imke told him what the locksmith had told her. Her anxiety was on the tip of her tongue, but why burden him with that? He couldn't help her.

He listened. He could do that very well: he was a good listener. It was as if he were laying his large hand on her head, and everything was all right again.

But nothing was all right. Nothing would ever be the same as before. Because nothing could bring Caro and the other murdered girls back to life.

* * *

At last she left the block of flats on her own for once. He waited until she was far enough away, then got out of his car, locked it and followed her. It could easily become an obsession, watching this girl in every spare moment he had.

Yesterday it had simply been amusing. Now it was more. He wanted to get to know Jenna properly. And then he'd decide what to do next. Every decision took time, and he would wait patiently until the right time came.

She walked with a light, springy step, her hair swaying. Like a model, he thought. That was how she moved. He imagined what she would smell like. Did she wear perfume?

It looked as if she was on a leisurely shopping expedition, for she kept stopping to look at the displays in shop windows, which made following her difficult. He felt like a detective in some American movie, except that he was nothing like good enough at it.

In the Old Town Jenna went into a bookshop. Nathaniel stayed outside, acting as if he were intent on the books in the window. Travel books – he noticed that much. It was the holidays, and books have their seasons too.

If he looked up he could see Jenna inside the shop. At most three metres away from him, she was picking up books and putting them down again. Then she started reading one seriously.

He looked around, feeling uncomfortable. He couldn't just stand here the whole time. Walking up and down was no solution either. He mustn't do anything to attract attention. He went into the bookshop.

Jenna was in the section devoted to books about animals and pets, and was holding a guide to cats. Nathaniel thought of his unexpected encounter with her cats last night, and remembered the sudden panic he had felt.

He didn't like the fact that he was beginning to get interested in this girl. At the same time he rather enjoyed feeling her slowly taking over his thoughts and feelings.

Like a slow poison, he thought. If he didn't get out of the shop now it would be too late.

He stayed. Knowing exactly what that meant.

* * *

Merle was at Claudio's. He had only to whistle and she came running. That guy was no good for her. He'd dump her sometime and go back to his fiancée.

His fiancée. How ridiculously old-fashioned the man was. Who still got engaged these days? For the first time I suspected that the supposed fiancée might be just Claudio's invention. So that he could keep Merle at a distance.

I'd thought a little shopping might take my mind off things. Calm me down. I'd look in a few shop windows, try some clothes on, have a coffee, leaf through books. That usually helped when I was upset.

Not today. It was getting late, just under an hour before closing time. People were hurrying from shop to shop in a busy way that gradually infected me too. I saw the bookshop at just the right time.

I took a couple of books off the shelves and promptly started reading. That was always likely to happen. And when I emerged from the book a little later I would feel bemused.

I felt bemused now. Colours were less intense, sounds less clear than they should be. I'd stay in this condition for a little while and then everything would be back to normal.

You somehow feel it when you're being watched. There's a small, cold sensation at the back of your neck. I looked up and met the eyes of a man at the back of the shop near the natural science books who seemed vaguely familiar. He quickly looked away. As if I'd caught him in the act of something.

If I've found myself absorbed in a book I usually buy it. And we needed a proper cat book. I went towards the cash desk, lingering briefly by the art books and then a stand of bookmarks. I usually bought bookmarks to give as presents, but this time I decided to get one for myself.

I chose another for Merle too. She was always dog-earing pages. It sent me wild to see anyone treat books like that. Perhaps a bookmark would help her to break the habit.

'Eighteen euros fifty,' said the woman at the cash desk. 'Would you like it wrapped?'

'No, that's all right.' I opened my handbag and realized I'd left my purse at home.

There's nothing more embarrassing than standing at a cash desk just before closing time, with a queue of other customers in a hurry behind you, and finding that you can't pay.

'Oh, I'm terribly sorry,' I faltered, feeling my cheeks burning. 'I forgot to bring any money with me.'

The woman at the cash desk could have taken it more calmly, but she probably had a long day behind her, and she looked tired. She glanced first at me and then at the cash desk. People were muttering behind me. 'But I've already rung up the sale.'

How was I going to get out of this?

'How much do you need?'

It was a pleasant voice. I turned and looked into his eyes for the second time. No, for the third time, because now I remembered him. The suntanned man in the nightclub who had been sitting at a table by himself.

'Eighteen fifty,' said the woman at the cash desk.

I wished there was a mouse-hole near me and I could disappear down it.

He put the money down on the counter, without a word. Just like that.

Instead of flinging my arms round him in relief or anything, I just muttered a 'Thank you', put the book and the bookmarks in my shopping bag, went out and waited for him. He had the book he was buying put in a bag, and came towards me, smiling.

'When can I pay you back?' I asked.

'Consider it a present,' he said.

His suntanned skin made his blue eyes look even brighter. His teeth positively flashed. He reminded me of the young Terence Hill. Except that he wasn't blond but had dark hair. And he was better-looking. More natural.

'Why would you give me such an expensive present?' I asked.

'Perhaps because I like you?' He looked at me thoughtfully. 'Or because I couldn't help you and your friend yesterday. Pick your answer.'

'Oh no,' I said. 'I really can't take it.'

'Yes, you can.' He smiled and turned to go. Then he turned back to me again. 'Would you like a coffee?'

I didn't answer, but just walked down the road beside him in search of a café.

* * *

They'd probably turned the ringtone of their phone down again. Or they were out. Imke tapped in the numbers of both their mobiles. '*The person you wish to speak to is not available at the moment.*' Why did they keep switching their mobiles off? Imke sighed. How many times had she asked Jenna and Merle to get an answering machine?

'Why would we need an answering machine, Mama?'

Why? 'Well, so that people can reach you.'

'And then we have to call everyone back, I suppose you mean. We don't have the cash for that.'

'As if money were a problem!'

'Not for you, Mama. It is for me. And it definitely is for Merle.'

Jenna and her pride! She wouldn't take a cent more than absolutely necessary. You only had to look at her car. Decrepit, dented, unreliable. A dangerous heap of rust. But Jenna refused even to think of a new car.

Imke made herself some tea and went to her room. She was going to try to write. All she needed now was to start fussing around like a mother hen. She wished she'd chosen a different subject. As she wrote, she kept seeing Caro in front of her. Every sentence reminded her of the poor girl's terrible death.

The superintendent who was to solve the crime in her book was getting to be far too like Bert Melzig. Imke realized that, but there was nothing she could do about it. Later, perhaps, when she was revising, but at the moment all she could do was follow her inspiration step by step.

Above all, she must distance herself from her murderer. It troubled her to realize that she had no difficulty in slipping into his skin and following his thoughts. It was important to adopt the right position. She didn't intend to justify a murderer's actions, even on paper.

She sat at the computer for an hour without writing a single sentence. She was exhausted by her unaccustomed housework, frustrated by the locksmith's phone call, and extremely anxious about Jenna and Merle. If she'd had a dog she'd have taken him for a run over the fields. As it was, she found a rug, curled up on the sofa in her study, and immediately fell fast asleep.

*   *   *

Merle despised herself for being so inconsistent. Claudio treated her sometimes like a princess, sometimes like an old dishcloth. Today he was very much the boss. Chivvying her here and there, snapping at her for the smallest thing.

The others working there didn't listen any more. They knew what Claudio was like and didn't interfere. As she saw it, that was just the way Claudio was, saying first one thing, then another. But he was a great guy at heart.

Merle had often come home in tears, swearing never to fall for Claudio and his charming ways again. Jenna and Caro had encouraged her.

'No man's worth crying over,' Caro had said. That was before she met the mysterious boyfriend, of course.

'Get a move on, girl,' said Claudio. 'I don't pay you to stand around.'

Merle untied the hideous green apron and dumped it in his hand. She was amazed by her own composure. She calmly looked into Claudio's fine eyes, which were now wide with bewilderment.

'*Ciao, bello,*' she said, and walked provocatively and slowly to the door.

'If you go now you needn't come back,' he shouted after her. He'd always been a bad loser.

She didn't answer, didn't even turn round. She just raised her arm and showed Claudio her outstretched middle finger.

Then the door closed behind her and she was free.

And alone.

Oh, shit. Now the tears were running down her face.

* * *

The alibis of the strawberry pickers who had left ahead of time couldn't be shaken. Some of them had skeletons in the cupboard, but none of them was responsible for the Necklace Murders. So what made Bert still feel so certain that the key to his cases lay with the pickers?

Pure intuition. No leads to justify going further there.

His work had seldom been made so hard for him. In the case of Simone Redleff there was a pitiful shortage of information because she had been so private – most of the people in her year had hardly known her.

With Caro the difficulty was that her family knew almost nothing about her. That included her brother, and they had questioned him now. The only people who might possibly be able to help Bert were Jenna and Merle, and they were set on investigating by themselves.

He stood up and opened the window wide. The noise of the street outside came in, and with it the sultry heat that had been weighing down on the town all day. It all suddenly got on his nerves. So did the constant background noise in his office – doors slamming, telephones ringing, talking and laughter in the corridor.

Caro's friends had been closely questioned, like her family and her earlier partners. Watertight alibis wherever you looked.

They had to find this unknown lover.

Bert closed the window again. Time to drive home. Demonstrate his good intentions to Margot.

He had a wife and children. There was life outside this room.

* * *

It was strange walking down the street with her. Now and then he sensed her searching glance. She was probably still asking herself whether she ought to accept the money or not. For the first time since Caro went he felt almost carefree. He almost wanted to burst into song.

His grandmother always used to hum to herself while she worked. Hymn tunes of some kind, not real songs. It wasn't an expression of the joys of life but an attempt to lighten her oppressive everyday existence. Or at least, that was how he saw it as a child. But somehow it never worked. Nothing was light about Grandmother. Even her movements had been slow and ponderous.

Nathaniel took Jenna to the big café on the market square. There was always so much going on there that no one would notice individual customers. He realized that he was running a risk, but didn't all gamblers do that? And he loved to gamble. Even with his freedom. With his life.

The girl was silent. He had the impression that she didn't feel uncomfortable about her silence. At last, someone who wasn't chattering all the time, he thought. You didn't meet people like that very often.

He looked at her out of the corner of his eye, and liked what he saw. Liked it far too much. She had thrown down the gauntlet, and he'd picked it up. He had planned to answer her challenge, but so far he hadn't stopped to think exactly how.

It would be easier for him to come up with a plan if she left him cold. But she didn't. Far from it. He dug his hands into his trouser pockets and tensed all his muscles so that she wouldn't notice the way he was shaking.

* * *

In Imke's dream she was running down a long tunnel with a faint light at the end of it. Her feet were splashing through ankle-deep water. The splashing and her own gasping for breath were the only sounds she heard.

Somehow she knew that this was a dream. Her legs, her arms, her sides – everything hurt, and she thought: What more do I have to do to reach the end and get out of here?

Her trousers were smeared with mud, her hair was wet with sweat. When she coughed the echo came back to her from all sides. For some reason she was mortally afraid. She tried to wake up, but she was stuck in the dream.

* * *

To make it even worse, Jenna wasn't at home. No one there to talk to, no one to console her or anything. Morosely Merle went into the kitchen and turned the espresso machine on.

The cats rubbed round her legs. They needed a little petting, a few kind words, and of course food. Merle poured milk into their bowl and cut two slices of cooked ham into small pieces. She might be feeling miserable herself, but at least the cats shouldn't suffer for it.

She lay down on the bed in her room and switched on the TV set. She mustn't think. Mustn't let Claudio back into her head, certainly not into her heart. Early-evening television was just the thing. So stupid and empty and pointless that it sucked all the ideas out of your brain.

* * *

I liked it that he didn't try chatting me up. He didn't say any of those stupid things that are such a pain. He was very calm and reserved, just like me.

It was too busy for me in the café, too plush and noisy. That didn't seem to bother him. His calmness communicated itself to me, and I felt safe, like when I was little and sitting in the kitchen with my mother, or in the car with my father driving through the dark.

We both ordered a white coffee, and only as we were stirring the froth on it did we start talking. 'There aren't so many people you can just be quiet with,' I said.

'And there aren't so many people you can talk to,' he replied.

His smile found something hidden deep inside me. Tiny little lines appeared round his eyes. I wanted to touch them, very gently. Of course I didn't. Instead I tore open the wrapping of the biscuit that was served with the coffee.

He was about thirty, far too old for me. So what was I doing here? Sitting with him in a place that was anything but cool, loving the look of his laughter lines. All we needed was for a Palm Court orchestra to start playing for a tea dance.

'Did you have any luck with your search?' he asked.

'I'm afraid not,' I said.

'Do you want to talk about it?'

I shook my head. No, I didn't. I wanted to forget everything to do with Caro's death for a while. Not think about anything sad. Just sit at this table with him, look at him, listen to him or sit in silence with him – any of those.

'Why don't we sit outside?' I asked, looking at the white tables and the bright sun umbrellas on the terrace. It was all shining, as if it had a glow inside.

'I've been out in the sun all day,' he said. 'I'd rather stay in here if you don't mind.'

OK. No problem. Perhaps he would tell me why he'd been out in the sun all day. Or perhaps not. It wasn't important. Nothing was important, only the moment.

* * *

He would have liked to go on just looking at her.

A new episode had begun.

He hadn't wanted it. It had just happened.

He could still simply get up and go.

He looked at her. And knew that such a possibility no longer existed for him.

17

It was just after nine when Jenna came home. Merle switched off the television. Perhaps they could cook something. Only now did she notice how hungry she was. Her stomach was as empty as her head. She shouldn't have watched that stupid TV series.

Jenna was standing with her back to the front door of the flat. 'Hi,' she said, smiling as if she'd just drunk three glasses of wine. Oh, marvellous. Just the right moment to go and fall in love!

'Who, how, when and where?' Merle led her away from the door and into the kitchen. 'And don't leave anything out. I want to know all about it.'

'Home already?'

'Trouble with Claudio.'

Merle hoped Jenna wouldn't probe any further. She'd spent all evening carefully keeping up a façade of composure. One misplaced word and all her efforts would be wasted.

'I'm hungry,' said Jenna. 'Shall we order something from the Chinese takeaway?' How easily she found the right tone.

'If you're paying. I'm skint. And out of a job.'

'Never mind that. You're my guest.'

They ordered, and then Jenna began telling her story.

*   *   *

Imke woke in the middle of the night in pitch darkness, and for a moment

214

didn't know where she was. She sat up, with difficulty, stretched, put her shoes on. She'd slept the whole evening away!

She felt very, very old as she went downstairs to look for something to eat. Her head hurt. She had a bad taste in her mouth, and her left eye was streaming.

She felt so unbearably alone in the soundless night that she sat down in front of the television set with some leftover chicken salad and a glass of milk, and gave herself up to the usual round of sex, violence and ads until she couldn't stand it any more. Without stopping to think, she picked up the phone. A sleepy voice answered.

'Tilo?'

He replied with a sound that was a mixture of a grunt and a groan.

'Would you like to finish your night's sleep here?'

He yawned very loud, and she was preparing for a cross answer, but then he said, 'OK. Be with you in twenty minutes.'

She got a bottle of red wine out of the cellar and put bread, cheese and fruit on the kitchen table. By now she was wide awake. She needed Tilo to listen, to talk, to hold her and make love to her. In that order. She'd always known she was born lucky. Only a lucky person could have found Tilo.

* * *

Just talking about him made me happy. I didn't even have to close my eyes to see his face before me.

'Good heavens,' said Merle. 'You're a really bad case!'

'You know him, anyway,' I said. 'From yesterday.' I tried to describe him. Merle didn't remember him clearly.

She wanted to know everything. His name. His age. His job. Where he lived.

I shrugged. None of that had mattered in the least. We hadn't talked about it.

'So what did you talk about?' asked Merle.

Yes, what? He'd told me about his childhood. How he grew up with his grandparents, and his grandfather had been violent to him. I'd touched the little pale scar on his chin with my fingertip. And seen other scars. On his throat and his forehead, half covered at his hairline.

He had twitched nervously when I touched him, and I had promised myself I would never, never hurt him.

I'd told him about Caro. I talked about her more than anything else. 'He had tears in his eyes,' I said. 'Can you remember when you last saw a man crying?'

Merle shook her head.

'He's a real man, though.'

'Tried him out already, have you?'

'Oh, don't be silly! I just mean he's not . . . he's more like . . . somehow or other he . . .'

Merle listened to my stammering and grinned. 'So let's sum up,' she said. 'His name is Nat, he may be around thirty or maybe not, had a hard childhood, is a real man but isn't ashamed to cry, and he's wound you round his little finger in less than three hours. Right?'

'You make it sound like a soap opera.'

'Because it's the same with love as sunsets,' said Merle. 'You think they're just plain soppy, but they take your breath away all the same.' And she began to cry.

Claudio. With luck he was finally in the past now.

I gave Merle a handkerchief and prepared for a long night.

* * *

He couldn't sleep. The moonlight was too bright, and it was too hot. The attic stored up the heat of the past few days. Opening the windows in the evening did no good. It just attracted gnats.

Jenna's voice had accompanied him to his room. He still had it in his head. Deep and soft. A wonderful voice.

She had talked about Caro. He had held back his tears with difficulty. He managed it only by concentrating on looking at Jenna and drinking in everything about her. The little mole on her temple, the dimple in her chin, the swirl of hair over her forehead.

Jenna wasn't pretty, she was beautiful. In her own way. Her beauty was of a different kind. Influential women in history had been beautiful in that way.

You recognize true beauty at first glance, he thought, and you don't forget it.

He could see every feature of her face before him. And he remembered how difficult he had found it not to touch her cheek, her neck, her ears.

Slowly. Take it slowly. The time would come.

He had told her true things and he had told her lies. That couldn't be avoided. Sometime he'd be able to confide everything to her, and she would understand and wouldn't reject him.

He had killed her friend.

A fit of shivering attacked him without warning. He curled up and wrapped his quilt tightly around his body.

Nat. That was the name he had told her, and he must remember it. Not too difficult. Just an abbreviation.

He must be sure to remember it, though. He mustn't make any mistakes. This girl had it in her to be the love of his life.

* * *

As soon as Tilo left Imke had called the girls and invited herself to breakfast. She had got Jenna out of bed – she could tell from her voice. 'I'm sorry,' she said, 'but I was afraid you'd elude me again.'

The girls seemed glad of her visit. And the warm rolls that she brought with her. Two cats were running about the kitchen chasing dust-fluff. Imke wished they had been dogs, large, strong, reliable animals.

She had hoped the girls would tell her their secrets, so that she'd know what they were doing and not feel so dreadfully helpless. But they didn't. They talked about this and that, two people who were good at avoiding delicate subjects.

Jenna was different from usual, radiating an aura that Imke recognized at once.

'That young cameraman?' she asked.

It was as if her daughter were bathed in happiness. She wore it like an invisible garment that made her invulnerable. My golden girl, thought Imke. But then it struck her that Caro had been in love too. And love had not protected her, might even have killed her.

It wasn't the young cameraman. It was someone else. Jenna said she didn't know much about him yet. They'd only recently met. Anything was possible, there were no reservations, nothing to slow them down.

He wasn't a boy like Jenna's previous boyfriends. That slightly bothered Imke. He was about ten years older than her daughter, a grown man. Only the other day Jenna herself had still been a child.

Living with her daughter, Imke had learned above all that if you tried to persuade her not to do something, you were just about certain to achieve the opposite. So she listened, and restrained herself.

'But do be careful,' she said as she got up to go two hours later. 'Now of all times you mustn't trust anyone blindly. Will you promise me that?'

Jenna nodded. But her nod meant nothing. Her smile told the old, old story: girl meets boy. Jenna had fallen in love with this man, and nothing would change her mind.

* * *

'Mama, I'm in love.'

'Nathaniel! My boy! Where are you?'

Why could she never listen?

'Did you hear what I said, Mama?'

She started crying. He hated it when she cried. He wasn't prepared to be responsible for her in any shape or form. Am I my mother's keeper? he asked himself.

Grandmother had made him learn the whole damn Bible off by heart. Now he could come up with the right quote for all occasions. And he liked playing about with the biblical quotes, twisting them round. Perhaps it was a late revenge.

'Are you listening to me at all, Mama? I'm in love.'

As if it mattered whether she listened to him or not. She never had, not once in his entire childhood, and that had lasted a hell of a long time.

'Oh, you've told me that so often, Nathaniel.'

He couldn't stand that whining tone of voice. Did she still think there was any point in appealing to him for pity? And those constant reproaches. How dare she keep criticizing him?

'Nathaniel? Nathaniel! Are you there?'

He hung up and put the phone card in his wallet. A young girl was standing outside the phone box, smoking. He ought to get a mobile. That would be practical. And anonymous. No one would be able to eavesdrop when he made a call any more.

Outside he tried to get control over his emotions. Conversations with his

219

mother always left him upset. He had never finally broken with her, that was the trouble. A neat line drawn under that part of his life, and he'd be free.

As he walked through the village, a place where he had never been before, he relished seeing buildings and people in the streets who were new to him. It gave him a sense of security.

He thought of Caro and realized, to his surprise, that there was no pain connected with the thought. She had retreated into the background. She'd become a memory that would fade more and more from week to week, from month to month. It had always been like that.

Although he had really loved Caro.

He walked all round the pretty village with its stone houses, explored a park with tall old trees, studied the inscriptions on the gravestones leaning sideways in a little cemetery. Until his feet hurt, and he sat down in a roadside café and ordered an espresso.

He was enjoying this half-day off work that he had decided to take for relaxation, just so that he could let himself drift. Now and then he needed that. Working so hard wore you out soon enough.

Girls strolled by, young women. Summer shone out of their eyes, cast a spell over their movements and their hair. Nathaniel watched them, appreciating the sight the way you might appreciate a picture.

He felt no desire for them, which took a weight off his mind. Relaxed, he leaned back and put his sunglasses on. Everything looked even more peaceful through the tinted lenses.

Life lay before him. A wonderful life. Just as he'd always dreamed of it. Life with a woman at his side who put all others in the shade.

'Jenna,' he whispered, and tenderly let the name melt on his tongue.

* * *

Merle fed the cats and then got ready for the meeting of the animal rights group. Jenna was out with that man again. This had been going on for three days. Every evening. By the time she came back Merle was already asleep in bed.

They didn't meet until midday at the earliest. A few times they had half-heartedly wondered how to go on with their search for Caro's murderer. And that had been it.

This wasn't the way Merle had imagined the holidays. What they'd undertaken to do wasn't going to resolve itself just like that.

She was so annoyed that she stopped asking about Jenna's love-life. Let Jenna wallow in her cosy togetherness with this man. Merle didn't mind.

you are
my all
I need
no more

It had been the same with Caro. Surely Jenna couldn't have forgotten that. Or had she just seen it all differently? Merle shut the door of the flat behind her. She suddenly felt like crying.

* * *

ARE THE POLICE SNOOZING?

They couldn't have picked a better lead headline. Even first thing in the morning the boss had been at a temperature of a hundred and eighty degrees, and he swept through the meeting like a textbook illustration of the choleric personality.

He had sweated, roared and waved his arms about. His face had turned bright red shading into purple. Once he had vented his feelings he stormed out of the room, slamming the door behind him so violently that the glass in it developed a hairline crack.

Bert was unimpressed by this performance. He had seen it all too often before. At times he thought such outbursts conformed to some natural law in his profession. You sat them out and then got back to work.

In his case that meant another expedition to Arno Kalmer's farm. During the first interviews he had paid most attention to the men, leaving the women aside. He was going to question them next.

He felt he was on the right track. At the same time there was nothing, nothing at all that he could point to. He couldn't sell the boss a mere feeling that he was right. The boss wanted results, and if there weren't any then some must be delivered.

Bert had spent another evening with Caro's diary and poems, and was furious with his own intellectual failure. It wasn't possible for a girl not yet twenty to code the truth so perfectly that he, with all his experience, couldn't decipher it. Every poem laid a trail. He just had to look at it the right way.

Easier said than done.

Investigations always consisted mainly of routine. And all that was going on as usual. But still there were no results, nothing the police could build on. Even the publication of a photo of Caro in the newspaper hadn't produced anything concrete. The policewoman who took calls from the public was in despair. Any amount of information had been phoned in, but none of it led them anywhere near the murderer.

Perhaps they really were dealing with a highly intelligent, extremely clever killer. Or perhaps the man had just had outrageous luck.

But sometime, thought Bert grimly, turning into the strawberry farmer's yard, sometime or other you too will make a mistake. And I'll be there to pick it up.

* * *

His favourite thing was driving me around and showing me villages that particularly attracted him. He had a good eye for things. And people. But he never got very close to the people.

On these drives it was like being on holiday, where you can see a place at a kind of a distance, without really being part of it. Now and then I thought: I'd like to write that down. Perhaps to decrease the distance that way.

He showed me the world, or rather the part of the world that mattered to him. And he told me about his past life. I could see his childhood like a film.

It was obvious to me that a man like him wouldn't do any steady job. You don't tie such people down. You have to let them spread their wings.

I was fascinated by the idea of working now here, now there, not having to decide today what you'd be doing tomorrow. What did I have to show that could compete with it? I just went along the path my parents had set out for me like a good girl.

He was one of the strawberry pickers I'd seen in the fields while I was driving out to see my mother. He knew our mill house; he'd often admired it when he went for walks. He'd even read some of my mother's books. He told me all this in his calm, deep voice, and every time he touched me I almost stopped breathing.

I told him about my mother and my father. About my grandmother, Tilo and Merle. I even told him about Angie and my little brother. And I thought: How can he be interested in anyone as ordinary as me?

He took my hand and kissed each fingertip separately. I went hot and cold, and buried my other hand in his hair.

'Sssh,' he said close to my ear, like a father soothing his child. 'Let's take our time. We have our whole life ahead of us.'

Our whole life. Yes. That was all I wanted.

* * *

Many friendships between girls cool off as soon as a man turns up. Merle could never understand it. Above all, she would never have thought it possible that Caro, Jenna and she could be like that. And now Jenna was acting like a love-sick goose.

Merle had tried broaching the subject with her a couple of times, but Jenna just didn't understand what she was talking about. 'My God, Merle,' she had said, 'don't begrudge me my happiness.'

That had been too much for Merle. 'Are you out of your mind?' she had shouted at Jenna. 'Do you really think I'd begrudge you that?' She had swept the fruit dish off the table with a single movement of her arm, registering with satisfaction the way it broke into a thousand pieces, while the apples rolled this way and that. 'If so, you're the silliest cow I ever met!'

She had left the flat and wandered aimlessly through the streets, until she suddenly found herself outside Claudio's place. She stood there undecidedly, but the next moment Claudio had spotted her.

He came out to meet her, full of contrition, put his arms around her, kissed her, shed tears, swore eternal love and took her into the café. Then he made her sit down, lit candles and served her a reconciliation meal.

'Now, little one, tell me what the matter is. What's depressing you, eh?'

Merle didn't want to talk about it to Claudio. But she did all the same. Because she had to shake off her disappointment and anger.

Claudio rolled his eyes, enraptured. 'But she loves him, Merle! How can you expect her to be sensible?'

Yes, how could she? She wasn't even being sensible herself. How often had she promised herself she was going to break it off with that devil Claudio? How often had she tried it? And she'd always gone back to him.

She saw the delight in his eyes, reminded herself of their last quarrel, and felt that she loved him in spite of his waywardness, or perhaps because of it. And suddenly it wasn't difficult to think of Jenna without indignation any more.

'Will you stay this evening?' asked Claudio.

Merle nodded. She would put on the horrible green apron and work for Claudio again. She would stay as long as he wanted. And although it was wrong, it seemed somehow right too.

* * *

It was dangerous to go so far. He had given away his identity to her. A proof of his trust in her, but she didn't know that. If she talked, anything could happen. The superintendent was not a stupid man.

But he couldn't ask Jenna to keep quiet about it as he had asked Caro. If Caro happened to have said something to one or other of her friends in spite of him, Jenna would see a connection at once.

He'd have to tell her everything at some point. At the latest when it was time for him to think up a new name again.

Bonnie and Clyde. Would she stand by him?

He had shut himself in his room and taken out the box with his mementoes. Carefully he took off the lid.

He had tied the locks of hair together separately with thin gold ribbon. He let one after another slide through his fingers. Then he put them in a plastic bag.

After that he looked at the necklaces for the last time. It had been coincidence that they were all wearing necklaces. A helpful coincidence which had put the police on a false trail.

He was not a fetishist. He had taken them only as souvenirs. They still meant a lot to him, and he could hardly bring himself to get rid of them. But he must. They put him in unnecessary danger.

But he decided not to destroy them. He couldn't bring himself to do that. He'd bury them. Somewhere out in the country, where no one would see him, where no one knew him.

With the plastic bag in his jacket pocket, he left the house, got into his car and drove away. He would make a new start. He would literally bury his past. To be free. To be free at last. For ever.

* * *

It always amazed Bert to see how different people's powers of observation were. Some took in almost nothing outside their own small world, some were fascinated by everything that went on around them. Some stored up their observations for a short time, others forgot them at once. And there were others again who remembered every detail. Police work would never function without these people.

Women, Bert had found, were almost always more precise in what they saw than men. But their accounts often departed from the essentials, turned rather woolly and random. Then you had to bring them back to the subject.

Margot thought this view of his was typically male. She had only recently thrown that up at him, and she had hurt him, because she hadn't been prepared to argue about it.

Bert didn't see what was so typically male about the fact that he thought women were better at observation than men.

'Because you just don't listen!' she had snapped at him. 'Unless someone's committed a murder or at least is involved in a murder case.'

Kalmer the farmer had given Bert the use of his office, a dark and cheerless room. The best thing about it was the fragrance of strawberries drifting in through the open window.

One by one the women strawberry pickers entered the small room where Bert was waiting with his questions. They all wore their work clothes, a motley assortment of lightweight summer garments. Some of them seemed quite glad of the short interruption to their work, others were in a hurry to get back to the fields. They were paid by piece work, not by the hour.

Bert thought it was best to question people in the surroundings they knew. He had police colleagues who saw it differently, who put their interviewees under pressure so as to make faster progress. And it was a truism that pressure was best generated in an unfamiliar setting.

'You'll never be a real cop,' Margot often used to say, and it had sounded loving, like praise. It was a long time since he'd heard her say so, and today she would probably have a disappointed note in her voice.

He asked his questions, and listened. His main interest was in the women who had arrived here before the strawberry harvest. Simone Redleff had been murdered at the beginning of June.

In April there had been only eleven male and ten female casual labourers on the farm. Kalmer had given Bert a list of their names.

Bert had talked to the men already. None of them had noticed anything that made him take further steps.

Are you on friendly terms with the other workers? Is there anyone you don't like? Do you know of any tension between particular individuals? Did you see anything that seems odd to you in retrospect?

He hadn't asked those questions the first time round. He had not gone into detail then, hadn't touched on the personal level. That was a mistake. He ought to have trusted his instincts from the first. But then again, in this case his instinct had confirmed a common prejudice.

Take your washing off the line! The circus folk are coming to town!

Two names came up several times in the women's statements: Malle Klestof and Nathaniel Taban. The former was described by most of the women as weird, the latter as nice but sometimes rather irritating.

The two men were on friendly terms with each other, the women said. Not really close friends, but they were mates: they had a drink together now and then, went to the cinema or a bar the way mates do.

'But somehow they don't really fit together.' He heard that more than once as well.

Bert relaxed. His interviews weren't finished yet, but he had the unmistakable feeling that he had found a lead at last. It might end nowhere, but it was the only lead he had.

18

He'd done it. The past was dead and buried.

A man's gotta do what a man's gotta do. John Wayne or some other big shot in American Westerns had said that in a movie. Although it was rather too theatrical for Nathaniel's liking, it perfectly described his feelings at the moment.

He'd done what he had to do. In a small wood out in the country. His grandmother would have called it the back of beyond.

Now he was on his way to the strawberry pickers' hostel. He could see Malle from some way off, sitting on the low wall reading the free advertising paper delivered to all households every Friday by a stout fair-haired boy.

Malle always studied the advertising paper thoroughly. On the side, he did shady deals in used electrical parts. Nathaniel didn't know anything about them in detail, and didn't want to.

'Long time no see,' Malle spat. 'Except at work, I mean.'

'I've had this and that to do,' said Nathaniel briefly. 'How about a beer now, though?'

That brought Malle to his feet. 'Hey, that cop was back,' he told Nathaniel on the way to the village pub. 'He was questioning the girls for a change, not us. Something new, I suppose.' He grinned, and scratched his belly under his T-shirt.

No one can know anything, Nathaniel mentally reassured himself, fighting down the rising panic. Not even smart-aleck Malle knows anything important about me. Take it easy. Very easy. Of course they'd go on asking questions. It doesn't mean a thing.

He congratulated himself on getting rid of the incriminating material. Sometimes he really did have a sixth sense. Now he just had to dispose of the key to the girls' flat. Perhaps he'd find a way of leaving it somewhere he could still lay his hands on it easily. You never knew. He might need it again sometime.

In the pub Malle poured a lot of liquor down his throat in double-quick time. Nathaniel drank moderately. He couldn't afford to befuddle his brain. He must have his thoughts straight, just in case he came into that superintendent's orbit. He heard Malle babbling away without really listening to a single word of it.

Think clearly, he told himself. Don't get careless. He had found the girl who was right for him, so he mustn't risk anyone coming across his trail. He had a duty to look after himself, keep safe. For Jenna. For their life together. And the children they'd have some day.

He had thought he'd reached his aim with Caro too. And had been so bitterly disappointed. Fundamentally, he thought, everyone has always disappointed me. Anger rose in him again. He went over to the pinball machine to play it out of his system.

Malle watched him, and finally turned off the flow of chitchat. Sometimes Nathaniel found him hard to take. Like he found most people. Everyone, really. Except for Jenna.

* * *

We'd come up against a blank wall. We couldn't move any further. We had no idea where we could go looking for Caro's boyfriend now.

'Suppose we just ask people in the street and in shops?' Merle looked at me hopefully.

'You want to go about showing Caro's picture to total strangers and asking them questions?'

'We didn't know the people in the clubs and cafés either.'

'That was quite different, Merle.'

'Oh yes? Like how?'

'There at least we had a starting point. Caro went to those places.'

'And I suppose she didn't walk about the streets or go into the shops here – is that what you mean?'

Merle was really getting me down with her know-all attitude. I wasn't comfortable around her just now anyway. She was carrying on like Joan of Arc. How could she say I'd let Caro down? How could she say I'd forgotten what we were planning to do? Just because I'd been out with Nat a few times. I hadn't let Caro down. I needed a little break, that was all.

'Maybe we should keep out of each other's hair for a bit,' I suggested. 'To clear the air.'

She took a deep breath to come back at me with a sharp reply, but then thought better of it, turned on her heel and left the flat.

I hadn't meant to hurt her feelings. But I couldn't bring myself to run after her. I decided to run a bath, lie in the tub and read. And think of Nat.

Perhaps this evening I could persuade him to come and have a meal in the flat with us sometime, as soon as possible. If Merle got to know him she was sure to like him. And then she'd understand me.

I'd have liked to introduce Nat to everyone ages ago, if only he wasn't so reluctant. No wonder, with the sad childhood he'd had. His grandparents wouldn't let him have any friends. He'd never invited a school friend home, even for his birthday. Experiences like that are bound to leave their mark on anyone.

The foam tingled on my skin as I stretched out in the water. It smelled of orange blossom. I closed my eyes and pictured Nat's face.

I'd be patient with him.

And love him, love him, love him.

Until . . .

In my memory I heard Caro saying what I didn't want to think through to the end. And now I saw her face too. It had made its way into my mind, in front of Nat's face. Her face the way it looked in the mortuary.

Suddenly a shudder ran down my back, right there in the warm water.

* * *

Merle didn't take refuge in Claudio's arms, and was proud of it. Instead, she went to see Dorit and Bob, her closest friends in the animal rights group. She felt like company and being alone at the same time. That wasn't a contradiction in terms with Dorit and Bob.

They'd been living together for the last six months in a flat where each of the tiny rooms led to another, so that in the end you were back in the room where you'd begun the round trip.

'Tea?' asked Bob, picking up the kettle to fill it.

Merle nodded, and sat down on the battered kitchen sofa.

'If you want to talk . . .' Dorit left the sentence in the air and opened the cupboard where they kept biscuits and so on.

Merle shook her head. She looked at the two of them moving round the comfortable, well-lit kitchen. Wasn't it odd that so many people preferred to sit in their kitchens? Everyone she knew did. Perhaps that was why she couldn't shake free of Claudio. Almost his whole life was inevitably spent in the kitchen.

'Would you like us to have tea with you,' asked Dorit, 'or would you rather be alone for a bit?'

'Alone,' said Merle. 'If you don't mind.'

'Don't be daft,' said Bob, blowing her a kiss.

They took their cups and went into another room. Merle didn't feel guilty about it. She'd do the same for her friends. She had to think. And at the moment she could think better here than anywhere else.

* * *

Bert remembered Malle Klestof the moment he saw him coming into the room. The strawberry farmer's wife had let him have the office again for interviews. She moved provocatively in her summer dress, which was almost see-through and had a low neckline. She probably turned the heads of many of the seasonal workers.

Bert wasn't attracted to her himself. It was her voice he didn't like, a toneless, flat, one-dimensional voice that sounded almost mechanical. How such a body could harbour such an unsensuous voice was a contradiction, and he thought about it until there was a knock at the door and the man Malle came in.

After the first few sentences Bert remembered that this man was the gossip among the pickers. Malle Klestof seemed to know all the dark secrets that people carefully tried to hide. He knew who was chasing who, who owed money, and how much. He knew everyone's family circumstances, their hopes and their deepest fears.

He didn't volunteer this information. He had to have it wormed out of him, apparently reluctant to give answers. But Bert suspected that he secretly loved every minute of it. Being well-informed, to him, might mean he got respect. It certainly meant that he had power.

He was a yes-man, Bert thought, someone who felt at ease in a crowd and probably had a new set of opinions every day.

His alibi for the murders of Caro and Simone had already been confirmed by the strawberry farmer's wife and his friend Nathaniel Taban. Malle Klestof had been working in the office on both days. Towards evening he had gone into Bröhl, where he had been in a beer garden until late at night with his mate Nathaniel Taban.

'This Nathaniel Taban . . .'

'Nate?' Malle thrust his chin out aggressively. 'What about him?'

Nate. Bert noticed the abbreviation. 'You tell me about him.'

'Tell you what? There's nothing to say about Nate.'

'There's something to say about everyone.'

'He's a lone wolf, same as me.'

You, a wolf? Bert thought. More like a hyena.

'And he's my friend.'

Did hyenas live in packs, or were they loners? Bert had a few images from wildlife films in his head; that was all he knew about them. Didn't hyenas pick up the scent of a wounded animal nearby?

Half an hour later Bert was sure that Malle knew almost nothing about his alleged friend Nate. 'Where is your friend at the moment?' he asked.

'Got today off,' said Malle. 'Going around the place. Cowboys in Westerns saddle their horses, Nate takes his car.'

'Just going around? How do you mean?'

'Like I say. He must've driven hundreds of kilometres since he's been here. I took a look at his speedo once or twice. Didn't let him know, of course. Nate hates people poking their noses into his business.'

Half an hour later Bert ended the interview. Malle had turned suspicious. As if he was afraid he'd given too much away. He shut up. It was like a roller blind coming down over his face.

'Till next time.' Bert offered Malle his hand.

'Next time? What more do you want?' Malle's handshake was soft and limp.

'A solution to this case,' said Bert. 'I hate to think of the murderer of four young women going around free, still not punished for his crimes.'

'What's it got to do with me?' Malle's tone of voice showed that he felt safe. He had an alibi for all the murders. Nothing could happen to him.

'It's possible that you know him,' said Bert. 'It's even possible that you know him well. You may be working here with him day after day, who knows?'

Malle's eyes went large and round. He opened his mouth and shut it again. Wheels were beginning to go round in his head. Bert registered the fact, and realized that he had taken a step forward.

At last, he thought as he drove back to the office. At last we're getting somewhere.

* * *

Show me your room, I'd have liked to say to him. Show me where you live. So I can imagine you when I'm not with you. Take me to see your mother. You don't talk about her, but I'm sure we'd get on well because we both love you.

Come home with me. See the flat that I'm so proud of, talk to Merle for a bit. And then I'll take you to the mill with me. You'll see the inside of our lovely house. Meet my mother and Edgar and Molly. And Tilo, of course, if he happens to be there. Tilo is the best thing that could have happened to my mother.

And if you're really brave we'll go and see my grandmother. She has X-ray eyes: she can see beneath the façade to a person's real character. Perhaps she'll give you her seal of approval. And if not I'll only love you all the more, I promise.

But of course I didn't say any of that to him, I just thought it while I looked at him sitting beside me, changing gear, steering the car, looking in the rear-view mirror and doing all that the way no one else had ever done before. Every movement he made was perfect. Every movement he made increased my addiction.

He liked to be quiet with me. So I stayed quiet. Although my heart was almost overflowing with love and longing and I really, really wanted to say so.

So why didn't I?

He gave me a dark look, as if he were thinking of stopping the car this minute to kiss me and put a hand inside my blouse. But then he just turned up the volume of the radio.

We were on our way to a little village, very old, where almost all the houses were under a preservation order. He loved the place. It was a dream of his to buy an old house like that and be able to renovate it some day.

I knew so much about him, and yet so little. He had told me about his bad experiences with women, and the therapy he'd had. 'Give me time,' he had said. 'I have to get my confidence back first.'

I'd obviously let myself in for a really complicated love affair. Like Caro. And Merle.

I touch you
fearing
you'll fall
to pieces
in my hands

As if Caro had foreseen this moment. My fear of touching him and suddenly finding that he was all just in my imagination.

'What are you thinking of?' he asked.

'Caro, and you and me.' I would never lie to him.

He asked no more questions, just took my hand and squeezed it, and drove a little faster.

* * *

Imke had been working hard, wouldn't let anything distract her, just did a little cleaning, washing and ironing now and then, so that when Mrs Bergerhausen came back after the holidays she wouldn't entirely lose her faith in human nature.

Yet she didn't know why she was in such a hurry with the book. She had plenty of time. And she was never keen to reach the end of a novel, because that meant she had to say goodbye to its characters. She was always afraid of leaving her perfectly constructed microcosm and going back to the well-trodden paths of everyday life again.

'I'm unfit for life, I really am,' she told Edgar, who looked at her as if he understood, but was really just waiting for something to eat. Molly was out and about. She was a good hunter and ate the mice she killed. 'Molly is a proper cat,' said Imke. 'Not a paper tiger like you.'

She rang Jenna and Merle's number. No one answered. She tried reaching Jenna's mobile. '*The person you wish to talk to . . .*' Blah blah blah.

It's the girls' holidays, she told herself. It's perfectly normal for them not to be at home in this fine weather. But another part of her wanted to know just where they were. The fictional murderer in her novel would soon be arrested. Caro's murderer still hadn't been caught.

She called the police. Bert Melzig was out. Could she give the superintendent a message? asked the friendly woman at the other end of the line. No need, replied Imke. She'd ring again.

So as to make at least one successful call, she rang her mother, who was just back from the hairdresser's and spent a good five minutes complaining

237

about her failed perm. 'Well?' she asked then. 'Would the girls like to come and stay with me for a while after all?'

'There's no getting Jenna to do anything at the moment, Mother. She's just fallen in love.'

'In love? Who with?'

That was just like her, always came straight to the point, no beating about the bush. Imke appreciated that feature of her mother's character, even if it was often uncomfortable.

'Except that he's around thirty and absolutely wonderful in every respect, I don't know anything about him.'

'Ask him to coffee. And me too. Soon, do you hear me?'

How urgent that sounded. They were all beside themselves with worry about Jenna and Merle; they just hid it well under the masks they wore every day. Masks worn so that they could endure life, thought Imke. Life and death.

She didn't even feel embarrassed about bursting into tears in the middle of her conversation with her mother.

* * *

He wouldn't tell Nate about it. The season wouldn't last much longer now, and then their ways would part in any event. Why risk annoying him?

Nate was nervous. There was something on his mind. You sensed it when you were with him. As if he were all tensed up.

But that didn't necessarily have anything to do with the murders.

A man who's a good mate of mine, thought Malle, can't be a murderer at the same time. Impossible. I'd notice that kind of thing. Couldn't just be hidden, not when you're working side by side day after day, crawling around the fields in all weathers.

They had sweated, toiled, eaten and drunk together, sat in silence together, laughed together. You get to be like two sides of the same coin, thought Malle. And some police superintendent couldn't just pop up and come between them.

But wouldn't it be better to tell Nate about the questions he'd been asked in the interview? Several people knew it had taken place. And they knew that the superintendent had come back specially for this one talk with him. By keeping quiet Malle would be making a mountain out of a molehill. He'd be giving his conversation with the superintendent a significance that it hadn't had at all.

So why was he bothered about it? Why did he feel so uncomfortable? He wasn't one of those who were afraid of Nate, was he?

Sure, Nate's manner could sometimes be intimidating. He often gave you a penetrating look that left you feeling guilty, although you'd done nothing wrong. And his voice could be so cold and cutting that you felt like making for the wide blue yonder.

But afraid? Not of Nate. Not his good friend Nate.

Malle decided to spend the evening in Bröhl. He needed to have people around him. Strangers who wouldn't ask him any questions. He didn't feel like brooding any more. He just wanted to be left in peace and have a few beers.

And he had no desire whatsoever to cross Nate's path this evening.

* * *

Jenna sat beside him in silence, looking at the road ahead. She obviously sensed that he didn't feel like talking. A good woman always sensed what her man wanted.

He felt as if his nerves were stretched to breaking point. Somehow this was all getting too much for him. It was not the right moment for a new love.

But did love ask before it overwhelmed you?

Having to think exactly what he would confide to Jenna and what he wouldn't was putting him under enormous pressure. But he must remain cautious. He still couldn't entirely trust her.

Time, he thought. We need time.

And that was the problem. Soon he'd be moving on. Then what? Jenna was still at school. How was he going to stand it without her? Weekend visits? Seasonal workers didn't have weekends off.

For the first time in his life he wanted to settle down. He looked at Jenna and met her eyes. She smiled, and touched his hand on the steering wheel.

I love her, he thought. Heavens, I love this girl so much.

She would help him to forget all the bad things. To be a better person. Above all, however, she would stay with him. For the rest of her life.

19

Merle heard Jenna come home. She looked at the alarm clock by her bed. One in the morning. Never mind. She hadn't gone to sleep yet anyway.

The light in the corridor crept through the narrow crack under the door into her room. Merle very much wanted to get up, go into the kitchen and have a midnight feast with Jenna. Or at least a cup of tea. They'd often done that when Caro was still alive.

Jenna probably wouldn't be hungry. Her prince was bound to have invited her out to dinner. At some trendy place in the country. It annoyed her a lot that Jenna told her hardly anything about him. She was never usually the type to make a mystery of everything.

And I, thought Merle, am always stupid enough to wear my heart on my sleeve.

She imagined it – her heart outside her and pinned to her sleeve. Figures of speech could be ridiculous if you took them literally.

She had spent all evening with Caro's poems, looking in her photo albums, writing down her own thoughts. She'd worked it out that the pressed flower and the leaves must be a clue to Caro's boyfriend. He'd probably given them to her. That would be the only reason why Caro would press a flower.

But it was a very small, ordinary sort of flower. So it must have had some special meaning, or Caro's boyfriend would surely have gone for something like a rose instead.

Merle had puzzled over the scarf too. It had probably belonged to a man. It wasn't a woman's scarf – not pretty enough. Caro had definitely never worn it. Merle would have remembered.

Old men in light-coloured suits often wore scarves like that as cravats round their necks. But Merle had looked at the little tag sewn inside it – it wasn't a silk scarf, not even viscose; it was plain cotton.

Instinctively Merle had thoughts of pirates. And then she had gone on working on that picture. What kind of man would wear a scarf like that on his head?

Young men following some kind of fashion. Chefs who had to cover their hair at work. Who else?

You could wear a scarf like that to protect your hair. From dirt. From damp. Or from sunlight.

Merle was beginning to feel certain that Caro's boyfriend had worn the scarf to protect his hair. She had examined it, centimetre by centimetre, under the light of the desk lamp.

She had found a few marks. Of course they had dried up long ago and smelled of nothing now. So they didn't tell her much.

Why had Caro kept the scarf? Presumably because her boyfriend often wore it and it was a part of him.

She'd have liked to talk to Jenna about all these ideas now, but the hurt was still too deep. Jenna wanted to keep her distance? No problem. She was welcome.

When Jenna softly opened the door, put her head into the room and whispered Merle's name, Merle pretended to be asleep.

* * *

I lit the candle on the kitchen table and put out the light. I drew a chair up to the window, sat down and looked out at the street. I loved the town by night. The grey shadows of the buildings with a few rectangles of yellow light.

Since I'd known Nat I loved the town even more. I'd explore it all over again with him. Take him to all the places that were important to me. Later, when he was ready for that.

I looked forward to showing him the castle. The castle park with its geometrically laid out flowerbeds and the little maze behind the water-lily pond. The winding alleys of the Old Town. And of course the Christmas Market.

I wouldn't take just anyone to the Christmas Market with me. It had always been special to me, something I wasn't prepared to share with anyone who wasn't very much part of my life.

we will
never see
the holy
lights together

Why did I think of those lines now?

Caro, I thought, you've been setting puzzles for us the whole time. What lights did you mean? Who were *we*? And why are all your poems so terribly sad?

At Christmas Nat would have gone away long ago; he'd be somewhere else.

I dreamed of Caro that night. We were strolling through the Christmas Market and we passed a Santa Claus giving presents to children. Only when we were opposite him did I recognize Nat's face under the cotton-wool beard.

I touched his arm. 'Nat,' I said, 'meet my friend Caro.'

When I turned round Caro had disappeared, leaving her coat behind. It lay on the pavement, as small and empty and lost as if it belonged to a doll.

* * *

Bert immediately remembered this man too. Nathaniel Taban, the tall, silent man with the fierce eyes. That was how he had noted down his impressions after the first interview.

And indeed, the man seemed to think about every word before he uttered it. His eyes were fixed on Bert, noticed every detail, didn't move away from him for a second.

He was more reserved than Malle Klestof. And considerably more intelligent. His calm, deep voice was deceptive. Underneath it he was strung up very tight. Bert could feel the tension he was under almost physically.

That needn't necessarily mean anything. Most people were nervous when they had to talk to the police, particularly in a murder case. No one acted in a police interview as they would while having a friendly chat on the living-room sofa.

No, he'd never heard the name of Carola Steiger before the murder. The name Caro meant nothing to him either.

It struck Bert that Nathaniel Taban held the photograph of Caro a moment too long. He put the pictures of Simone and the other two girls down again quickly, as if he were afraid they might burn him. Or make his hands dirty.

'You've asked me these questions before,' he said.

Bert had shown him the photographs before too. Nothing about the way Nathaniel Taban looked at them had struck him then, although he was taking careful note of everything. The smallest hesitation could be an important clue. 'We have further information now,' he claimed.

Nathaniel Taban leaned back and folded his arms. A relaxed attitude, Bert wondered, or was he stonewalling? It had become so much a natural part of him to register every tone of voice, every gesture of the person he was questioning that he couldn't shake off the habit even in his private life. It was like a curse.

'Stop looking at me like a cop,' Margot often snapped at him. But with the best will in the world he couldn't do it.

It was particularly difficult to read taciturn people. It took great self-confidence simply to remain silent and let things take their course. This man had that self-confidence. He said nothing, looked at Bert and waited.

Once Bert would have been slightly thrown off balance by such behaviour. He would have talked too much himself, thus decreasing the pressure he wanted to put on his interviewee. He had learned better now. The man wanted to stay silent? Fair enough. Bert could keep quiet too.

Suddenly and surprisingly breaking a silence was a good method at times. Following an impulse, Bert read one of Caro's poems aloud:

'*my prince*
and beggar
charlatan
wise man
I never
touch you
you never
stay you
hate
enclosed spaces'

Under his suntan Nathaniel Taban turned pale. Bert noticed that without batting an eyelid. 'A poem that Caro wrote,' he said. 'Shortly before her death. I'm asking myself who this prince, beggar, charlatan and wise man might be.'

Nathaniel Taban steadily met his gaze. 'I don't know anything about poetry.' The colour was coming back into his face, but only slowly.

'That's a pity,' said Bert. 'We might have tried to interpret the lines together. Do you know anyone who writes?'

Nathaniel Taban shook his head.

Bert had nothing concrete against him. A vague suspicion and unpopularity among his colleagues at work were not enough. A murderer needed a motive, and Bert couldn't see one here.

Were there any signs that Nathaniel Taban was a psychopath?

Bert tried to imagine Caro with this man. He couldn't do it. He was sorry he had never known her when she was alive.

'Did you kill the girls?' he asked, entirely out of the blue. It was a shot fired from the hip, against all his experience and his reason.

Bert was ready for a number of different reactions. The man could be indignant. He could be baffled. He could burst out laughing, give an ironic answer. Raise his eyebrows. He could say, 'Me? Don't be ridiculous.'

Nathaniel Taban did none of those things. He looked right through Bert, and his face took on an expression of extreme grief. For a long moment he seemed to be entirely absorbed in himself.

Bert watched him, fascinated.

Then, quite suddenly, Nathaniel Taban shook himself. He looked at Bert. His eyes turned cold. 'I am not a murderer, Superintendent,' he said. Short and sharp. I. Am. Not. A. Murderer.

Bert couldn't rid himself of the feeling that the man was lying.

* * *

'How was it?' asked Malle. Of course he had heard that the superintendent had been back. Everyone knew that.

'How do you think it was?' Nathaniel grinned derisively. 'He was poking about, acting as if he had a lead.'

'Exactly!' Malle laughed his bleating laughter. It sounded a little thin, and Nathaniel wondered if Malle could suddenly be feeling afraid of him. He was keeping more of a distance than before. Normally he would have slapped Nathaniel on the shoulder now.

Nathaniel knew that Malle too had been questioned again. Everyone was talking about it. But not Malle, who couldn't usually keep anything to himself. He wasn't saying a word. There could be only one reason for that – the same reason as for his sudden fear. Malle suspected him, and was desperately trying to avoid the delicate subject.

Cowardly bastard, thought Nathaniel. He picked up his crate, turned his back on Malle and went back to work. He had left his scarf in the washroom; his hair was falling over his face and sticking to his sweaty skin. An unpleasant sensation.

Nathaniel faded out the sounds of his surroundings and thought. The superintendent couldn't have anything definite on him. He had used a different name and forged papers in north Germany. They couldn't trace him back there.

But what would happen if the police had a saliva test done? Then he'd be found out. A life on the run. With Jenna. Would she be prepared for that?

Why was he bothering about this, though? The superintendent had left again. He didn't know anything at all.

Nathaniel smiled. His love protected him. Nothing could happen to him as long as he loved her.

* * *

He was a strawberry picker!

Merle hurried home at a run to think about it in peace. For once she was thankful to Claudio for being so mean, or he wouldn't have sent her off to a pick-your-own field for strawberries. And Merle had realized all of a sudden that the pressed flower and leaves among Caro's things were from a strawberry plant.

Suddenly it all made sense. Merle had often seen the strawberry pickers in the fields when she went to the mill house with Jenna. Many of them wore scarves to protect their hair from sunlight and sweat.

on your mouth
a terrible red
sweet smile

She could suddenly understand those lines too. When Caro's boyfriend had eaten a strawberry his lips had been red and tasted sweet. And perhaps the smile had seemed terrible to Caro because the whole relationship had turned so dark and baffling.

She had begun self-harming again. That had always been an alarm signal with Caro.

'Oh, shit!' said Merle, her breath coming short. 'Shit, shit, shit!'

They hadn't been able to help Caro because Caro herself had gone along with the man's game. She hadn't said a word to anyone about him. Except for that one last conversation with Jenna. But even then she hadn't really given much away.

who are you?

all those
unasked questions
all those
songs not sung
nine lives
unlived

Suddenly it all sounded like a prophecy. Caro couldn't ask any more questions. Or sing any more songs. Or live her life to the end.

Merle ran on. She felt the sweat breaking out of every pore. She struggled for air. And she was crying. People made way for her. They looked at her face with alarm.

* * *

Bert called Imke Thalheim back. He hadn't done it immediately because he had promised himself he was going to keep his distance. But at the sound of her voice his good intentions wavered. He needed to be with her, sit beside her, hear her and look at her as she talked.

Was there any news? she asked.

'I think we're on the right track,' said Bert. 'But you know that I can't give you any information.'

'I'd hoped you might make an exception in . . . in my case,' she said.

In her case. His heart was beating unreasonably fast. Did her mind work the same way as his? 'That wouldn't be correct,' he said.

'You're right,' she said after a few moments of silence on both sides. 'Forgive me. It's just – well, I'm dying with anxiety about the girls. And I have a feeling . . .'

He usually took the vague feelings people sometimes had seriously – the indefinable fear that seemed to indicate danger.

'What kind of a feeling?' he asked.

'That Jenna's in danger.'

'Is there anything I ought to know?' he asked.

'She's in love.'

'But that's good news.'

'Are you sure? Caro was in love too.'

It was high time they put a stop to the man's activities. That would bring a whole series of fears to an end. And make grieving possible. All those affected by these murders needed to be able to draw a line under them. Then perhaps they could look to the future again.

'You mustn't brood over your fears,' he said. Good advice, but she wouldn't take it. She couldn't. She was entangled in her fears already.

'He's much older than Jenna. And there's something odd about the whole thing. My daughter's usually bubbling over with happiness when she falls in love. Not this time. She hasn't told me anything about him yet.'

Bert thought of Caro. She too hadn't talked about the man she was in love with. Nonsense, he told himself. Was he starting to imagine things?

But the parallels were there. And so was the inner tension that he always felt when a new door opened in a case.

'Have a quiet talk to your daughter,' he suggested. 'Ask her for details. Try to find out his name.'

'I'll try.' He was right. It was the only way to get rid of this gnawing anxiety. 'Although she's almost never at home.'

After this conversation Bert sat there thinking for a while. He had the impression that he was holding a tangled ball of threads which might suddenly unravel. If only he could find the right one to pull.

* * *

He was sitting in his car, waiting for Jenna. They were going out to Blankenau again, the little town with the beautiful old houses. Somehow he drew strength from these historic sights. And courage.

He really belonged in a different period. He'd always felt that. Perhaps it was all true about reincarnation, and Jenna and he had met before in an earlier life.

Had they been in love then? Had they even maybe lived together?

He'd ask her if she believed people were reborn.

He would ask if she loved him. He'd ask if she had ever loved anyone before as much as she loved him.

And he would ask her if she'd go away with him when his job here came to an end.

Impatiently he looked for her. He mustn't do anything in too much of a hurry. He mustn't frighten her. He must go carefully.

Midday. He had taken the afternoon off. 'I have to go to the doctor,' he'd said, and that was what he had told Malle too.

So far he had managed to cover all his traces.

* * *

There was a letter lying on the kitchen table.

Dear Merle

I'm sorry, I was really horrible to you. Please don't be angry any more! It's not that I wouldn't like to tell you things. It's just that Nat and I have talked about so much, but we still know very little about each other.

I know it sounds funny, but it's as if I've known him all my life. As if I know everything important about him. What difference does it make whether he's a doctor, an accountant or a strawberry picker? I love him. That's all that matters.

251

*Couldn't we get together tomorrow and have a nice long talk? And clear up
all this stupid stuff that's come between us? I'll look forward to it!*

Love and kisses

Jenna

*P.S. We're going out again to one of those little medieval towns he likes so
much. Imagine me looking at old walls and not being bored! Women are really
silly when they're in love — yes, I know, I know!*

Merle read the letter several times. Each time, a couple of words leaped
to her eye. Doctor. Accountant. *Strawberry picker.*

How high were the chances of both Caro and Jenna falling in love with
a strawberry picker? About zero. Unless the strawberry picker was the same
man, and had known how to up his chances a little with Jenna.

Next moment Merle had the superintendent's card in her hand and was
punching in his number.

He wasn't in his office, and his mobile was obviously switched off. How
could he be out of reach now, when Merle needed him?

20

I was a little late, and I'd been afraid he'd be annoyed. He was very keen on punctuality. I'd noticed that already. But then I saw the real anger in his face, and it scared me. I mean, a little delay was nothing. How would he react if he had some real reason to be upset?

'One of the cats left a puddle in the hall. I had to mop it up.' I saw the expression on his face change. Saw the anger disappear and give way to a hesitant smile.

'That's all right.' He drew me close, or as close as we could get behind the steering wheel, and kissed me. At last he was himself again.

He seemed to be thinking about something during the drive. When he was thinking he frowned; he already had fine lines on his forehead. I didn't mind. I was with him. That was all I wanted.

The landscape flew by outside: woods, meadows, fields, arable land and pasture. I was glad I lived in a small town with real country still around it. 'Can you imagine living in a big city?' I asked.

'I could live anywhere with you,' replied Nat, without taking his eyes off the road. 'Just so long as we're together. Nothing else matters.'

'Except our families and friends,' I said. 'My mother, my grandmother and Merle are the most important women in my life. I think I'd feel somehow incomplete without them, only half of myself, as if I'd had an amputation.'

He didn't reply to that. His hands tightened on the steering wheel.

I put my head back and closed my eyes. Thought of my bag. And the condom I'd tucked into it. I'd been carrying it around with me ever since I met Nat. Would I be taking it out today?

* * *

Nate at the doctor's? Pull the other one! Nope. He was skiving off. Malle carried his full crate to the trailer. Sweat was running down his neck. It was a real slog, this work, but it made money. Not a lot of money, but enough to live on.

Malle had never been able to imagine anything but a free life. It got to the point where he felt he was stifling in enclosed spaces. He had to be out of doors, feel the sun, wind and rain. It was the same with a lot of people he'd met on his various jobs.

When a seasonal worker skived off it must mean something. They weren't in regular employment, when you just had to hand in a sick note to your boss and still get your salary. And they were seldom ill. They were tough, could stand up to any virus.

Perhaps Nate had some kind of business deal on and hadn't said anything about it to him. He was so secretive, kept his lip tightly buttoned. But just now, with the cops sniffing around again, it was important for each of them to know what the other was doing. So that they could lend each other a hand if necessary.

No one understood why Nate had palled up with Malle, if that was what you could call it. Malle didn't understand it himself. They had nothing, absolutely nothing in common except for liking a beer in the evening. But even there Nate held back. Malle had never seen him drunk.

As if he had to keep in control, thought Malle. As if otherwise his life would fall apart. He took the empty crate back and returned to where he was picking. He realized that he knew next to nothing about Nate. Nate, on the other hand, knew pretty well everything about him.

*   *   *

Someone calling her at last! Imke laughed out loud with relief. 'Merle! Where are the pair of you? Why didn't you ring?'

Merle started crying. Imke felt her whole body freeze. 'What's the matter, Merle?' Please, she thought, please, please. Don't let anything have happened to Jenna!

Sobbing, Merle told Imke about her suspicions. How she thought Jenna was in love with the man who'd been Caro's boyfriend just before she died. She explained, briefly, how she'd worked that out.

'But that's far from meaning . . .' Imke's mouth suddenly felt dry. She swallowed convulsively. 'Where's Jenna?'

'Out with him,' said Merle, so quietly that Imke could hardly hear her.

'Wait for me,' said Imke. 'I'll be with you in ten minutes.' She flung the telephone down on the table, snatched up her handbag and ran to the car. She didn't go to the trouble of closing the garage door, but went down the drive at a speed that sent the gravel spraying up behind her.

*   *   *

He wasn't annoyed with Jenna for being late any more. It had just been a brief spurt of anger that quickly died down. You couldn't be angry with Jenna for long. And she hadn't kept him waiting on purpose.

She sat beside him, humming along to the music on the radio. As if there were no problems. She didn't know what storm clouds were gathering.

The police were not to be underestimated, particularly not this man Melzig. When he first saw the superintendent he'd known at once that you couldn't fool the man easily. Something told him that the crunch had come. That he must react. Melzig was on his trail.

Jenna stroked his arm. 'I'm so happy,' she said.

He squeezed her hand. He would never let anyone make her sad.

* * *

Yes. Merle would wait. For Jenna's mother and for the superintendent's phone call. She had left a message asking him to ring and saying it was urgent.

She found it difficult to trust cops. She would never have dreamed that she'd be asking one for help some day. But she couldn't do any more herself. She had no option.

The cats seemed to feel that she was nervous. They were avoiding her, even hissed if she came too close to them. Merle could understand that. They'd had enough upheavals in their lives; they wanted peace and quiet now.

Merle had put the pressed flower and its leaves, the black scarf, Jenna's letter and Caro's poems on the kitchen table. She had to keep looking at them. She had to keep thinking it all over.

'So what?' she said out loud. 'Suppose he really is a strawberry picker? That doesn't make him the murderer.'

But she knew he was the murderer. If he'd just been Caro's boyfriend he would have got in touch with them. It had been in all the papers that Caro had been murdered. And even if he hadn't read about it – surely he'd have missed Caro and tried to find out about her.

'You total bastard,' said Merle. 'She loved you!'

* * *

Bert had been out to Kalmer's farm again to talk to Nathaniel Taban. To tighten the noose he had put round his neck. He did not for a second doubt that he was on the right track now.

The strawberry farmer's wife told him Nathaniel Taban had taken the afternoon off to see the doctor. Alarmed, Bert had asked if the man had seemed unwell.

Not really, said the farmer's wife, unruffled. He was sturdy as a tree and had seemed the same as usual. She was tidying some papers as she talked to Bert. He got the impression that her composure wasn't real.

Was there something between the two of them?

'I'd like a word with Mr Klestof,' he said. 'Would you fetch him, please?'

Reluctantly she went out to send someone for Malle.

Damn! He'd alerted the man. That had been part of his plan, yes, but he hadn't foreseen that things wouldn't go just as he planned. He could only hope that this time his instinct had let him down, and Nathaniel Taban really had taken the afternoon off for a visit to the doctor.

*   *   *

After her moment of horror on the phone, Imke felt nothing. She drove her car in her usual cool, routine way, observing traffic signs and red lights, noticing every pedestrian, every car, every bicycle. I'm probably in shock, she thought. Like after the accident. She had failed to give way to an Audi, and it had caught her on the passenger side. There was a terrible crunching sound, and the right-hand wing of her car had looked like crumpled foil. She'd been in shock then too. She had felt nothing at the time, only after-wards. That was how she felt now.

As she approached Bröhl she wondered what she could do if Merle's suspicions were correct. Not much. She could only let Bert Melzig know. And hope and pray.

She couldn't find a parking place, and left the car on a double yellow.

A little later she was running up the stairs.

Merle was standing at the door of the flat waiting for her. Her face was tear-stained, and she was crumpling a handkerchief.

257

Imke took her in her arms, held her close for a minute, and then went into the kitchen with her.

'There, you see?' Merle pointed to the table. 'A strawberry plant. And he must have used the scarf to protect his hair. They work in the full sun, so you can imagine how they sweat.'

Imke had so often driven past the strawberry fields. She had so often gone to the strawberry farmer in the village to buy berries. Day after day she'd seen the pickers with their scarves and their hats.

So close.

He had been so close all the time.

Yes, the evidence that Merle had put together made it likely that Caro's friend had been a strawberry picker. But was he her murderer too?

'Would he have ignored her death if he wasn't?' asked Merle, as if she had read Imke's thoughts in her face.

She was right. It was a very simple conclusion to draw. And it made sense.

'Read that.'

Merle picked up the top sheet of the pile of paper and handed it to Imke.

hello
black man
you belong
to darkness
not to me
hello
darling
come up

with me
into the light

'When he wasn't actually picking strawberries,' said Merle scornfully, 'he hid away like a rat. Caro wasn't to know anything about him, and what little she finally did get to hear she wasn't to pass on. It was a sick relationship from first to last.'

Had he made Jenna promise to keep quiet about him too? Imke remembered another of the poems.

you promise me
your life
yet you give
nothing away
while you
know
all about me.

Tilo had refused to look more closely at the poems and help her work out what they meant. First, he said, they were literary texts, and not the kind of thing you could simply apply to real life. Second, he didn't feel he was in a position to say anything about someone he had never known. 'And third,' he had added, 'I'm not prepared to interfere with police investigations.'

But didn't this poem say a lot about Caro? Couldn't you conclude that she was so upset by the man's reserve that she was starting to harm herself again?

'Here,' said Merle, handing Imke another poem. 'The last three lines.'

on your mouth
a terrible red
sweet smile

'A strawberry smile,' said Merle. 'Red and sweet. And terrible. Perhaps Caro was afraid of him.'

'Take it slowly.' Imke massaged her forehead. She had a headache. 'Take it slowly. So that I can grasp it all.'

Could a serial murderer fall in love? Had he had a relationship of some length with all his victims? Had something perhaps gone wrong with each of those relationships, something that drove him to kill?

Imke wished she were only asking herself these questions as part of her research for a new book.

Suddenly her fear came back. The shock had passed off. And although her stomach was churning with anxiety she was glad to be feeling something again. 'The superintendent. We must call him.'

'He's not in his office, and I couldn't reach him on his mobile either.'

'Then let's leave him a message.'

'I've done that already. We can only wait now.'

Imke sat down at the table. She stared at the things Merle had set out on it. Wait.

'Do you know where they were going?' It was hard for Imke to mention Jenna and this man in the same breath.

Merle shook her head. 'They wanted to go to some little medieval town, but Jenna didn't mention the name.' She showed Imke the letter.

When she saw her daughter's handwriting Imke burst into tears. This time it was Merle who comforted her and soothed her. She put her arms round Imke's shoulders and rocked her gently back and forth. 'We'll find them,' she murmured. 'We'll think of something.'

* * *

It was really beautiful in that dreamy little town, even if I couldn't entirely share Nat's enthusiasm. Hump-backed old houses crowded round a small market square paved with cobblestones. Women were once burned as witches in places like that.

'The Middle Ages were a cruel time,' I said. 'We shouldn't let the sight of these pretty houses make us forget that.'

'Every time is cruel.' Nat put his arm round my shoulders. 'Modern man has refined his methods, that's all.'

He was such a mixture of contradictions. He could be happy as a child looking at something beautiful, and the next minute say a thing like that. Perhaps it was because he was older. He'd seen and done so much more than me.

We had an espresso in a street café and watched the people strolling past. Nat's face was soft with contentment. I leaned over and kissed him on the cheek.

I'll be patient with you, I promised him in my mind. And I'll do anything to make you happy.

* * *

The call came as Imke and Merle were poring over the map. There were so many old towns in these parts. How were they to know which one Jenna had gone to with this man?

His name was Nat. Jenna had told her friend that much at least. Imke had never heard the name before, but that wasn't why she disliked it. She would hate anything to do with the man, even if he turned out not to be the murderer. If only for what he had done to Caro when she was still alive.

'I'll be with you,' said Bert Melzig when he had heard what Merle had to say. Half an hour later he was sitting at the table with them, getting them to explain exactly how Merle had reached her conclusions.

'His name is Nat,' said Merle, 'he's around thirty, and—'

'His name's what?' Bert leaned forward.

'Nat. And he—'

'There's a Nathaniel Taban among the strawberry pickers. His friend calls him Nate.'

Imke started. Merle stared at the superintendent as if she'd had an electric shock.

'I've just been out there to talk to him, but I didn't find him. He'd taken the afternoon off. Allegedly to visit the doctor.'

Imke had heard enough. 'Didn't Jenna mention the name of the town at all before today?' she asked. 'For heaven's sake, try to remember, Merle!'

Merle propped her head in her hands. She closed her eyes. But she couldn't remember anything. The likelihood that Jenna had ever mentioned the town name to her was very slight. Jenna had turned quiet and secretive. Like Caro.

* * *

The plain beauty of the buildings cast its spell and calmed him to some extent. Yet his mind was still working away. They would get him sooner or later. And although nothing at all had happened yet, he felt as if the super-intendent's hand were already on his shoulder.

Jenna didn't seem to guess at the turmoil inside him. When their eyes met she smiled. The sun shone on her face and her hair and made her eyes shine.

Driven into a corner like a wild beast – that was how he felt. He had realized very early that he was powerless in the grip of his feelings. His mind could do nothing about them.

They still don't have anything definite against me, he thought, to give himself courage. I have time to react.

'Shall we go for a little walk?' asked Jenna. Her face was so young, so carefree. Not a single line to speak of any bad experience.

He waved to the waitress for the bill.

* * *

On the way to his office Bert called Arno Kalmer and asked if Nathaniel Taban had a car.

'Yes, a dark Fiat Punto,' replied Kalmer briefly.

'Can you tell me its number?'

'Just a moment.' Bert heard sounds: something clattering, footsteps, then paper rustling. 'No, sorry. Didn't note it down. Shall I ask around?'

'That's not necessary, but thanks.'

It would only take Bert a call to find the number. And then? What evidence against Nathaniel Taban did he have? A pressed strawberry flower and three leaves. A black scarf. Poems by a dead girl. Her diaries. The name Nathaniel, Nat or Nate was nowhere in them.

Nothing to prove that Nathaniel Taban was the murderer.

Nothing to prove that he was out with Jenna now.

Bert was relying on pure speculation. And his instincts. Yet again.

Nathaniel Taban was in the records as resident in a village in south Germany. A police officer there had interviewed his landlady. Mr Taban was usually away, she had told him. When he was at home he was quiet, made no trouble. A good tenant; she'd never had any difficulty with him.

Nothing against him. Made no trouble. Quiet. No difficulty. The perfect citizen. But Bert had started things rolling on less evidence than this in his time. He'd have a police search organized for him. Him and Jenna. The danger that something could happen to the girl if he hesitated was just too great.

Never again, he promised himself, would he switch off his mobile so as to be left in peace during lunch. The thought of Merle trying in vain to reach him brought him out in a sweat.

He punched in a number and, back in his car, began giving instructions to start the hunt for Nathaniel Taban.

21

'Come on,' he said. 'Let's drive home.' And then he would pack his things and leave, he thought. With her. But immediately he had doubts. Was that the right way? Might there not be other possibilities?

'Home?' Jenna looked at him in surprise. 'But we've only just arrived.'

'Jenna! Please!' He couldn't think clearly. How was he to make the right decision?

'Well, if you really want to.' Jenna looked around again. As if saying goodbye to all the other things she'd have liked to see.

He sensed that she was thinking about things. But she kept her thoughts to herself. In one way he liked her reserve. On the other hand it maddened him. He wanted to know what she was thinking. He wanted to know what she was feeling. There were too many places in her head to which she could withdraw. And then she was alone. Where he couldn't reach her.

On the way back to the car he took her hand. So that she would stay with him and not disappear into her own thoughts again.

She must never leave him.

* * *

They had stayed in the flat so that they could be reached on the phone. Imke was sitting by the window looking down at the street. Merle had decided to bake a cake. When Jenna got home she would lay the table and cut the cake. Jenna loved surprises.

The cats were gambolling around the room, playfully growling and

265

spitting and chasing each other. Merle was glad to have them there, making cat noises. Imke had said nothing since the superintendent left. And silence was a breeding ground for ghosts.

Three hundred and seventy-five grams of flour, some baking powder, eggs. Merle was using honey to sweeten it. The honey was thick and hard to mix in. She stirred the nibbed almonds into the cake mixture and dropped the cherries in. Soothing manual work.

But she couldn't switch off her thoughts. She thought of Caro. Of her laughter. And then of her dead face. She thought of Jenna and their last quarrel. She had put Jenna's letter in her trouser pocket. It was good to know that she could re-read it any time.

Then the thought of this man Nat pushed its way in. A dark, menacing thought, like the man himself. Merle quickly dismissed it from her mind.

* * *

Perhaps he should try to talk to her. Now. At once. After all, he had no choice. He couldn't go on living as he had until now and just wait for whatever was coming to him.

But how was he to begin? And how far could he go? Jenna wouldn't be able to cope with the truth. Not yet.

He could try some kind of pretext. Suggest an adventure.

No. It wouldn't work. She wouldn't burn all her bridges and go away with him without speaking to her mother and this friend Merle first. She wasn't like Caro. Caro would have enjoyed a game like that.

Time was running out for him. What was he to do?

* * *

There was something the matter with Nat. His hands were shaking and he was driving too fast. I'd have liked to ask him what was wrong, but I didn't dare. He seemed quite different from usual – stern and cool, really strange.

I didn't dare turn on the radio either. I just sat there looking out at the road. Now and then he glanced at me without smiling. Where had the tenderness in his eyes gone?

I had never before thought so long about how to act. I had never before felt so unsure of myself. I longed to hug him, but I was dreadfully afraid of being pushed away.

Be kind again, I thought. Love me again.

I often used to feel like that. My father used to withdraw his love to punish me. Usually I didn't even know what I'd done to make him angry.

I sat up very straight. Took a deep breath. And then I looked at him and asked, 'Nat, what's the matter?'

* * *

The search was on. Everything was moving. Two police officers in an unmarked car were watching the boarding house where Nathaniel Taban was lodging to arrest him if he came back there. Another car was stationed outside the block where Jenna and Merle lived.

Bert faxed his colleagues in north Germany a personal description of Nathaniel Taban and the registration number of his Fiat Punto, and asked them to check up.

A few minutes later an officer there called back. None of the seasonal workers on their lists drove a car with that number. He himself would check the description.

That was pretty much what Bert had expected. No mention of the Fiat in the records of seasonal workers in Jever and Aurich, and no mention of the name Nathaniel Taban either. Perhaps because Taban hadn't been there, but perhaps because he'd used a false name, false papers and a different car.

Bert got himself a coffee. Now he could only wait and hope he'd made the right decision.

* * *

The waiting was getting Imke down. Fascinated, she watched the way Merle dealt with it. First she baked a cherry cake. Then she tidied up the kitchen. Watered the plants. Fed the cats. Took the rubbish downstairs. And in between she kept making fresh coffee.

'Are you hungry?' she asked now.

Imke shook her head. 'Sorry, Merle, I'm not very good company just now.'

'It's this damn uncertainty.' Merle sat down, rubbed an invisible mark off the tabletop and stood up again. 'Enough to send anyone crazy.'

'Do you think . . . ?' Imke felt the tears coming to her eyes. 'Do you think she's all right?'

'I'm sure she is.' Merle put her arms around her. 'Jenna's strong. She knows how to defend herself. And perhaps we're all wrong. Perhaps there's nothing in my stupid theory at all, and she's having a nice walk in the country with him and would laugh herself to death if she knew we were worrying like this.'

Laugh herself to death. Dear God!

'Laugh herself silly, I mean. Oh, shit! I wish she were back now.'

Imke felt the situation was all wrong. She was the older woman, she was senior to Merle, she was the one with wide experience of life. She ought to be comforting Merle, not the other way round. Hesitantly she began caressing Merle's back. 'Hush,' she said. 'Hush.'

And Merle clung to her.

* * *

'Do we have to go home at once?' I asked.

Nathaniel looked at the time. Then at me. Still in a strange way.

'I'd love another little walk.' I stroked his arm, saw the little dark hairs stand up. 'Somewhere in a wood, maybe. Wouldn't you like that too?'

It was a long time before he answered. Almost as if he hadn't heard me. 'I'll turn off at the next exit,' he said at last.

I could hear my heart thudding.

* * *

After about an hour another call came from his north German colleague. There was a seasonal worker who fitted the description. At the time in question he had been working in the Jever area, for a farmer who sold strawberries and raspberries. His name was Kurt Walz. He had driven a car, but no one remembered it very well, certainly not its registration number. That seemed to be because Walz kept himself very much to himself.

He hadn't stayed on the farm with the other workers, but had rented a small holiday flat. He'd only had written contact with the landlords, who didn't live in the area themselves. Nor had he made friends locally. He came and went, and hardly spoke to anyone more than was absolutely necessary.

He had seemed weird to a number of the women workers, and they kept away from him. Most of them had decided he was a loner, and didn't try to get to know him better. Walz went out with one of the men now and then, that was all.

He had done his job conscientiously and never gave cause for complaint. Yet everyone still remembered him. He had never come under suspicion during the murder investigations. He had been out drinking at the time of the crime with the only friend he'd made, and the two of them had given each other an alibi.

Just like Nathaniel Taban and Malle Klestof. The same pattern. Possibly, thought Bert, I've been underestimating Malle. He called the strawberry farmer and left a message for Malle to come to his office. No more polite skirmishing. Now he wanted to know the truth.

269

He stood at the window and looked down at the street, bathed in sunlight. People were hurrying busily back and forth. Women. Men. Children. Lovers walking hand in hand. And somewhere out there, somewhere far away, were Jenna and Nathaniel Taban. A girl and a murderer.

* * *

The cake was baked, the kitchen was spotlessly clean. The cats had been fed, the plants had been watered, the rubbish taken out. What could she do now? The phone kept ringing, but it was only someone from the animal rights group every time.

Everything was happening all at once there. Two of her friends had been picked up unexpectedly during a police check. For how long would they manage to remain silent?

Merle quickly got rid of those callers. She had to keep the line free. For the police. For Jenna. Please, thought Merle, dear God, please let Jenna call! Let her have forgotten something and call about that – oh, please!

Imke's mobile was switched on. 'But suppose she calls me at home?' she suddenly said in alarm. 'I didn't think of that.' She tapped in a number. 'Tilo? Listen, I need your help.'

Merle went out so that Imke could speak in private. She stood in her room, not sure what to do. Then she sat down at her desk, propped her elbows on it and buried her face in her hands.

Maybe if she thought really hard of Jenna she'd manage to reach her. Telepathy had been proved ages ago, hadn't it?

Jenna, she thought. Jenna, can you hear me?

* * *

It was a picture-book wood, not too tidy but not completely overgrown. The ground was soft with spruce needles and moss. The sunlight sparkled down through the tree canopy high above our heads.

'Isn't this lovely?' I let go of Nat's hand and ran a little way along the winding path. Then I flung my arms into the air and let out a loud cry. The trees caught it and swallowed it up.

'Beautiful.' Nat was standing behind me. He kissed the nape of my neck. 'But stop shouting now. You have to be quiet in woods.'

'Do you?' I turned to him and looked into his eyes. 'When you're in love you can do anything. You have licence to do as you please.'

He took my head in both hands and kissed me as he had never kissed me before, hard, passionately, almost desperately. But then he suddenly let go of me. He rubbed his face, wiping all the emotion off it, and said, 'Didn't you want to go for a walk?'

I didn't like his voice at that moment. It didn't sound like Nat. It sounded like a stranger.

* * *

Tilo had cancelled all his engagements and driven to the mill house to wait by the telephone there. He had never heard Imke in such a state before. Her voice had been hoarse with fear.

He'd had a key to the mill for a long time but had never used it before, because they had always made a date already when he came. The key meant a great deal to him, though.

Imke had dedicated a book to him, had introduced him to her circle of friends; he had even become a part of her family, but a key to her house was the best present she could offer him. With it, she was giving him access to her private sphere, and he would never have dreamed of misusing the privilege.

As always, he felt the peace of the house, and imagined what it would be like to live with Imke here. Perhaps the time for that had come. He shook his head at himself. Wasn't he too old for romantic dreams?

He spread out the books and papers he'd brought on the conservatory table. He would pass the time by working. If he could concentrate. He had taken Jenna to his heart, and was more afraid for her than he would ever have thought possible.

* * *

Was he wrong, or was she really different from usual? She seemed somehow reserved. Like a woman you've only just met, and you don't yet know how to act with her.

He took her in her arms and kissed her again. This time he was in control of himself and kept his eyes open, looking at Jenna. She closed her own eyes as she returned the kiss. That was all right. She was the same as ever. His imagination had been playing tricks on him.

'If I were a spy,' he said, putting his arm round her shoulders and strolling on with her, 'if I were a spy and had to leave the country, what would you do? Would you come with me?'

'Bond,' she said theatrically. 'James Bond. With a licence to kill.' She grinned. 'I've always wanted to go to the South Seas. Or Timbuktu. No problem.'

He squeezed her shoulder. 'Would you or wouldn't you?'

'That's a game we often used to play,' she said. 'If I were a tree, what tree would I be? If I were a flower. If, if, if.' She kissed the tip of his nose. 'You're not James Bond. You're not a spy.'

'Would you?' He stopped and stared at her.

'Yes, kind sir, I would.' She drew him on. 'But only if we could live in a pretty little house by the sea. I'd go swimming every morning before breakfast, and buy fresh rolls on my way home, and wake you with a kiss and never, never go to school again.' She laughed. 'And you'd paint pictures or write books under a new name, and not be a spy

272

any more, because if you were I'd be much too scared for you.'

'And we'd have children,' he said, because what Jenna was saying suddenly came very close to his own dream of their future. 'Two boys and two girls.'

'And the boys would look like you. They'd have your nose and your eyes.'

'And the girls would have your lips, your hair and your smile.'

'We'd have a dog too, of course, a dear little dog with a curly coat, not at all dangerous. And cats on the sofa and all the windowsills.'

'And you'd be my wife for ever and ever.'

'And I'd love you, love you, love you.'

She broke free and ran along the path. Laughing. Happy.

It was just a game to her. She hadn't taken his question seriously.

* * *

Malle sat on the chair like a defiant child with a guilty conscience, twisting his worn baseball cap in his fingers. He'd never been asked to provide anyone with an alibi, he said, no, not Nate either. 'We were out having a beer. I give you my word.'

As if your word was worth anything, thought Bert. 'Witnesses?'

'Not so far as I know. We were pub-crawling. We often do. Lots of people see you, but no one would bet on it afterwards because most of them are already drunk.'

'And Mr Taban was with you the whole time?'

Malle nodded, and crumpled the cap in his shovel-like hands.

'All evening? And all night?'

Malle nodded again. 'We didn't get home until the small hours.'

'Drunk?'

'Sure.' Malle grinned. 'We'd been out boozing.'

'How drunk?'

'Well, pretty well sozzled. Both of us. Nate and me.'

'How did you get home?'

'In Nate's car.'

'When you were falling-down drunk?'

Silence.

'Who was at the wheel?'

'Nate, of course. He won't let anyone else drive his car. It's sacred to him.' Malle straightened out his cap again. 'He can always drive, even when he's been drinking. Nate has a good head for liquor.'

'Thank you. That will be all for today.'

'For today?' Malle made a face. 'Do you mean . . .?'

'That more questions might come up? Yes.'

Malle rose and put on his cap. He made his way to the door awkwardly, a man who moved more freely in the open air than in enclosed spaces.

'Oh, Mr Klestof?'

He stopped as if caught in the act of something and turned to Bert, prepared for more unpleasantness.

'You really don't know where your friend is at the moment?'

'No. Nate never takes me into his confidence. If I knew I'd tell you.' He opened the door and made his get-away as quickly as he could.

Bert noticed the smell that Malle Klestof had left behind in the room, a disagreeable mixture of soap, sweat and a sweetish aftershave. He opened the window wide and took deep breaths of fresh air.

Malle Klestof had been drunk. Very drunk, as he admitted. He had more than likely had a mental blackout. Which meant that Nathaniel Taban's alibi fell through. It would have been easy for him to persuade Malle of anything he wanted next day.

You're clever, Nathaniel, Nate or Nat, thought Bert. But not so clever that no one can be on to you.

He felt a sense of elation. A presentiment that he was very near his quarry now. But he couldn't enjoy it. Not until Jenna was safe.

22

I didn't like the game. He was taking it too seriously. So seriously that suddenly it wasn't a game any more. I laughed my uneasiness off. I could do that when Nat was with me – I couldn't feel uneasy for long.

I wasn't going to stop and wonder why he was acting so oddly today. We hadn't known each other long; there was a lot I still had to find out about him.

And he had to find out a lot about me. He didn't yet know, for instance, that I craved peace and harmony and couldn't stand quarrels. That any little thing would make me cry. That my self-confidence sometimes let me down.

He'd find all this out sometime, and have to accept it. And I'd have to accept the fact that he sometimes acted strangely.

'This really matters to me, Jenna,' he said, stopping again. Light and shade danced over his face. 'Would you . . . ?'

I kissed him and put my hand under his T-shirt. Don't say anything, I thought. Just feel me.

It was very quiet. A few birds were singing, that was all, and even their voices sounded muted. This was the ideal place. The ideal time. We'd waited long enough.

'Let me show you how much you mean to me,' I whispered.

He seemed to freeze for a moment before pressing against me.

* * *

Imke thought back to when Jenna was a baby. She remembered it as clearly as if it were yesterday. Even the scent of the baby cream, shampoo and powder lingered in her nostrils.

In the evening she would often sit by Jenna's cot and listen to her breathing. Her perfection sometimes brought tears to Imke's eyes.

Imke's instincts had been purely animal. She sensed what her baby needed and provided it as well as she could. She'd have fought like a lioness for her child if Jenna had been in danger.

So was the lioness old and toothless now? Why was she sitting around here waiting instead of doing something?

But what? Her child was grown up and went her own way. Imke didn't know what way it was just now.

She felt an urge to call her husband, even though he wasn't her husband any more. He was the only person who would really share her fears.

She rang his office number. Heard his voice, and fought back the urge to weep. Very briefly she told him about it. 'Would you stay by your phone?' she asked. 'Just in case Jenna rings you.'

He seemed to hold his breath, and then gasped. 'My God,' he said. 'My God.'

After they had spoken Imke prowled up and down the kitchen, wondering whether this situation would ever have arisen if she'd managed to keep her family together. She covered her ears to silence the voices inside her head.

* * *

He hadn't wanted it to be like this. Not this way. He hadn't really wanted it at all. It was too soon. He hadn't been ready.

She was like the others. Like the others. Like . . .

Tears were running down his face. He didn't wipe them away.

And with grief came the anger. Red, raging, incandescent anger.

The girl had buried her fingers in his hair. She was murmuring tender words that he didn't hear. He had loved this girl. How could she stab him in the back like this? Disappoint him so much? Soil his feelings, his body, his thoughts?

He heard a scream in the distance. A scream of torment and of rage.

'Jenna,' he whispered. 'Why?'

* * *

The cats were asleep, curled up together on the kitchen sofa. Imke was leaning against the window frame, standing motionless as she looked down at the street. It was so long since she'd moved that Merle had almost forgotten she was there.

Merle had cleared away the things she'd laid out on the table. She didn't need to be reminded of them. She would never forget them as long as she lived. Instead, she had laid plates and cups and brought out the cake. The candles were ready too. All they needed now was for Jenna to come home.

'A good thing it isn't winter,' said Imke suddenly. 'Waiting would be much worse then.'

'Could be.' Merle doubted whether the time of year made any difference, but she saw no point in contradicting Imke.

'I was always worrying about Jenna,' said Imke. 'Most of all I was afraid she might go off with some stranger.' She laughed bitterly.

And now the nightmare's come true, thought Merle. She *has* gone off with a stranger, and she hasn't told anyone where to.

'All these years and nothing happened. And just as I was beginning to let go, trying to grasp the fact that my daughter's a grown woman now and my fears are simply ridiculous, just now she does it. She goes off with a stranger.'

'He isn't strange to her,' said Merle.

Imke turned to her. 'She hardly knows him! And she obviously knows nothing at all about him. No one knows anything about him.'

'The police will find them,' said Merle. 'Nothing will happen to her – I'm sure it won't.' She joined Imke at the window and looked out.

Outside it was summer. People wore light, frivolous clothes, just the thing for a lovely day like this. And none of them knew that they were really moving over glass, and it could splinter into pieces at any moment.

* * *

His cry sent the birds flying up from the trees. It exploded in the silence and in my head. It wasn't a cry of orgasm, it was a cry of despair. And rage.

I didn't move.

'Why? Why? Why?'

I lay perfectly still. So as not to provoke him even more. What did he mean?

Fear crawled down from my head into my body, until everything about me felt dull and heavy.

What had happened?

Nat was weeping, his face against my throat. His tears rolled down my skin as if they were my own. He was calling me horrible names. He went on weeping.

I couldn't make him out. I didn't look into his face. My racing thoughts made no sense.

He shook me, pulled me close, pushed me away, embraced me again.

I ventured to look at him. I regretted it at once. He was going to kill me. I didn't know why, but he was going to kill me.

* * *

'What was that?' Heinz Kalbach asked his wife.

Rita Kalbach lowered the newspaper. 'Sounded like someone shouting.' They lived in a very isolated spot, and noticed noises. 'Young folk again, maybe.'

Only last weekend a group of teenagers had invaded the wood and rampaged around for hours. *Having fun* – that was what they called it these days.

'I expect you're right.' Heinz Kalbach picked up the sports section again. Now that they'd retired they had all the time in the world to read. After finishing the paper he'd go back to the thriller he was enjoying at the moment.

And then, before supper, they'd take a nice walk. The dog was getting lazy, just like them. And fat. Heinz Kalbach looked at the black and white cocker spaniel sleeping on his blanket.

He obviously hadn't heard the cry. Or he'd simply ignored it. He was an old dog now, eighty-four in dog years. At such a great age even a watchdog could retire.

Rita Kalbach smiled at her husband. He smiled back.

* * *

'Why don't you girls carry a pepper spray?' asked Imke. 'Or something else to defend yourselves with? And for goodness' sake, why switch off your mobiles when you're out?'

'We never thought anything could happen to us,' said Merle.

'So what happened to Caro? Didn't it change anything?' What happened to Caro. Imke had never put it like that before, but now she couldn't say the word *death*. She was afraid it might come true.

'Yes.' Merle bent her head. 'But we were so sad and angry, it was like a protection. We felt safe.'

Imke could have shouted at her, but at the same time she was sorry for this unusually subdued Merle, who could hardly bear her guilty feelings. 'Sorry – take no notice of me,' she said. 'It's just that I'm scared. Some people go quiet when they're frightened; I start rabbiting on – sometimes I really talk my head off.'

She called Jenna's mobile again. '*If you would like to leave a message . . .*'

The mobile had stored her message long ago. 'Jenna, darling, please ring. It's urgent! I'm with Merle. We're waiting for you to call.'

She didn't want to put it more plainly in case she made the man nervous. Or scared. Or aggressive. Anything might send a psychopath over the edge.

Merle was staring out of the window intently, as if that could conjure up Jenna in the street, inside the building, in the flat.

* * *

I felt around on the moss with both hands. I couldn't find a large stone or a stick, but my right hand suddenly touched something that felt like my mobile. It must have fallen out of my bag.

Nat had gone quiet. That scared me even more than his fury. I didn't stop to think; I just hit him as hard as I could on the forehead with my mobile.

He groaned and put his hands to his head. I turned to my left and pushed him off me. Then I jumped up and ran for it.

I hadn't taken off my skirt when we made love. It had all happened so fast. It was a full skirt, made of lightweight fabric, easy to run in. The front of my blouse was torn open. Nat had been in too much of a hurry to un-button it properly.

Branches whipped against my legs. Stones and roots hurt the soles of my bare feet. Then I was back on the path.

I didn't have time to try remembering which way the road was. I just kept running to the left.

My mobile hadn't survived the blow. It had broken apart. So why was I still holding it? I threw it away.

My panting seemed to be the only sound in the wood. Was there any point in calling for help? Probably not. Who was going to hear me? And it would cost me an effort, would use up some of my breath, and I couldn't afford that.

I mustn't stay on the path. I must turn into the undergrowth so that Nat couldn't see me. I had enough of a start now to risk it.

Only when I was about twenty metres from the path did I dare look round. Nothing. Perhaps I'd knocked him unconscious. I hoped so.

I was going more slowly now, because there were bushes everywhere catching at my skirt. And I didn't want to run straight into him.

'Caro,' I whispered. 'Dear, dear Caro!'

I knew who had murdered her now. And I was running away from him myself.

So this was what Caro had felt before her death. Naked panic.

* * *

The dog raised his head. He got up with difficulty, trotted over to the door and sat down.

'Back to your blanket, old boy,' said Heinz Kalbach affectionately. 'It's only young folk amusing themselves.'

But the dog didn't obey. He put his head on one side. Then he barked.

'Perhaps you should go and see what's up,' said Rita Kalbach. 'He's acting in a funny way.'

Because he's a funny old dog, thought Heinz Kalbach, and we spoil him rotten. Although he sometimes shows sense. He put the dog on a leash and went out with him.

* * *

Where was she? His head hurt. There was blood on his left hand. She'd broken the skin!

Whatever happened now, she'd brought it on herself.

He went back to the path and looked around. They'd gone a long way into the wood – there was no danger of her finding her way back to the road in the next half-hour.

He saw something black beside the path a little way off. Going over, he picked it up. Her mobile, or what was left of it. Good; at least she couldn't phone anyone now.

He was so sure he'd find her that he didn't hurry too much. A slow jogging pace was fast enough. He was fit, he was strong and he was furious.

He had sharp eyes too. He immediately noticed the tiny scrap of fabric that had caught on a bush beside the path. He plucked it off and rubbed it between his fingers.

A bit of her skirt.

It wouldn't be long now.

* * *

The dog really was acting strangely. He was tugging at the leash, whining, growling. Perhaps there was a wildcat somewhere near. The dog had encountered wildcats a couple of times before, and he always came off worst. All the same, he was ready to attack them again.

'Come on, Rudi,' said Heinz Kalbach. 'Do your business and we'll go home.'

As he waited for the dog to lift his leg, he looked at the house. It was like an enchanted place. Hidden among the beech trees, covered with Virginia creeper. When the old forest warden's cottage came up for sale they had bought it at once. They liked living in this remote place, on the outskirts of the woods and some way from the nearest village or town.

Heinz Kalbach had always loved the woods. He knew and trusted them. He felt safe and secure here. Only human beings were dangerous.

'Finished, Rudi?'

The dog ignored him. He growled deep in his throat, and then began tugging frantically at the leash and yapping.

* * *

My feet were burning, my legs hurt, I had a stitch in my side. I tried to breathe regularly to conserve my strength. I mustn't stop; I absolutely must not stop.

Leaves rustled and twigs cracked under my feet. My breathing was too loud. Suppose he heard me? He could be anywhere.

Where was he?

Don't turn round.

But suppose he was right behind me? Very close?

Fear paralysed me. I slowed down, stumbled.

'Caro,' I whispered, 'help me!'

I thought of her until there was nothing in my head but her name.

And ran on.

* * *

What on earth was the matter with the dog? He never usually acted up like this. However hard Heinz Kalbach pulled at the leash, he made no impression on Rudi. So much for the dog-training course.

Heinz didn't want to go the way the dog was pulling him. If Rudi had smelled a wildcat it was guaranteed to disappear the moment they turned up.

'Rudi! Heel!'

He'd often regretted giving the dog that silly name. It made commands sound less than serious.

The dog growled. Actually growled at him! And went on yapping.

* * *

He felt as if his head were bursting. The wound on his temple was still bleeding. Blood had run into one eye, and the additional pain made him even angrier.

His anger was no longer hot and red. It was black and cold.

He followed the girl through the wood. In spite of his pain and anger he was able to think clearly and logically.

First he must catch her. Then he would punish her.

* * *

Rita Kalbach had come out of the house and was now standing beside her husband. Like him, she stared at the wood without seeing anything unusual. 'Rudi doesn't sound like himself,' she said in her calm, thoughtful way. 'Let him off the leash, Heinz.'

He didn't argue. She had said only what he was beginning to think himself. He bent down and undid the leash.

Rita took her husband's arm. 'I think we'd better just wait, don't you?'

He nodded. What else could they do?

* * *

Suddenly I heard something. It sounded like – like a dog barking. I didn't stop, but in spite of my loud gasps I was making a great effort to hear more.

Yes, it was barking. And it was coming closer.

I ran towards the sound. If there was a dog somewhere near, there'd be people too. Tears were running down my face and collecting on my chin.

That cocker spaniel was the most beautiful dog I'd ever seen. It jumped up at me, barked again and ran off. Then it stopped, turned, waited for me to come closer and ran on again.

It wanted me to follow, and I did. Perhaps Caro had sent the dog to show me the way.

* * *

The dog arrived first, then the girl. She was barefoot and wore a ragged blouse and torn skirt. She could hardly manage to stand upright. Her face was dirty and tear-stained.

'Into the house,' she said between her gasps and sobs, and looked back over her shoulder at the wood.

They understood at once and took her arms, Heinz Kalbach on her right, his wife on her left. They half led, half carried the girl indoors.

Heinz Kalbach closed and bolted the front door. Then he went round all the rooms closing windows. Only then did he phone the police.

Meanwhile his wife had led the girl to the sofa and covered her with her shawl. Now she was sitting beside her, dabbing her face with a damp flannel. 'Look at her poor feet,' she said softly. 'Raw flesh.'

The girl was weeping, so hopelessly that Rita could do nothing but sit perfectly still beside her.

The dog on watch by the door began to growl. The girl sat up with a start, clasped the shawl to her breast and stared at the door, wide-eyed.

* * *

She was in there. He felt it.

He heard a dog bark and was on his guard. Quietly he stole around the house. There'd be a window open somewhere.

They had barricaded the house, made a fortress of it. What should he do? Break the glass of the patio door?

He tried to judge how large and how dangerous the dog was from the volume of its bark. Coming to no conclusion, he looked around the front garden for something he could use as a weapon.

There was a small pond between the fence and the garage, with a border of decorative stones. Each stone was the size of a honeydew melon. Perfect.

Whenever you think you can't go on, there's a glimmer of light coming from somewhere. So his grandmother had been right after all – sometimes, anyway.

I ought to have stopped her mouth, thought Nathaniel. Back when I was finally stronger than both her and Grandfather put together.

No one would see fear in his eyes again. No one would ever dare hit him again.

Certainly not the girl hiding from him in there.

He went round the house again, stepped onto the patio, took aim and threw the stone through the glass of the patio door. Then he saw the dog.

Nathaniel grinned. Too small and too old to be dangerous.

But a nuisance. He raised his arm.

23

Late yesterday afternoon, following a major search, the police succeeded in arresting their suspect in the case of the serial killer known as the Necklace Murderer, who has been terrorizing the local population for weeks.

Nathaniel T., a seasonal worker, has confessed to the murders of Carola Steiger of Bröhl and Simone Redleff of Hohenkirchen, and also to the earlier murders of Mariella Nauber of Jever and Nicole Bergmann of Aurich.

The police, says Detective Superintendent Bert Melzig, cannot rule out the possibility that he will face charges for further murders. The motives of the alleged murderer are still unclear.

Information leading to the arrest, as Melzig told the press conference, came from a friend and flatmate of the murder victim Carola Steiger. The police, he added, ultimately owe it to her that they were in time to prevent another murder from being committed.

* * *

Bert put down the paper and got himself a coffee. He sat down at his desk again with the steaming mug and put his feet up. He was tired – he was exhausted, but he was very content.

He had tried to call Imke Thalheim immediately after the arrest. A man had answered the phone, sounding self-confident, friendly, firm-voiced.

Then Bert had called Imke's mobile number and found her at her daughter's flat. She had wept and laughed with relief.

So that story had ended before it even began. But that was how it should be.

The boss had lavished praise on Bert and his team. In the course of the morning that would change, because Bert should never have let it be known at the press conference that the success of the search was not due exclusively to the police.

That was how it should be too.

He finished his coffee and rang his home number. 'Hello, darling,' he said. 'Just wanted to find out how you are.'

* * *

Jenna was still asleep. Merle went around the flat on tiptoe. The least she could do for Jenna now was to watch over her sleep. There'd be plenty of time to talk later.

The poor thing had been in a terrible state. She could do nothing but stare straight ahead and cry from time to time. Merle had offered her cake, Imke had made tea, but Jenna didn't want to eat or drink anything. They had seen to her feet, got her into a pair of pyjamas and put her to bed.

Merle quietly opened the door of Caro's room. She sat down at the desk and looked around. Everything was still the way it had always been. She could sense Caro everywhere.

'They caught him,' she said. 'He'll never hurt anyone else again. You can rest easy now.'

Sometime perhaps they'd get around to letting Caro's room to someone else, but at the moment Merle couldn't think that far ahead. Caro would always be in their hearts, of course, but as long as her memory still needed a room to live in it was too soon.

Merle listened at Jenna's door. Nothing. Not a sound. Jenna still seemed to be sleeping soundly.

It would do her good to rest. Merle and she had all the time in the world.

* * *

It had been hard for Imke to go home. She would have liked to sit at Jenna's bedside, watch over her sleeping daughter and never leave her again. But then she had reminded herself that it was time to let go. It's only if you let people go that they come back to you.

Tilo had been waiting for her and took her in his arms, and she knew it was time for that too. She would live with him at last.

He had cooked a meal and kept it warm. He was a terrible cook, but she didn't show what she thought of the mushy spaghetti and over-salty meat sauce when she ate it in the middle of the night.

'I believe I really do love you,' she said now, to his back.

Tilo didn't hear, because he was asleep. She stroked his hair, and then he turned, gave a comfortable little grunt in his sleep and put his arm round her waist.

Imke lay perfectly still and listened to his regular breathing.

* * *

Heinz Kalbach was asleep too. His wife was sitting at the window, watching the shadows in the room. The dog lay on his blanket, licking his paws.

They were both wide awake. Too much had happened for them to sleep.

Rudi had a cut over his left eye; her husband had bruises on his chin, his throat and his arms.

But the girl was safe.

Rita Kalbach smiled in the darkness. She'd never forget the surprise on her husband's face when he found out just who it was they had helped. Imke Thalheim was his favourite author. He'd read every one of her books.

Perhaps they might feature in one of her next novels?

No. Rita Kalbach shook her head. She felt sure that Imke Thalheim wouldn't exploit her own daughter's deadly danger in a book.

Quietly she stood up and went out of the bedroom. The dog followed her.

'A little extra treat, Rudi?'

He wagged his tail. She went down to the kitchen with him. He was old and he was brave. He had earned an extra dog treat.

Nathaniel lay on his back with his hands clasped behind his head, his eyes closed.

They had suddenly come running at him from all directions.

They had been shouting at him.

He had let go of the old man and turned to them. No one was going to shout at him any more. No one!

The dog had bitten his leg again. The animal had been incredibly tenacious. Nathaniel had given it another kick and sent it sailing through the room.

The girl had been crouching on the sofa, with a blanket or something like that clutched over her breasts. Her eyes had been so wide, so full of horror.

The police had overpowered him and put the handcuffs on. And even though his hands were now cuffed behind his back they held him firmly by both arms.

'Jenna,' he had said. 'Don't be frightened of me.'

They had dragged him out of the living room and onto the patio, and the stupid dog had run after him and tried to get at him again. One of the police officers had picked it up and taken it back indoors.

On the way to the police car Nathaniel had called her name – nothing else. 'Jenna! Jenna! Jenna!' The woods had swallowed up his voice like a huge, dark animal.

* * *

When I woke up I was so sad. I didn't feeling like getting dressed. Everything about me hurt. Outside and inside.

I could still hear him calling my name.

Merle seemed to have been waiting outside the door, listening. She came in, sat down on my bed and beamed at me. 'Hungry?'

I cautiously shook my head.

'Not even for my super-duper cherry cake? With whipped cream?'

I began crying again.

'Move up.' Merle lay down beside me and put her arm round me. She didn't ask any questions, and I was grateful to her for that. I needed time.

I thought of Nat. Where was he now? How was he feeling?

He had murdered Caro.

And he'd been going to murder me.

So why couldn't I hate him?

I'd been afraid of him, dreadfully afraid. And now that I was safe I still loved him.

'It'll get better,' Merle murmured. 'Wait and see, it'll get better.'

She meant something else, but she was right. It would get better in time.

Probably.

Some day.

A Swift Pure Cry
by Siobhan Dowd

A heartbreakingly beautiful tale of loss and discovery

Life has been hard for Shell since the death of her mam. Her dad has given up work and turned his back on reality, leaving Shell to care for her brother and sister. When she can she spends time with her best friend, Bridie and the charming, persuasive Declan, sharing cigarettes and jokes.

Shell is drawn to the kindness of Father Rose, a young priest, but soon finds herself the centre of an escalating scandal that rocks the small Irish community to its foundations.

'Beautifully written and deeply moving'
Guardian

'By far the best novel I read in 2005'
Tony Bradman

Available now as a Definitions paperback

ISBN 978 0 099 48816 3

The Hand of the Devil
by Dean Vincent Carter

When Ashley Reeves, a young journalist working
for freak-of-nature magazine Missing Link, receives a
letter promising him the story of his life, *his life* is
exactly what it might cost him.

The letter is from Reginald Mather, who at first
seems no more than an eccentric collector of insects,
happy to live in isolation on a remote island. But
when Reeves finds himself stranded with Mather and
unearths the horrific truth behind his past, he is
thrown headlong into a macabre nightmare that
quickly spirals out of control. His life is in danger
. . . and Mather is not his only enemy . . .

'It scared the daylights out of me. Better than
Stephen King'
Andy McNab

'Sensational'
Daily Express

Out now in CORGI paperback
Not suitable for younger readers

ISBN: 978 0 552 55297 4

The Garden
by Elsie V Aidinoff

Love it or hate it, you will find this novel irresistibly gripping!

In the beginning there is God. Magnificent, all-powerful, fascinated and excited by the things he can create, but dangerous.

And there is the serpent, a wise, loving and seductive teacher, ready to nurture Eve's every moment.

And then there is Adam, lithe, beautiful and physical.

And finally comes Eve. Enchanting, passionate, lively, always questioning as she wrestles with the dictates of God, the whims of Adam and the problem of free will.

This compelling debut novel brings controversial insight and inspiring freshness to one of the oldest tales on earth, exploring questions of personal responsibility, justice and freedom.

'Intriguing, absorbing and touching'
Guardian

'This is a remarkable, morally complicated, provocative novel. I don't think teenagers should be allowed to keep it to themselves'
Observer

Available now as a Definitions paperback
Not suitable for younger readers.

ISBN: 978 0 099 48407 3

The Angel Collector
by Bali Rai

A missing girl. A web of clues. A race to find the truth . . .

It's been eight months since Sophie went missing at a music festival and Jit is tired of waiting for answers. He once made a promise to Sophie to come and find her if she ever went away – a promise he is determined to keep.

With help from Sophie's best friend, Jenna, Jit starts to unravel the events of that weekend to follow a trail of clues that will lead him into more and more danger. What were the members of the strange cult doing at the festival and could they have anything to do with Sophie's disappearance? And what about the other girls who have gone missing – is there a serial killer on the loose?

As Jit's desperate search leads him all over Britain, he comes closer and closer to the horrifying and devastating truth . . .

Praise for Bali Rai:

There is a vitality and freshness about Rai's writing that engages the reader . . .
Books for Keeps

Bali Rai deals with important and controversial issues not because it is fashionable to do so, but because he is compelled to. Long may he continue!
Carousel

Available now in CORGI paperback
Not suitable for younger readers

ISBN: 978 0 552 55302 5

Set in Stone
by Linda Newbery

Love and possession. Art and immortality. Ambition and desire.

When naïve and impressionable artist, Samuel Godwin, accepts the
position of tutor to the daughters of wealthy Ernest Farrow, he does not
suspect that he's walking into a web of deception. He is drawn into the
lives of the three young women who live at Fourwinds: Charlotte Agnew,
the governess; demure Juliana, the elder daughter; and her passionate
and wilful younger sister, Marianne, who intrigues Samuel to the point
of obsession.

And it is not just the people who entrance Samuel. The house, Fourwinds,
holds mysteries of its own. What lies behind the disappearance of the West
Wind carving and the gifted sculptor who created it? Soon Samuel and
Charlotte start to uncover horrifying and dangerous secrets . . .

This thrilling novel, set in the late nineteenth century, will hold you in its
grip until the very last page.

'Wonderful descriptions . . . Newbery writes with grace and immediacy'
Daily Telegraph

'A powerful page-turner, gripping to the end'
Celia Rees

Available now as a Definitions paperback

ISBN: 978 0 099 45133 4

Noughts and Crosses
by Malorie Blackman

*A totally absorbing novel set in a world where black
and white are right and wrong*

Callum is a nought – a second-class citizen in a
world run by the ruling Crosses . . .

Sephy is a Cross, daughter of one of the most
powerful men in the country . . .

In their world, Noughts and Crosses simply don't
mix. And as hostility turns to violence, can Callum
and Sephy possibly find a way to be together? They
are determined to try.

And then the bomb explodes . . .

'Dramatic, moving and brave'
Guardian

'Will linger in the mind long after it has been read'
Observer

Available now in CORGI paperback
Not suitable for younger readers

ISBN: 978 0 552 55570 8